THE
STORMWATER
DRAINS
in CANBERRA

PAUL JOHAN KARLSEN is a Norwegian-born writer, editor, and research-oriented psychologist. He holds an MA in psychology from New York University and a PhD in psychology from the University of Oslo, Norway. He lives in Oslo and New York City.

THE
STORMWATER
DRAINS
in CANBERRA

PAUL JOHAN KARLSEN

KRUTT&PLUTTPRESS

KRUTT & PLUTT Press
New York 2015

Cover design by Heidi Larsen. Interior design by Patricia Capaldi

Library of Congress Control Number: 2015917743

Publisher's Cataloging-in-Publication
(Provided by Quality Books, Inc.)
Karlsen, Paul Johan, author.
The stormwater drains in Canberra / Paul Johan Karlsen.
pages cm
LCCN 2015917743
ISBN 978-0-9969272-0-8
ISBN 978-0-9969272-1-5
1. Teenage boys—Fiction. 2. Gay teenagers—Fiction.
3. Male homosexuality—Fiction. 4. Gays—Identity—
Fiction. 5. Norway—Fiction. 6. Bildungsromans.
I. Title.
PR9144.9.K37S76 2015   823'.92
QBI15-600208

Krutt & Plutt Press
75 East 4th Street, Str. 1 Ste. 4006, New York, NY 10003
www.kruttplutt.com

Visit us online at **www.kruttplutt.com** or call us at 212.400.7631

ISBN 9780996927215
E-book ISBN 9780996927208

Manufactured in the United States of America on acid-free paper

Oh, time to get ready
Time to get ready
Time to get ready
For love

Hal David / Burt Bacharach

CONTENTS

Prologue

THE AUSTRALIAN CAPITAL was founded in 1913, twelve years after the formation of the country itself. "There's no such thing as a soft drizzle there," Tim Høiby said. "Only hard downpours. The sky collapses over you and takes everything with it."

Because of the harsh climate, vegetation was sparse. The dried earth stretched firm and solid across the landscape. Hence, rainwater didn't easily penetrate the ground. Yet Canberra was awarded the title *capital* after a careful examination, at several competing locations, of landforms, climate, and water supplies. Following Washington, D.C.'s example, the future city was given its own inland territory, a limestone plateau 550 meters above the Pacific Ocean.

Soon Canberra, the maturing capital, needed electricity. The surrounding farmland—future vineyards included—could also do with some drought relief. Selmer, a Norwegian engineering company, held the necessary expertise on the construction of waterworks. They pioneered a project in the Snowy Mountains, south of the federal territory, to dispense the rainwater and snowmelt.

The high altitudes near the great ocean proved ideal for gathering water. The mountains forced the sea air upward, cooling it and producing a massive release of rainfall. One needed only to collect it. The natural rivers ran *eastward*, releasing their runoff back into the sea a short distance away. By redirecting the precious resource *westward* instead, to dry land around Canberra, electricity would be created in the process, for here the steep inclinations necessary to spin the turbines, coupled with the cold temperatures that would reduce evaporation from the dams above, could be found.

The endeavor started in 1949 and lasted twenty-five years; it was to become the world's largest hydroelectric and irrigation system. The Snowy Mountains Scheme, consisting of sixteen major dams, seven power stations, and one pumping station, eventually became the Earth's greatest artificial funnel. Only 2% of the mammoth construction is visible above ground. The tunnels proved wet and dangerous to work in—121 workers lost their lives in the effort, out of 100,000 workers who actively participated in the venture. They sailed in from more than thirty countries.

By now Jonny had declared his intention to write a feature article of some sort for his sponsor, *Aftenposten*. He'd borrowed a pen and was taking serious notes on his paper towel.

And as Jonny worked, our meal took shape—the first course, our host Tim quickly explained, consisted of smoked ham wrapped around asparagus and Parmesan cheese. Tim poured red wine—a vintage 1996 Australian Shiraz—into fresh glasses at each place setting on the dining room table. "It's from the Australian Capital Territory," he said.

There was so much space there, he went on. But the city planners foresaw that whenever it rained, Canberra would be vulnerable to flooding, dragging away topsoil every which way. So before the suburbs were established, thousands of eucalyptus trees and pines had been planted. Separated from ordinary sewage pipes, stormwater drains had also been built to absorb and disperse immense amounts of runoff.

The stormwater wasn't cleansed though. These drains dragged cigarette butts, used syringes, dog turds—all kinds of filthy trash—along with them into the dammed-up Molonglo River nearby. The issue of contaminants and pollution arose. For that reason, it was illegal to wash one's car on the capital city's streets. Yet most of the time, the drains were indeed deemed safe. Kids, roaming about, would scavenge in the cement gullies. A secret society, the Cave Clan, even encouraged trespassing into the off-limits tunnels deep under the city. But whenever rain set in, no one wanted to loiter anywhere near those drains.

After overseeing various parts of the Snowy Mountains project, one Selmer director returned to Oslo with a new wife, an Australian musician from Canberra. Now a wealthy, art-collecting widow, our host explained, the elderly woman sought the advice of a select group of art historians, music critics, and fellow artists before she approached young talent. Then she'd take the emerging artist or musician to dinner in a luxurious restaurant. At the end of the meal, she'd write out a generous check, for the beneficiary to spend however he or she wished. "Oh, I wish she was here today," Jonny said.

The subsequent year, a follow-up dinner would take place, during which the lady demanded a status report. If she saw promise and progress in the artist, she'd start buying. Since 1991, she had methodically acquired many of Tim Høiby's works.

Following an exhibition of his photos in Sydney, Tim had taken a series of Australian stormwater pictures as a tribute to his faithful collector. The pair of photographs hanging by the piano came from that set. "Ah ha," my fiancé said cryptically, as he filled up the last white space on my paper towel with his scribbles.

PART ONE | *Stormwater*

ACT I (1996–1999)

1

LOOKS-WISE, I wasn't anything to write home about. The owner of a huge, swelling Adam's apple, I rued my skinniness almost as much as my cracking voice. Despite having an abnormally large appetite, I assumed that I didn't put on weight because I burned so much nervous energy. On my way to school, I kept swallowing and muttering phrases like "Hello, hello, this is a test" to make sure my voice still carried, because every moment it felt like it was about to vanish. People could hardly understand a word I was saying. I caused pain for everyone in class.

Indeed, the mere sound of me struggling to speak proved piercing and intolerable, and I wanted to spare us all the excruciating torture. Taking cues from whatever kid the instructor called upon first, from where he sat in the room and how late in class the questioning began, I'd predict whether I'd have to speak out loud or not. Then I usually knew when to relax, which was bliss.

I treasured mathematics, the most peaceful subject. While some of the instructors in Norwegian, English, and German moved systematically along the rows, always starting on the same end, others launched their reading sessions from a different angle each time, yet in a foreseeable manner, from one chair to the next. A select few even made each pupil read for so long that they never got to more than a fraction of the class. The scariest of all were the exacting teachers who, perhaps to keep us alert, selected their victims at random.

While a few teachers tolerated or even understood my condition and didn't ask, others—usually the young, male substitutes—accepted no excuse. "I can't hear you. What did you say? You have a sore throat? But that's okay. Just give it a go, like everyone else." At that point, the lump in my throat would jolt up and down—its strange mobility was pointed out by a couple of classmates who nicknamed that particular body part my yo-yo. Dad later taught me this was my larynx. After a few agonizing paragraphs, the substitute teacher might say, "Please, try to read a little louder," and then, without further comment, he'd give up and move on to another kid.

Afterward, in the corridor or in the gym changing room, the more inquisitive classmates who demanded equal treatment for everybody would invariably pursue the matter. "Hey, yo-yo! Why can't you read? Why should you be excused from something no one wants to do, when the rest of us can't get away with it? When's your voice *ever* going to work? Hey! Don't get so close to my face when you talk—it's creepy."

I couldn't argue with their off-the-cuff observations. I stretched my neck much like a pigeon and tended to step too close to people's ears before speaking. It was my way of ensuring they heard me. For then I wouldn't need to repeat myself. Even on the handball court, an occasional parent, after clearing his throat, would ask why I never spoke up. Yet for the most part, I was allowed to be the stealthy, quiet team member—I signaled with my head, hands, and shoulders—and that, too, was bliss.

Slowly, things got worse. A teacher reprimanded me for whispering to my seatmate: "Kurt, you're not paying attention."

I blurted out "yoh"—Norwegian for "oh yes"—to deny the charge, but I'd been caught off guard. I even made the instructor blush. Oh, the pain. Consequently, boys in my class probed the astonishing range of the male pitch with each "yoh." They started outlandishly high, ended absurdly low, and closed off with, "Oh look, the pigeon turned red."

Needless to say, preparing for compulsory theatrical performances or, even worse, musical recitals in front of an audience at confirmation camp proved utter misery. To escape the agony, I had to either build up the courage to merely torment everyone or else ask to be excused and have to explain myself—by now something I detested equally. No, my vocal cords weren't breaking right. I had no control over my own voice.

I fantasized about all the things I'd set in motion the moment my voice carried. I'd be well prepared by then. I'd hit the ground running. I was working under cover and things were well underway. Once a week, at most, I made a trip to the post office, either during mid-session or straight after school. I had no legitimate business there and always dreaded Mum's subtle interrogation at dinner later: "Kurt, I didn't know you had a mailbox." So I took precautions, planned out different scenarios. If I ran into relations, I'd pretend I was buying stamps. Perhaps I was collecting them, who knows? And before retrieving my correspondence, I always made a detour into the main room to check whether anyone I knew was in line. If a friend of the family were to see me leaving the mailbox room and ask, "Is that you, Kurt? Do you have a mailbox?" I'd smile serenely and answer, "Oh, I was only taking a look—you know, just curious to find out what was in there." Plus, I had another backup plan if someone caught me in the act with my mailbox open. "Oh, it's not mine; it belongs to the handball club," I'd deadpan. Made-up stories like that.

For a period, Dad had been the club accountant and held a key to a mailbox. I'd been there with him a time or two and knew how the whole process worked. As fate would have it, there had been no waiting list when I'd signed up for one in my own name. Fortunately, the letter containing the bill had appeared in the box itself. I embraced efficiency, never wasting much time on my jaunts, for my gravest concern was that Mum would discover me herself, with my hand indisputably thrust inside the mailbox. I knew that I wouldn't be able to explain *that* away. But if someone ever saw me, they made no direct comment to me. And if my parents ever heard anything, they didn't bring it up.

Thus uninterrupted, I carried on.

If I found a big, brown envelope addressed to the fictitious Thomas Larsen among my junk mail, I immediately tore it up and buried the debris in the bin, shoving it deep into the accumulated trash by the sorting table. The desirable contents within that outer envelope—smooth, white, smaller envelopes—I hid in my pocket. I suspected that the people working behind the metal compartments understood what I was up to. Hearing a postman hum as he passed out his mail, I wondered how many lockers contained suspicious material like mine. In my mind, any big, brown envelope from an unknown sender screamed ILLICIT CONTENTS.

Barely able to maintain my nonchalance, I brought the letters to the park across the street. Not to the wide-open area in front of the building, but the overgrown and quiet part on the side. There, I'd read each and every reply, savoring each word, convincing myself I was laying down the foundation; I was learning about what was out there; I was drafting a master plan—so I could strike when readiness overtook. I didn't want to meet anyone until my words would carry properly, until I sounded manly. Because otherwise, few would seriously entertain the idea that I was of legal age.

Consumed by pubescent desire, I'd wanted to speed up my sexual coming of age. Unfortunately, the small Northern-Norwegian town in which I lived, north of the Arctic Circle, presented me with few viable candidates—although the readers of *Aktuell Rapport*, my chosen porn magazine, stretched the interpretation of the wording "seeks local lad of similar age" much further than I did back then, in 1996. Indeed, the replies came mostly from out-of-towners who'd hit their thirties, forties, or occasionally fifties.

Some traveled the country and were willing to meet the next time they visited Bodø. One in particular wanted me to recommend a good hotel with spacious rooms, huge beds, and mirrors, because a trip lay not necessarily that far in the future. Others offered to pay for flights to their hometowns. Even to these men though, it was imperative that events remained off the books, for some were married, had girlfriends, or even male partners.

Several enclosed snapshot cutouts anyway, usually from vacations to warmer places, so I could examine their bodies, if not their faces. They weren't attracted to the 'scene' as they put it; they wanted no part of that. They were looking for 'outsiders'—people living in the *real* world, like themselves. They longed for that normal, masculine boy who hadn't acquired the mannerisms, self-limiting predilections, and moral corruption of those who 'only hung with each other.'

But I didn't understand. They were mostly of similar age so why couldn't these older guys just play with each other? I shredded their letters to pieces and threw them into random trash bins on my way home. I kept only a precious few inside my notebooks, in my desk drawer, until my emotions sufficiently cooled. Then I'd rid myself of the evidence. I didn't want family members or friends who might sneak through my things to assume I was, in all earnestness, planning to meet men as old as my parents. I thought of myself as highly selective, as someone rather exclusive, a lifetime award of sorts. The bottom line: I was far from egalitarian when it came to desire.

Certain books, handed down from one class to another, suggested stirrings had long been rumbling under the surface of my scholastic predecessors. Erect penises had been etched, in pen or pencil, on most of the disciples in my junior-high Christian knowledge textbook. Their names handwritten inside the cover, all of the previous owners had been boys. I wondered who'd been responsible for the defacing yet, in comparing ink types, couldn't make any definite conclusions. And then, more blatant evidence surfaced. In my home-cooking group, Otto, a soccer player, confided that during a tournament sleepover a teammate had not only let the others see his hard-on but had even inquired, casually, if anyone wanted to touch. The story rendered me flabbergasted—why didn't such things happen at handball tournaments, to me? Another enriching life experience—missed.

I'd seen the free-spirited athlete around with his friends. He didn't look half bad, but he was in a class above me at school and we lacked common ground. More importantly, perhaps, he seemed a bit full of himself and rather dimwitted. I wanted someone I found more stimulating, more than half decent. No, I wasn't for everyone.

I'd worked out the numbers—they were available in the public library and in certain school texts, even Dad's medical books: approximately one candidate existed in each and every class. So my odds were acceptable. Although with so many classes, year levels, and schools to work my way through across Norway and beyond, I had a lot of exploratory research to do before smoking out my prey.

So there you go, Ragnar; you obviously hadn't entered the picture yet, but that's how it started. I wanted to find out what was out there. I wanted to investigate the secret thoughts of my peers. I wanted adventure, to be a sex pioneer.

Idly hanging around, waiting for *something* to happen, that strategy would be self-inhibiting, for I might very well be the only contender in my own class and on my handball team. Nevertheless, what were boys my own age willing to do, in secret, given the right circumstances? How does one find oneself an adventurous Bodø boy? The most systematic approach, I determined, was to arrange an open call, requesting interested parties to respond anonymously, in sealed envelopes. Then I could simply sit back and wait.

I smelled of saltwater the day I first laid eyes on a real porn magazine, after an end-of-school-year celebration. My class had lingered by a lagoon-like pool protected from the deeper sea by a weathered concrete barrier. It was still too cold to swim so we played soccer instead, and during the match, a girl pushed me into the frigid water. I tried to do the same to her, but she didn't like it much, and after some struggle, our teacher told me to stop. He offered me a lift home with the kids who didn't catch the bus, but that was out of the question, for I, my soccer-playing friend Otto, and another classmate—a redhead who was known for expressing his desire to build a bomb—wanted to race back to town on our own bikes. We had our own plan—not as hazardous as manufacturing explosives, but risky enough. Seagulls glided overhead all around us as we closed in on the community dumpsite, Bratten, in a hillside just north of Bodø. Bulldozers shuffled, rolled, and flattened the refuse too. New layers with fresh sand had recently been poured, the deposits sagging slowly toward the sea, and a few deserted houses had been sucked into the mass.

Making the diversion had been my idea; I'd plunked my peers with the suggestion on our way out to the lagoon. The year before, Dad and my little brother, Kåre, returned from the dumpsite with an entire carload of mint-condition comics, the unrecycled garbage from Magazine Central. Trucks and cars occasionally drove past, so we hid our bikes in the bushes that day. My soaked underwear left a damp spot on the foam seat.

My classmates and I weren't lucky enough to find any free comic books, but we snagged a handful of porn magazines that had barely survived the rain. Black boxes obscured hints of male excitement on the water-damaged pages, but the female body could be studied in detail. "Who's taking them?" the scrappy redhead grumbled before shoving them into his backpack. Even though I sometimes dreamt of wrestling around with him, I didn't dare to ask to borrow his magazines.

Summer vacation continued and turned into one long daydream. Black boxes visited me in my thoughts, making me feel weird and dizzy, and my white briefs turned a mortifying shade of yellow. Startling orgasms woke me up at night, so I had to change underwear every morning and hide the old pairs in the laundry basket.

Impatient for Kåre to finish up his computer game in the basement so I could have my go, I'd paced the wooden stairs—pounded my way to Dad's basement office and back upstairs again—one time too many. Disturbed from her nap, Mum yelled from the sofa, "Kurt! Don't lock yourself indoors; it's a clear blue sky outside."

Careful not to bother her, I left a note in the kitchen that I'd gone on a bicycle adventure. I then emptied my school backpack, jumped on my bike, and drifted through the streets of Bodø. Mum was right about one thing. It was so deliciously warm I could wear shorts. Nuzzled by the late sun, I made it up the hill above the shimmering ocean to the trash heaps at Bratten and, without attracting any attention, sniffed out four new porn magazines. I hid in the bushes along the road to absorb the fresh pages.

Unlike the others, these magazines were in perfect condition, and for months I kept them in my drawer among my notebooks. I worried constantly that my nosy brother would come across my stash though. In the fall, when the novelty wore off and my anxiety finally grew unbearable, I threw the inky pages into a public bin on my way to school, but only after I'd memorized the address to the periodical I liked best.

From my own experience, I knew aching desire builds until it bursts and fizzles away. One moment you're ready for anything, imagining yourself with just about anyone—a certain red-headed classmate, for example; then, for an achingly long time after, you wonder what came over you and swear to higher standards in the future. Hence, I had to reach my conquest at his ripest, most vulnerable moment—when he was most likely to surrender.

Even before my own advertisement appeared in *Aktuell Rapport*, I recognized a way to enhance my chances further. I knew that whenever a boy from my area came across the copy containing my advertisement, he wouldn't necessarily read it or, if he did, wouldn't necessarily think much of it. By submitting the same ad more than once, my call became louder, more insistent. Although I never actually saw any of those calls to action in print, I can't forget their gist—a blend of other advertisements that had made a memorable impression on me. My ads read something like:

BOY FUN

Bodø boy, 16 years old, seeks local lad of similar age for boy fun. One hundred percent mutual discretion and one hundred percent hygiene is a must.

I made the rather reasonable assumption that my ad would be rejected if I didn't meet the criteria for legal sexual conduct, so I put a stopgap on that possibility by faking to meet the requisite age. In any case, I found myself admiring certain boys from high school, the fit ones, the ones in white socks and gray fleece pants, the ones a couple of years older than me, the sixteen-year-olds. I told myself my attraction stemmed mostly from the fact that I wanted to be like them when I came of age.

I also didn't want to get caught. A false age and a mailbox provided a less traceable identity. I didn't want Mum or Dad knocking on my door saying, "Kurt. Here's another big, brown, anonymous envelope for you—what's in it?"

Now you see. I was fourteen at the time—two years under the age of consent—and also a full-blown sucker for secrecy.

2

MY ABSENT-MINDEDNESS could be a problem though. You see, a year later, one day after school, Otto, the soccer player from class, paid me a visit. I'd closed the door to my room and was tidying my bed so we could sit on it when he made a startling observation on my desk. The mailbox renewal bill begged for an explanation.

Otto exclaimed, "Hey, Kurt, I didn't know you had a mailbox."

Okay, so the bill was a little steep. I'd delayed making the payment for a few days. But I was shocked at my lack of caution; I couldn't for the life of me remember why I'd left the bill in plain sight. Mum might bring in fresh clothes, and Kåre often picked up comics from my floor. Taken aback, I blurted out the first excuse I could concoct on the spot—that the lease was for the handball club.

My tall friend held up the sheet of paper, as if preparing a cross-examination. "Have you gotten yourself a board assignment or something?"

Had he only known what lay down by his feet, inside my desk—a letter from a middle-aged Swedish farmer. I'd stowed the envelope into the old pile of completed notebooks where I'd hid my first porn stash. I had no idea whether the Swede realized this was, in fact, his second reply, but I liked the photo of his lover—an

educated Thai chef and masseur who, in his early twenties, was only
a few years older than me. Together in Härjedalen, they ran a wild
boar–breeding farm that was surrounded by forest and lakes.

The photocopied invitation, in Swedish, read like a tourist bro-
chure—they tried to evoke an enchanted place, a country home
where one brought together the finest sexual fantasies of all ages. A
traditional sauna cottage sat in the woods, and near the barn they'd
recently installed an outdoor Jacuzzi. Wanderlusting men, it tanta-
lized, were encouraged to explore, relax, and expect surprises in the
form of room guests. For this particular farm disguised a male-only,
secret sex hotel, a place for carnal Bacchanals to run wild in the forest, as often as every night. Indeed, apart from the one on the wine
cellar, the establishment boasted no locks; doors could be opened
and closed at anyone's discretion.

The farmer had scribbled a note on the flipside of an airplane
photo: "This is your lucky call … Travel and accommodations are
free for roaming satyrs from the north. Just let us know if you need
a summer job. We'll teach you how to pour wine and play the pipe."

Me, a satyr? Yah, Ragnar, I had to look up the word in the
encyclopedia and think for a while. A roguish, seductive, yet timid
creature of the untamed woodlands, instinctually able to defend itself against threats, prepared to help or hinder travelers at a whim,
and ready for any physical pleasure? I wasn't so sure…. But I was
flattered.

And parental knowledge would be the spoiler, wouldn't it? To
make a short visit, all I needed to tell Mum and Dad was that I was
going on a cabin trip somewhere in the forest outside of Bodø. It
was a believable enough excuse and almost true; Otto's parents did
have a log cabin. But so did many parents of my classmates and
teammates, and I tried to think of a human cover I didn't see on an
everyday basis, someone my parents knew by name but weren't likely
to bump into at the wrong moment. Mum might ask for the exact
location of a cabin. She might even demand the telephone number
of my friend's parents in case something came up.

So I considered inventing a camping trip instead, perhaps convincing Otto into believing he was illicitly covering up so I could be
with a girl whose name I couldn't yet reveal to anyone. I'd make him

pretend he was going with me two trips in a row—once for real. That way, a phone call or the question, "So how was the camping?" wouldn't catch him completely off guard. I knew he owned a decent sleeping bag and so did I. A couple of roll-up mattresses I could borrow from home.

But what if something serious happened to me, or to someone in my family, while I stayed in Härjedalen? I knew how to nurture my unquestionably precocious talent for worrying, foreseeing complications. There was no fast return—I'd checked. The trains didn't go often. The journey took more than twenty-four hours. I needed to make several changes. Furthermore, at the time I didn't yet own a cell phone—neither did my classmate. No, I didn't have the nerve to carry out such an elaborate scheme. I wondered instead if I should claim to have found a summer job at a wild boar farm through some thrown-away magazine or newspaper.

I struggled with my words, tried to buy time to think. Otto must have sensed my discomfort. "I opened a mailbox for Dad," I said. "He's running the accounts."

"Really? Why didn't he do it himself?"

"I don't know… He asked me to. I volunteer at the club sometimes, you know."

"But the box's in *your* name. Shouldn't it be in the club's name?"

"Oh, is it? That's a mistake. I hope it doesn't matter. I haven't really looked that carefully at that paper."

I sounded defensive, yet I was grateful that I hadn't taken my secrecy another step—because a year ago, when the post office clerk had failed to ask for identification, I almost faked my name. If the lease had been issued for Thomas Larsen, I'd have had more explaining to do now. I would've had to profess that Thomas Larsen was my granddad or something, claim that I was taking care of his mail.

I wasn't entirely sure whether my classmate simply decided to be tactful, but he finally let the subject go. He couldn't have been aware of the fact that Dad had handed down his charitable task at the club long ago. Otto dropped the bill and sat down next to me, then mindlessly stroked his massive ankles, the way he always did. A sensible guy, he never returned to the question of the bill. I think my soccer-playing friend understood, somehow respected, that I didn't like to talk too much about myself.

I wanted to learn what was out there without anyone finding out about me. All the secrecy—my forming a private life—was part of the attraction. Back then I already loathed the idea of having to explain myself. Prying eyes and second-guessing. That's not for us, Ragnar. We're similar in that sense, aren't we?

3

ONLY A FEW days after coming so close to giving myself away, I discovered a better and much closer choice, in an overdue letter. I abandoned the intricate Swedish summer job plot straightaway. Just a year older than me, my newest correspondent, Jonny Larsen, was a sixteen-year-old Bodø boy who played the euphonium in the school marching band. He liked jogging and audaciously invited me for a run. Evidently, he was braver than I—either more at ease with opening up to strangers or given to sheer recklessness—for the local lad proceeded to offer his home address *and* phone number. I'd even be able to recognize him on the spot!

The enclosed photo, apparently an official confirmation portrait, showed a chubby boy in a blazer, his face covered by acne. And his last name, so common in Scandinavia, was the same as my own, hence strikingly simple to memorize. I found his parents in the phone directory, among the many hundred Larsens listed in Bodø, under the address and phone number he had so boldly provided. I learned his name by heart and discarded his letter along with that of the farmer too—the very last proofs of my affair with advertising—for now I knew where to find my adventure. Thus, my jaunt with post office secrecy came to a close. I didn't want envelopes for Thomas Larsen forwarded to the house though, so I needed to renew the one-year lease. Wasting money on a safety buffer was necessary, just in case delayed replies arrived from still more unacceptable candidates.

My plan was to call Jonny as soon as I possessed a proper masculine voice. Much to my chagrin, on the phone people mistook me for a girl. Unquestionably, something about my voice still remained out of tune. Although a voice break, I reasoned, couldn't last forever. Before the end of 1997, while I was still fifteen, this whole weird and embarrassing struggle would be over—or so I decided. I gave myself deadlines: "Just a few more months now. A few more months, that's all...."

But nothing happened; nothing changed. A few more months to wait always remained. I'd read somewhere that the average Norwegian male made his sexual debut around the time he turned seventeen. Thanks to my croaking tone, my prospects as a sex pioneer were quickly deteriorating.

Soon enough, my deadline shifted to the summer of 1998 and the time I finished ninth grade. And then it changed again to the end of summer, in time for high school and new classmates. By then, well past sixteen years of age, I'd obtained my first part-time job— I'd become a fixture among the graphic designers who were employed at a local printer. I assisted in the production of the matchday program for the senior handball team, and I did the layout for a journal at the hospital where Dad worked.

The deadline for the first program of the 1998–1999 season loomed. On my way to school, I stopped off at the printer with my last illustrations. The designers helped me scan pictures, turning them into low-resolution black dots so that Xerox machines could properly replicate them. The woman who usually looked after me wasn't there, and when I approached her coworkers, a portly male, the obnoxious type, immediately burst out with, "Tell me, what's wrong with your voice?"

Totally unprepared for his frankness, I squirmed. "I know; it's a little weak."

"So I hear.... It sounds awful. I can hardly understand a word you're saying. You really should see a doctor—as soon as possible."

He was so blunt and forceful that I promised to go—he wouldn't really accept any other response. I'd never felt as embarrassed. While he scanned my images, he cleared his throat. Yah, Ragnar, in my presence, adults would constantly swallow or clear their throat. Such acts proved contagious; around me vocal cords constantly went gruff, and I wondered why no one—including myself and Doctor Dad—had reached this conclusion before. My voice had been breaking forever. The transformation wasn't going to happen on its own; an unfamiliar graphic designer had to kick me into action. He was absolutely right. I'd been waiting for my voice to work itself out when plainly it wouldn't. I'd been stalling.

Once Dad got home from work, I ordered him to look down my throat. I didn't even give him time to put down his briefcase. He seemed a little bewildered by my resolve but told me to wait on the sofa while he fetched his old medical bag from the basement. Grabbing several tools—a wooden tongue spatula, an angled mirror, a handheld lamp—he made me lean backward and say *aaah*. While I struggled to suppress my gag reflex and the flow of spit, he took a long look. I wiped my chin and fastened my eyes on him as he packed up his equipment. Was everything down there the way it was supposed to be?

"Your throat looks fine," he finally said. "There are no knots on your vocal cords."

Knots? "But something's wrong."

He was about to offer some soothing words but, seeing my expression, hesitated. He then said, "If you'd like, I could refer you to an ear-nose-throat specialist."

And so, a few days later, Mum picked me up at school and accompanied me to the specialist's office. Even she swallowed as she explained the issue. I was so self-conscious I could hardly open my mouth. Yet Dad's colleague came to a similar conclusion. "You have normal vocal cords, boy. There's nothing to worry about. It's natural for your voice to be cracking."

Apparently there was nothing wrong—no cysts, no knots. But I wasn't easily consoled and could barely sit still.

For a while, Mum had kept to the background. A hefty silence weighed over the three of us, and the man in white garments took his turn and swallowed. I glanced at Mum. "It's been going on for some time," she admitted.

I finally raised my voice. "My brother's a year younger than me and he went through this thing two years ago. I'm sixteen and a half, and it's been going on nonstop since I was thirteen."

Everything about me was one big knot! That nothing was wrong was utterly wrong!

Rather awkwardly, the doctor grabbed my shoulder. "I could write you a referral."

Mum looked puzzled. "To where?"

"To a speech therapist at the hospital."

4

WAS IT OKAY if she turned on a tape recorder? The audio, she explained, would be treated confidentially, to document progress. She dealt mostly with stroke victims suffering from paralyzed speech muscles, and cancer patients who'd undergone substantial mouth or throat surgery—although she was well aware of boys who'd experienced prolonged periods of voice deepening, even cases of mutational falsetto, or puberphonia.

She knew of instances that, left untreated, had lingered into adult life, because everyone, including the affected speaker, had taken his voice to be naturally feeble. Anxious to deflect such a fate, I agreed to become a documented case, as long as she promised I wouldn't have to listen to the recording.

Her own, exceptionally low-pitched, voice proved strangely calming. She asked me to close my eyes, breathe in deeply, and slowly exhale. Behind the closed door of the speech therapist, with her hospital air conditioner droning monotonously, I finally began to relax.

"Straighten your back. Let your shoulders fall. Feel your cheekbones loosen; let your jaw relax, your Adam's apple sink. Now ... don't forget to breathe. No, not from your chest. From your *stomach*;

from the bottom of your rib cage. Rest your hands, palms in, on the sides of your body; there, between your waist and rib cage. Feel them move in … and out."

She asked me to breathe slower, to count from one to ten while I inhaled, then back down to one while exhaling. "Come on. Make sure you have enough breath to count all the way back to one."

She insisted that this way, the volume and force of my voice would increase dramatically. And then, after all the breathing and relaxing, she wanted me to blow out harder, adding the sound *hmm*. We repeated this exercise many times, yet what came out of my mouth audibly registered altogether different.

This circumstance had arisen a few times before, I realized, in winter. If I didn't wear a scarf and a cold wind blew down my neck, sometimes no voice emerged at all, and I'd be struck temporarily mute. Hence, on entering an empty, steamy changing room before handball practice, I'd hum softly to myself, repeating the standard phrases: "Hello, hello, testing, testing." If others were present, I'd remain quiet until my vocal cords steadied themselves. In the event I let my guard down and spoke without thinking, my voice would modulate wildly, like a trombone sliding out of tune.

The changing room turned dead quiet after such episodes. One particular coach, when alone with me, had nagged me about it. "Try to speak *clearer … clearer!*" Feeling powerless, I'd tried, at the very least, to steer clear of the cracks. To keep my pitch pure and avoid any further embarrassment, I'd stretched my neck and whimpered on, whispery and hoarse.

As I left the hospital building, I continued to sigh and hum. The only possible conclusion I could make, riding the streets of Bodø, was that my voice breaking had been completed long ago. When the cold stunned my beleaguered larynx, I'd found my natural grown-up pitch. I roared on my bicycle, startling an old lady resting on her rollator. I couldn't help but laugh at myself. This pigeon could speak with a deep, masculine voice! Heading home, I even started singing Mum's music: *It's time to get ready. Time to get ready. Time to get ready for love.*

For the time being though, I mumbled on with the more arti-ficial voice whenever I got off my bike—so much growing increasingly clear to me. I'd basically been handed a new personality and I wasn't prepared for the attention. I felt unsure of everyone's reactions. When I found myself away from people, or in traffic, I'd sing, chant, and even *shout*, "Hello, hello!"

And so at my second speech therapist appointment, the question became: "How do I go about using my deeper voice permanently?" The specialist countered with a question of her own: "Would you mind if a colleague of mine, from Oslo, listened in at the subsequent session?"

Ganging up on me, the two therapists dared, "Would you like to try it out on a few people, or just go ahead exercising your fuller, more natural voice nonstop?" They claimed matters should improve within weeks if I chose the latter. The thought of a completely new pitch, overnight—at home, school, and handball practice—was almost unfathomable, and the insecurity crept in. What about my character? What about the impression I made on others? What if I still couldn't keep my voice steady?

Dad arrived home second, after me, and stopped in the kitchen to say hello. He missed a beat when I replied. Coming in third, Kåre took a seat on the sofa, settling in with the newspaper, before Dad said, "Kåre, I think you're failing to spot something in the kitchen."

My brother stood up. "Huh? In the kitchen?" Striding in, he casually tossed out a "Hey, what's up?" to me.

I was frying fishcakes, said hello, and kept my composure. Today Mum was the last to arrive. Dad filled the water glasses on the dinner table and my brother sat nearby, alert for her reaction. And then I did what I did each time another family member came home and entered the room: I merely answered "hello." Explanations were hardly needed.

On the way to school the following day, I rang Otto's doorbell and repeated my trick. Surprises resulted in class and between classes; I even got a few "congratulations." During lunch, kids hung around me, amused, as more people reacted to the news of the pigeon with the bass voice and dared me to say something, anything.

Though a little coarse at first, the new voice steadied itself. The novelty of shocking people with it eventually wore off. I went to the printer. I bicycled to handball practice. And I visited the speech therapist, for one last time. On the surface of things, my years of puberphonia were a thing of the past. At long last, I was ready for that much-delayed phone call.

5

SEARCHING THROUGH THE phone directory under the name Larsen, I looked for a street in the right part of town that would trigger my memory. I came across a man and a woman at the same address, the Bodø boy's parents, presumably. More than a year had passed since Jonny sent me his letter. I assumed he'd given up on hearing from me and put the whole thing out of his mind.

As I was scribbling down their phone number, my brother slouched into the living room, stopped, and asked, on a whim, if I wanted any spaghetti.

I tensed up and told him no. It didn't take him long to start a pot though. He threw in the pasta and, before the water began to sound, returned to the basement. He asked no other questions. Relieved, I memorized the number, tore up the note, crumpled each piece, and threw them into the kitchen bin.

Dad's workstation stood right next to the most secluded phone outlet in the house. Kåre would hear a beep if I picked up the living room phone. For almost three years, I'd rehearsed my secret to-do list. And so I'd grant myself one final night of figuring out what to say.

There wasn't such a thing as one's own sweet time; that much had been proven to me. Ambition, goals, and—most importantly—purposeful, persistent effort were necessities.

Nineteen hours later, I rushed back from school through the blue snow, for now my turn had arrived to occupy Dad's office chair in the basement. In the future, this would be the time to meet—unmonitored, free from parental intrusions. The only obstacle I could think of now was that Kåre liked to play computer games in the mid-afternoon and could show up at any moment.

There I sat, going over my lines. No, it wasn't like me to wait for things to happen in their own due course—how *does* one thing lead to another? I left the electric heating fan off. It produced a steady murmur that might hide the sound of my brother's approach. I picked up the receiver and, losing the dial tone, cursed myself for taking so long. I had to prepare haddock gratin for dinner. It needed to be served at 3:45 p.m.

Another twenty-three hours went by. As usual when I trotted home in the snow, landing lights lined up in the far distance—passenger planes closing in from the south along the rugged coastline. It was, once again, that peaceful, private hour after school, full of anticipation and endless possibility. I didn't fear the prospect of the boy's siblings answering the phone—if he even had any. I believed I could talk my way out of smaller questions like "Who are you?" and "How do you know my brother?" Unless Jonny had a late class, he too was probably home from school. His parents were most likely still at work; it was that sweet, unmonitored time of day.

I tried to whip up my courage. In the process my tracksuit pants landed on the floor. I tried to keep my feet warm on a piece of lamb fur under the desk. I eventually raced back and forth between the downstairs bathroom mirror and the phone. I kept that frenetic pacing up until I thought I heard someone outside—maybe Mum or Dad parking the car. I pulled up my pants and shoved my boxers inside my pocket, and just in case it was my brother, I turned on a computer game.

I couldn't concentrate, not even at a computer game. Through the tiny basement window I saw nothing but snowdrift and frozen branches. So I ran upstairs, two steps at a time, to inspect our lot from the kitchen. With each step, the pressure of the waistband forced my foreskin aside a little further. Through the exposed slit, a shiny pearl emerged. The overpowering odor matched the sensation of the waistband movement. I saw nothing in the front yard but my own fresh footsteps in the violet snow.

Back downstairs, I dialed his number without delay. A youthful sounding, masculine voice answered.

"Larsen," he said.

Taken aback by his brisk tone and use of the family name, I couldn't remember his first name. "Hi, this is Kurt. Can I talk to … the seventeen-year-old boy in the house?" He was probably seventeen by now, I reasoned, maybe even eighteen, so when he didn't answer, I asked the same question one more time.

Now speaking in a sensitive, almost hollow tone he said, "There's no such person in this house."

"Are you sure? Because I need to speak to him. I'm not a salesperson."

But no, he was positive. I asked if he was eighteen by any chance.

"Huh? You must have called the wrong number."

I apologized, hung up, and regretted my hasty reaction at once—I'd planned to mention the ad. "You know, the one you responded to." That would be neutral enough. If he asked, "Which ad?" I could answer, "Did you respond to more than one?" He might be the wrong brother though, so I had to be cautious. Who knows, perhaps I had a pair of skis to sell. First of all, I should ask whom I was speaking to. I was pretty sure I'd recognize his name if I heard it. Then I'd have him. Next, I needed to determine if anyone was listening in. In that case, I'd simply tell him to take note and meet me after dinner.

Fortunately, the same boy answered when I called a second time. "Hi, it's me again. Are you sure there's no seventeen- or eighteen-year-old boy in the household?"

A moment of hesitation ensued before he replied that a person who was sixteen lived there. I took that admission as an encouraging sign and asked, "Are you that person?" This he confirmed. I then asked if he had any idea who I was. He did.

He asked, "Are you the one I wrote to?" The words made me shudder with anticipation. He sounded friendly enough, but he didn't volunteer to speak.

We'd gotten one huge step closer, but an awkward silence suffused the air before I remembered my line. "I'm sorry, but I've forgotten your name."

"That's okay."

"Well, I'm Kurt."

He didn't answer and I couldn't get out the words to nudge him into revealing his name. Upstairs, the click of the lock told me Kåre was home. Changing my tactics, I cut to the chase.

"Do you want to meet?"

"When?"

"Today. After dinner."

"So soon? This comes a little out of the blue."

"Do you have a girlfriend?"

"No."

"So can we meet?"

"I don't know. I don't think it's so smart. It's been a while since I wrote that letter."

In Kåre's room, the backpack fell to the floor. Seconds later, he was stumbling down the stairs, whistling some made-up tune.

"I have to go," I whispered. "I'll call you later."

"No, you'd better not."

There was no time to challenge him. My brother, seeing me by the computer, sighed and retraced his steps. Pausing on the staircase, he shouted, "Are you going to be long?"

"I'll tell you when I'm done."

I struggled to collect my thoughts. What *was* his name? Jim? Jens? Jan? Jakob? Jon? Joachim? Jonas? The phone made a clicking sound. I gathered that Kåre, now in the living room, called Mum for dinner instructions. Moments later he returned downstairs for potatoes and carrots. Now, how could I make my fellow Bodø boy overcome his shyness? How could I get him to realize that he shouldn't let himself miss out on this opportunity? When Kåre was done in the food storage room, I called a third time. A young girl answered this time. That made it trickier. I tried to sound as nonchalant as possible.

"Hi, it's Kurt. May I speak to your brother?"

"You mean Jonny?"

"Yah … Jonny!"

How could I've forgotten?

A door closed; Jonny was back.

"Yah, hello?"

No, I wasn't going to let him off the hook easily. I had no intention of starting over, opening another mailbox, posting a new ad, and working my way through more letters from old guys all over Norway and Sweden. After all, he'd been the one who'd gotten in touch with me in the first place.

He might not know it yet, but I was certainly better looking than he! If anyone was supposed to be picky, it was I!

This time I asked him straight out, almost accusingly, "Are you sure you don't want to meet?"

More dreadful silence hung between us as Jonny fiddled with the receiver. And then he gave in. He didn't want to meet today, nor in the Glasshouse, the covered pedestrian street in the middle of town. Fewer people mulled at the bus station down by the harbor, he said, and he'd show up there tomorrow at six in the afternoon.

The whole conversation lasted less than a minute, but finally everything fell into place. It was really happening. I wouldn't even have to skip tonight's handball practice, or my homework, although I'd have a hard time concentrating or getting any asleep.

Tomorrow I'd meet a dark-haired boy just under my height. And soon afterward, I'd remove his blue and yellow all-weather jacket and get down to some serious boy fun.

6

THAT VERY NEXT day, right after school, Roy, another one of my classmates, called. We'd attended the same classes all day long and hadn't talked then. Now suddenly he wanted to catch up, go to the swimming pool together—this afternoon in fact.

"Kurt, what's on your mind? I'm ready whenever!"

Never before had we spoken on the phone; not once had we hung out in our spare time. The stark unlikelihood of it all struck me as incomprehensible and highly suspicious.

He wasn't particularly popular, but he assumed a superior air nonetheless. Relying on innuendo, he gave an impression of dislike and flirtation at the same time—a strange way to treat anyone, let alone someone you barely knew. Was there talk? I wondered. Was I being discussed? Were my classmates making unfair assumptions about me only because I had, until recently, sounded like a girl?

All day at school I'd struggled to hold my composure. I'd let apprehension twirl into hope, then charge into panic. Showering, followed by a dip in the pool after dinner, would freshen me up and keep my mind on track. Plus, I wouldn't need to talk my way out of any unexpected chores that popped up around the house—like doing the dishes.

Unsure of what he really wanted, I accepted his invitation.

Was he teasing me in the hope that I'd give myself away, so he could humiliate me in class? My parents knew Roy's name, so his company provided an entirely valid excuse for being away for the rest of the evening. I arranged to meet him outside the swimming pool no later than 4:30 p.m., which was early but fine with him.

As I prepared dinner—fish balls in white sauce—in my head the plot, much like the mixture in the pot, thickened. Roy had played in the school band in primary school; he and Jonny might actually know each other. What if more than a year ago Roy and Jonny had come across my ad and decided, out of mean-spirited curiosity, to flush out the local culprit, to downright embarrass him?

What if my classmate somehow knew I was busy at 6:00 p.m. and was attempting to pluck it out of me? If my number had shown up on Jonny's phone display, he could easily have checked with directory assistance and discussed the result with Roy.

I could always blame Kåre. In any case, it would be words against words. My restless mind wouldn't stop crunching through the possible eventualities and their consequences. Why hadn't I thought of using a phone booth when I called Jonny?

Our family dinner conversation proved unusually subdued, as if something—in me, about me—held everyone back. Mum and Dad might have questioned my rush, but having returned home late from the hospital and the bank and grocery shopping, they'd delayed dinner. So as soon as I'd eaten my serving of fish balls, I left the table. When I asked, Dad granted me change from the kitchen coin jar for the pool entrance fee and I grabbed a plastic bag, my swim trunks, and a towel.

Roy, waiting in the artificial lighting outside the cracked concrete building, thought I was crazy to bicycle through the November slush, but how else was I to make everything—dinner, swimming, sexual debut—in one go? Crawling immaculately in a separate lane, he didn't get near me once, and I had to remind myself that there was no reason for him to act so superior. Unless he had his own secrets, or I'd been set up, I'd soon, well ahead of him, become a member of that elusive club of sixteen-year-olds who'd actually had sex. Whoever they were.

He exited the shower quickly and expressed no interest in sitting in the sauna. Yet in the changing room, he invited me to follow him into the air-raid shelter in the adjoining hill, an old German bunker from World War II. "I know an entrance through the bottom of the building and practice archery in there," he explained, playing up the offer. I shrugged and turned him down—I had handball practice in an hour. For once, he looked impressed.

But I was out of time.

I rode away in the weak, flickering glow of my bicycle light, generated by my own pedaling, and prayed that Roy wouldn't make a trip into town on his own. I parked by the SAS Hotel near the harbor, well out of view from the bus station. Not wanting anyone to steal my swimwear, I carried it along, because the bike looked vulnerable on its own along the wall. Then I walked over to the single story station building, a rather provisional wooden structure by the look of it.

On one side of the metal staircase, directly opposite the door to the waiting room, stood a brightly illuminated news agency that was empty of customers. As the only person on the staircase, I could easily be seen from the road. Occasionally, cars passed by, or a lone figure trudged by in the dirty snow. Standing here was out of character for me. I never took the bus. I lived so close to everything that walking to places was faster.

If Mum or Dad for some reason drove by, they'd almost certainly wave me over and offer a lift home. I tried to anticipate their questions, prepare acceptable answers. What was I doing here, waiting for a bus? Okay, so I'd gone into town with Roy ... And I'd deemed it unsafe to cycle because of the slush! Or maybe I hadn't yet decided what to do?

I could tell them I was waiting for someone! But whom? I could come up with no acceptable answer. If they insisted that I jump in the car and I still wanted sex, I'd have to run back here as soon as I got to the house ... I'd have to argue that I'd forgotten something, lost something. No, this sort of overthinking had to stop at once.

My watch read 6:10. Perhaps Jonny had gotten cold feet and stayed home—or something had come up, some last-minute distraction.

A bus from his end of town came in without him. Along the half-frozen sidewalk across the street marched a scrawny town character inappropriately dressed as a soldier. He was a striking sight whenever he appeared and I knew him to be an incessant walker. Maybe my boy had slipped past earlier, over on that side, and not liked what he saw?

He could be a nervous wreck or an arrogant, unreliable snob. Lingering on, I decided I'd attract less attention below the lit stairs. If anyone I knew came by and my bus arrived, I'd waste money on a ticket and get off at the first stop—unless they planned to catch the same departure. Then I'd pretend to wait for someone from out of town.

I resolved to leave at 6:35 and find out what had come over Jonny by calling first thing after school tomorrow. Soon enough I was brooding over whether to extend my deadline by another fifteen minutes—and then suddenly a door opened, startling me. The toilet entrance, wedged between the other two doors, faced the parking lot. Since I hadn't noticed anyone walk in all this time, I instantly turned, anxious to see if it might be Jonny.

An elderly lady in a fur hat stopped in her tracks and asked if I was waiting to get in. To enter, you needed a five kroner key, available at the agency, but the woman was holding the door for me so I nodded in affirmation to see if Jonny might be inside. The men's room lay before me deserted—yet there were two stalls he and I could hide in. That meant privacy.

I shuddered at the stench of tobacco and urine so I walked back out but kept the door open with my foot.

Was I starting to look suspicious hanging here so long? Two older girls with shopping bags in tow threw me a quick look as they came out of the news agency. And then another bus pulled in, scattering its passengers across the parking lot, so I removed my foot from the door. The driver left the engine rumbling, and while he took a smoke in the slush, the fumes swirled toward me.

During that prolonged moment, a lone boy approached across the lot, from the town center. My own age no doubt. He wore a yellow and navy blue Helly Hansen jacket and, apparently not sure whether to proceed into the kiosk, slowed down before reaching the flight of steps. I spoke his name, cautiously.

There we stood, surveying each other without making eye contact.

His hair, sticking out from under his winter hat, was long and splintery. But what really caught my eye were his pigskin moccasins, the kind preferred by old alcoholics in the Glasshouse. He pulled off his mitten and offered me a piece of chewing gum. At first I declined, but then I thought better of it—clean breath was a good idea. When I proposed picking up the key to the toilet, he gave me a puzzled look. I explained that we'd be alone in the bathroom. No, he wanted to go somewhere nicer. "Okay … where?" He had no idea. As we stepped off the staircase, he asked if I'd done this before. "Absolutely not."

"Sorry … you just seem to know your way around this." He studied me. "Didn't you get many replies?"

"Apart from you, only from old pigs out of town. I threw them away."

Jonny had written only that one letter. He added that he hadn't, in fact, tried anything sexual before.

"Me neither," I admitted.

Walking on in the slush, we didn't discuss our school affiliations. Conversation, such as it was, came in bits and pieces. After months without a reply, he'd concluded that nothing would come of his letter. Needless to say, he grew a bit overwhelmed when I finally called. I asked if he marched in the May Seventeenth parade. He did, every year. He played wind instruments, mostly the euphonium, and National Day, he explained, was the year's biggest marching band event.

Did we absolutely have to go somewhere indoors? Jonny thought so.

The only indoor place he could think of, away from the Glasshouse, was the town library in Dronningens Gate, just a few blocks away. The library had a public restroom and was open until 7:30. I could come up with no better alternative and accepted his suggestion, even though it wouldn't leave us with much time.

We entered the stone building quietly. He waited by the restroom door while I picked up the key from the loans desk.

Although it wasn't really a place meant for two people, the

crammed toilet was clean and odor free. I stacked my plastic bag, scarf, and jacket on the sink. Following suit, Jonny uncovered a flannel shirt, the top button fastened. Pressed against his head were some thick, rather impressive curls. We stood on separate sides of the washbasin. I spat my gum into the wastebasket and couldn't help but glimpse his moccasins. He kept his gum and I listened to his chewing, staring at his fly now and then. Should I open it?

"They might get suspicious outside," he said.

"Why? No one saw me take the key."

"But what if someone knocks on the door?"

"Then be quiet."

No, he simply couldn't be quiet. "It's a bit impersonal in here. It's difficult to talk."

"We're not supposed to talk. Someone could hear us."

"What if they see us leave together?"

"You go first and I'll follow in a minute."

"Now?"

"No, not now. Afterward …"

I knew I'd regret it later if nothing happened. The tidiest solution, I decided, was to just spurt our loads into the toilet. But there really wasn't enough room for two people by the toilet bowl, and I didn't want to leave my clothes on the floor or the toilet lid. That made the sink option out of the question too. There was, of course, the trash bin or the linoleum floor, but that seemed dirty. That's not to mention the stupefied numbness I felt the entire time that completely killed any sensation of horniness.

A pool of melted snow slowly expanded between us and I couldn't get myself to meet his eye or make a move. Jonny must have felt the same way.

"Why don't we wait for a better occasion?" he suggested.

"Yah, maybe."

Reluctantly, I watched him get dressed, and he departed first, as planned. As I locked the door behind him and started to count down my sixty seconds, I spotted a hook for clothes and realized the sink option could've worked after all. I checked my watch: 7:12, barely time enough, but surely sufficient for a first experience. Jonny, however, had disappeared. Seeing nary a single person, not even a librarian, I hesitated: Should I hold on to the keys? I returned them to the counter and hurried down the stairs, anxious to find him. My surreptitious exit felt like I was departing a crime scene—yet nothing had taken place. Fortunately, Jonny hadn't left me behind; he was waiting outside, under the roof overhang. It had started snowing, and we watched the flurries for a moment. "Should we try one more time? For a few minutes?"

He burst out, rather curtly, "It's getting late." But I could think of other, less imminent opportunities—we should meet at home after school to listen to, or maybe dance tight to, Burt Bacharach instrumentals. Or we might go for a swim and then search for the entrance to that air-raid shelter. For now, I asked if he wanted to take me for a run sometime. "Only when the weather gets warmer," he offered.

Now, that called for some patience. He took off his mitten and wanted to shake my hand to say goodbye.

7

THE SENSATION OF his hand, in mine, lingered on as I scurried down Storgata. Making my way through the snowdrift, I guessed that Jonny too was heading back toward the bus station, along Dronningens Gate, one block up.

A single bus idled in the parking lot, lights on, ready to leave. I hastened to look for him, the lone boy among the few passengers who were staring blankly out the windows. Sitting there next to him, feeling his warm thigh against mine, and not talking—that could make all the difference in the world!

When I reached the bus entrance and realized I had the wrong line, the driver noticed my disappointment. He gave me a sympathetic look.

On the wall next to the toilet door a thumbtack held a timetable in place. His likely route, I discovered, left at 7:20—ten minutes ago. No wonder he'd said goodbye so hastily. Living that close to the edge of town, he probably knew the schedule by heart.

With an hour between each departure, it dawned on me that Jonny hadn't absolutely needed to walk down here at all. There was a stop right next to the library. There was, of course, the slight chance he had missed his 7:20 departure and still remained outside the library. Either that or he walked along the route to keep himself warm. Both possibilities crossing my mind, I had an urge to look for him on my bicycle. I prayed that no one had stolen it.

I wasn't wearing a hat, and the lingering droplets from the shower had frozen in my hair. A pain had begun to build inside my ears. I brushed the fresh snow off me. I couldn't get myself to go home. What if Jonny felt the same way and came to look for me one more time?

Trying to make up my mind what to do, I drifted into the bright light of the news agency. Once indoors, I came to the conclusion that one way or another I needed some sort of closure. Since no one knew my face here, I should at least make the best of the situation and feed my imagination, build courage by means of hormones. And if I read aloud to Jonny at our next rendezvous, I could strengthen his courage too. I had fifty kroner of my own as well as Dad's change from the jar.

When the salesperson, a middle-aged woman, disappeared into the back room, I took the opportunity to locate the porn magazines on a top shelf. I couldn't see *Aktuell Rapport*, but it didn't pass my notice that they even had *Playgirl*. By the looks of the cover, posing men filled its glossy pages. If we'd been a whole gang buying a copy together, it would have seemed like we were playing a practical joke. Right now though, I had to be extremely careful about my pick. Pictures of men only would be exceptionally suspicious; to avoid added attention, both sexes must be present in the magazine I chose.

It finally dawned on me: Why wait months for answers to my own personal ad when I could respond to others immediately? Yah, why mind a trip out of town, and why did the other person have to be my own age anyway, when inexperience only led to awkward inaction? From the doorway, the saleswoman examined me so I nervously turned to the paperbacks and then rushed out of the agency, startled by her scrutiny.

Sadly, there was no sign of Jonny near the parking lot. Holding hands, a man in large boots and a woman in a fur coat walked past me up the stairs—and headed straight for the dirty magazines! Moments later, with a flat plastic bag dangling from their clasped hands, they'd redirected themselves toward the SAS Hotel. To the salesperson, it must have been obvious what I was after. Yet I told myself that she didn't necessarily have to think I was building up the courage to buy porn, when I was really trying to build up the courage to have sex as soon as possible. Indeed, assuming that I wanted to buy porn would be sheer prejudice on her part, for if you were waiting for your bus there was nothing, really, to do around here but idle about.

All I needed to do was act on autopilot, grab a magazine, and pay for it—I hurried back inside and squatted over a handball magazine. Too heavily dressed and sweltering, I stood up and, getting dizzy, walked out once more. To cool down, I zipped open my jacket, loosened my scarf. I then returned indoors. With some rather belligerent movements, the woman busied herself by tidying the stand below the porn. Brushing her way past me, she burst out, "If you're looking to read the publications, you need to buy one." I headed to the counter with the handball magazine; at least there were plenty of photos of strong arms and well-built legs to look at inside.

I should have pursued the couple to their hotel room—why didn't I think of it in time? The fur-dressed woman might have been in her thirties, but the man was younger, in his mid-twenties, and good-looking. As long as he wasn't ugly or too weird or way too old, I'd be fine. The saleswoman took her time, but finally came over to the register to count my money. "I'm quite surprised," she exclaimed. "You didn't dare to steal it after all?" I met her eyes defiantly, unable to utter a sound. "Well then, do you need a plastic bag?" I didn't, and in any case I was utterly lost for words. What's more, I could feel my face flushing. When I left the magazine and my money behind, she too looked quite disconcerted.

The toilet door slammed open on the metal staircase. Ignoring the apologies of a bearded old man in huge rain boots, I pushed my way past him as I felt the tears building. Inside the stall—still hot from the previous occupant—I arranged my belongings on a hook, tracksuit pants and boxer briefs on top of my plastic bag and outerwear. I might be an emotional yo-yo, but I could take care of my own needs.

According to the trash on the floor, this was a place for drinking hard liquor, smoking hand-rolled tobacco, and reading piles of tabloid newspapers while one waited for the next departure—the public sort or the not so freely broadcasted sort. Despite the less-than-erotic atmosphere, my foreskin grew surprisingly sensitive and I quickly developed an erection. Spreading my legs to each side of the toilet bowl, I found myself dreaming of Jonny yanking away my hand and taking control. Proud of my appearance, I studied and massaged my strained muscles. No longer in a rush, I concluded that Jonny Larsen was missing out—because he was too hesitant. Shame on him! My sneakers squeaked and my flapping foreskin sounded like a dog lapping water from the toilet bowl. I'd delay the moment of shooting and flushing as long as I could.

A key entered the lock and I froze. Was there a tiniest chance Jonny had paid his way in here to look for me? By the sounds of it, another old man was the more likely intruder. His lungs sounded in ill condition as he strode into the adjoining stall and ripped off immense amounts of toilet paper. He sat down and let out a big fart, groaned gleefully, and flushed a couple of times. Then he turned disturbingly quiet. Resolving to wait him out, I made an effort not to squeak with my rubber-soled shoes. If I changed position, I might alert him to my guilt-ridden presence. I closed my eyes and tried to think of Jonny naked. My legs ached. Suddenly I felt something caress my crotch.

When I looked down, the man was eyeing me through a small hole in the lower wall: A bulging eyeball flicked back and forth, hunting for a better view. I had no idea how long he'd been eyeing me, but he started talking the moment he realized he had my attention. "Ooh, how nice! What a lovely cock!" I made out his mouth, recognized his white beard, and felt his warm breath once more. The man had entered the restroom a second time; he must have thought I was putting on a show. Dumbfounded, I turned away to hide my face.

I had to make it outside ahead of him—I didn't want him to get another glimpse so he'd recognize me later, and I certainly didn't want to create a public scene. Pushing my sneakers through my boxers and my pants, I spoiled both garments. As I grabbed my swimwear, I heard the door hit the wall between us with a loud bang. The effect was unintentional, but it might teach him a lesson I reasoned, splashing for my bike.

8

ANOTHER RISING FEATHER cloud exploded in color as I rushed home from school—up there, actual uninterrupted sunlight hinted of more pleasant jogging conditions elsewhere.

At that instant, I may not have been on the brink of becoming the youngest male sexual pioneer in the neighborhood, yet I wanted, at the very least, to be *normal* and *average*.

My standards had temporarily risen—for nearly two months I'd made no effort to get back in touch with that other Bodø boy. What a fine line there was between exploring the nature of things and reaching total disgrace. I'd needed time to regroup and digest the sequence of events.

Not until well into January 1999 had I made peace with those moments on my own. Once more I found comfort in the anticipation of possibilities. Whenever my tracksuit pants slipped to the floor of my room, Jonny Larsen was never far from my mind. I was, again, increasingly consumed by lust. Remember, Ragnar: he was the boy my own age—for a year and a half he'd been my token of hope. I longed to meet him, longed to hang out with him, longed to see what would happen when we were together and left to our own devices. Kåre would be away in Southern Norway the whole week with his class. It was the first day, in fact, since mid-term test-ing before Christmas, that I had the entire house to myself. Signifi-cantly, my seventeenth birthday—my self-imposed deadline for my sexual coming of age—was rapidly approaching. It was the perfect opportunity for inviting the boy over. 1999 marked the end of my patience. I wanted sexual gratification within the current millenni-um. Hence, I took the opportunity to work through my agonizing basement procedure anew. His sister answered the phone that day; yah, her brother was home.

My heart raced when Jonny picked up and I asked my one, much-rehearsed question: Could we meet again? He just snapped, "*Please*, no more phone calls."

"Okay," I mustered.

I just sat there, in Dad's office chair, and thought of very little. Then I began to fume. I was dealing with one self-inhibiting and off-putting teenager who for unclear reasons didn't want to be re-minded of my existence. Why he had written a letter, teasing me like that in the first place, and included a picture and an address and a phone number, now became a mystery to me, since he had proven to be so weak, cowardly, and ineffectual in person. How long did he plan to continue living in such a wretched state of self-denial? Yah, what was holding him?

January passed and Kåre returned from his class trip. And then February slipped by, too. Yah, for a long time—almost four whole months in fact—I resentfully obeyed Jonny's request.

Then came spring. I studied the marching bands intently during the parades on May 17, but there were just too many rows strid-ing past. The big instruments, uniform hats, and moving limbs ob-structed a glimpse of even the lankiest of boys.

Okay then, no more phone calls, but I still wanted to give my fellow Bodø boy one last chance to prove himself a worthy candi-date. Someone needed to teach Jonny Larsen a lesson or two about enjoying life to the fullest. I—the topnotch choice for some boy fun in this town—was eager to volunteer.

The following day, Mum's lined notepad with her latest memo lay on the bench together with that day's main course from the base-ment freezer, coalfish cakes. I tore off the note and grabbed a pen from the jar. All the things I'd been unable to say over the phone, all the things the stupid boy out there on the outskirts of town was missing out on, I put to paper. Spring had arrived; it was time to make our run, to take him up on his offer. Then, when we finally got sweaty together, in the forest or a deserted street, we'd see what happened.

I had a tendency of writing with a heavy grip when I was in a rush. Not wanting Kåre or my parents to decipher the indentations left by my pen, I tore the underlying sheets to pieces. My intent was to give the paralyzed coward the maximum number of chances to pull himself together. Then, when he eventually did, I'd show him the time of his life.

Playing his new computer game, Kåre made room so I could fetch an envelope and a stamp from Dad's desk. In the kitchen, I read through my enticing letter one more time, adding a final, tantalizing suggestion: "Meet me at 6:00 p.m. at the same place as the last time." I didn't specify the location further. You never knew whose hands a letter might fall into, and you could never be sure how an unintended reader would react. I signed off as Kurt only—I offered no return address. All he needed to do to bring the details on those sheets of ruled paper to life was meet at the specified day and time and then either walk home with me or catch the bus to his place. I bicycled to the post office to ensure next-day delivery, leaving a pot of potatoes to steam on the stove.

And then, two days later, I arrived at our intended meeting place, directly from handball practice, more than ten minutes early. A constant flow of people strode up and down the metal staircase, but no boy looking for fun.

I checked the waiting room, the news agency. No sign of him or the saleswoman from before. I hung by the toilet door and stole my way inside at the first free opportunity. The stench had grown unbearable but the bathroom was empty. I lingered on at the staircase in the warmth of the late sun. In the distance, slowing down at Bodø airport, a fifth successive fighter jet reversed its engines—today I kept track of every sight and sound around me. And it's then that it occurred to me: What if Jonny had mixed up the meeting place and expected me at the library?

I didn't find him there either, though maybe I'd arrived too late. And so that same night I wrote him one last letter, this one stipulating that we meet "on the original metal staircase, the place you suggested yourself, neither at the public library nor inside the Glasshouse." My practice of withholding obvious clues proved too strong; if only I'd added a return address, then at least he could write me a response if he couldn't make it. The letter might still make tomorrow's delivery if I posted it directly at the main post office.

On my way over there, I came across an unrolled condom lying on the ground. The item appeared new—I assumed a gang of high school seniors had played around, blowing it up like a balloon. To take a closer look, ahead of an older woman with uncontrollable limbs, I made a U-turn. Noticing no visible fluids in it, I picked it up by the tip and slid it into my shorts. The struggling woman, another unstoppable walker, didn't look at me twice.

Charged with anticipation, I pedaled on. Even if it were a used condom, I'd clean it thoroughly at home. I'd never owned a condom before, never tried one on, in fact. Now I'd be ready for absolutely anything.

9

WAS I TURNING into the staircase boy?

I tried my best to ignore a white-haired man in sunglasses and leather jacket. This wasn't the person I'd seen before, but he behaved suspiciously nonetheless.

The man entered the toilet whenever someone unlocked the door and each time threw me glances from inside, as if he expected me to follow. He clearly wasn't about to extinguish his hopes. He seemed to think he could win me over with his stares and heavy breathing.

Well, I had hopes of my own.

I'd even brought my condom in my right pocket, just in case. And it was past 6:30. I'd given Jonny more than a day's notice; I'd showed up with my bike and gym bag a quarter of an hour early. Here, enthusiastically waiting for him, was a fit and attractive guy— just ask the white-haired man in sunglasses and leather jacket. I'd even developed a tan from standing so much on the bus stop staircase.

I knew he was there, knew pretty much why he was there. Struggling to pretend otherwise was ridiculous and wearisome. Drifting down the stairs, the older man turned around, eyeing me. I could stand his wooing no longer. If he tried to strike up a conversation, I'd flare up in anger and demand to learn what he was up to.

Across the street from the bus station, a chubby guy in a beanie staggered past—another walker—wincing at the potent early evening sun. I decided this was my final cue to leave.

The moment the old pervert returned up the stairs and brushed past me, I walked off. I made sure he didn't follow. I didn't want my stalker to witness my meeting with Jonny and make his own biased, dirty assumptions about us.

In the end, I wanted my fellow Bodø boy to apologize for leading me on, for making me feel like such a nag, and for turning me into this pathetic staircase boy. At the SAS Hotel, I found a quiet phone booth that accepted coins and, ignoring Jonny's expressed wishes, dialed the memorized number without feeling the slightest bit apologetic. Indeed, I felt strangely relaxed, disturbingly entitled. I mean, what's wrong with talking on the phone? I wanted him to explain himself. If nothing else, I wanted to talk.

Her voice came across as husky. It wasn't his sister; this time his mother had answered.

I introduced myself as Kurt and then asked for Ronny. Bad start.

"You mean my son, Jonny? You said your name's Kurt?"

During the long wait, my own inexplicable lack of caution shocked me—my sentences had been spilling out too quickly. Lacking much of a plan for this burst of spontaneity, I now worried that I'd run out of coins.

Returning to the phone, she explained that Jonny was occupied, but she could take a message—another eventuality I hadn't planned for.

"Could you ask him to call me?"

"Certainly."

She sounded more astonished with each phrase that came out of my mouth. I mentioned that perhaps he didn't have my number, so to be on the safe side, I'd give it to her. Then, lastly, I blurted out that he'd better wait half an hour, because I was out of the house right now.

Although the older man was no longer there to observe me, I felt no less apprehensive as I hurried back to my bike. I'd given out my name as well as my phone number and undoubtedly left Jonny's mother with a pile of questions in the process. Bad finish.

10

THE MOMENT I'D removed my shoes Dad addressed me from the kitchen, his voice raised over the hum of the dishwasher. He said a woman had just been on the phone and was going to call back in a few.

I found him opening the window to air dry the wet casserole containers and dishes on the counter. Somewhere in the neighborhood, kids made noise. I even heard an early lawn mower. My heart sank with each print of my sweaty socks on the laminated floor. I couldn't just stand there. I grabbed a towel and began, almost feverishly, to put away the items. I couldn't bring myself to ask if she had mentioned what the call was about. I feared a peculiar conspiracy at work; I feared they'd engaged in a serious conversation.

Still washing up, Dad didn't say another word about the imminent phone call. He didn't even ask who the woman was.

If he'd been warned, or sensed something alarming, he could pick up in the living room and listen in if I answered the call from the basement. Anyway, it would seem guarded. And for all I knew, my brother was still playing computer games down there. I certainly didn't want *him* by my side. And it would look plain weird if I rushed back upstairs while the phone kept chiming. In other words, I had to answer in the living room, within listening distance of Dad.

Then there was the question of how to behave while on the phone. If I spoke too clearly, he'd be able to hear everything, and if I mumbled my answers, I'd come across as behaving strangely. Hence, I'd have to speak clearly without saying too much.

Should Dad inquire afterward, I planned to tell him that she was a mother in the handball club who wanted me to volunteer to sell waffles at the bingo. Perhaps it really was a mother from the club. It didn't absolutely have to be Jonny's mum.

But of course it was Jonny's mum.

I dried my hands on a terrycloth towel before answering her call. Water still streamed through the tap into the kitchen basin. Utensils clinked about inside the steaming bubbles—Dad's hands at work. If I hung up now, she'd likely phone back.

She took charge of the conversation. "Do you understand what this is about?"

I answered her questions, listened to her monologue:

"Jonny doesn't want to talk to you—do you know why? Are you the one who sent such letters? We want no more of those. Do you understand? So Kurt, can we come to an agreement? Let's agree that you will stop bothering Jonny: no more letters, no more phone calls. Do you hear me? Does it sound fair? Do we have ourselves an arrangement?"

During the conversation, I'd said nothing but *Larsen, yah, yah, yah, okay, goodbye* and I told myself I'd merely taken a message, possibly a bingo instruction. I retrieved the towel from where I had left it.

I knew that Dad—the former accountant—thought it ironic that the club would make the lion's share of its proceeds for the healthy pursuits of local youngsters from a smoke-filled room of retired people. He was unloading the dishwasher and proceeded to fill cold water into the kettle. I was taken aback when he asked, almost as an afterthought, "Do you want some coffee?"

"Dad, I don't drink coffee," I snorted. "You *know* that."

On my way to my room to absently stare at the wall, floor, and ceiling, I regretted my harsh reply. Yet how's a teenage son supposed to react? I'd run out of options and Jonny's mum was on to me.

ACT II (2002)

11

IT WAS FRIDAY the 13th—and I entered one of the tallest structures on campus, depriving myself of the fresh air to cool off with. Students who were smart enough to wear shorts crowded its interior. When I attempted to remove the hooded pullover I had on, the moist T-shirt beneath it got tangled up inside, trapping my head. The garments stuck to my body, and I inadvertently exposed my back.

I couldn't get it off, and I couldn't get it back on. Blinded and self-conscious, I struggled in vain until someone behind me, a boy, yelled, "Oh please, just give it up."

Okay then. I was the thin-skinned, over-interpretative, horny type—a roaming satyr, right? I decided I should just resign myself to remaining in line with my lower body out there and my head trapped inside a pullover.

Because I'd forgotten my belt and carried too much in my pockets, my new jeans were sagging—and my boxers were old, the waistband long ago having lost its elasticity. Hence I knew my ass lay exposed, because I could feel a distinct tickle of air down my cleavage. "No-o!" a girl whined, cracking her gum. "I want to travel. Let's go, let's go!"

"Please, don't nag! It's too late." That was the boy again. "We don't know if our student funding's ready. I don't know where my passport is either."

I clutched my jeans and was contemplating whether to ask for help, when the shock of an alien hand on my naked back straightened my spine. The boy behind me, tall and lanky, withdrew his palm, wiping his fingers on his shorts. The girl accompanying him, squinty-eyed and light on her feet, stepped onto his sneakers. To hold on to her, he grabbed her by the hips. She cracked her gum with her mouth open and stared him deeply into the eyes.

Muttering a barely acknowledged thank-you, I turned away, embarrassed by their unapologetic behavior and affection for each other. Yet I couldn't help but notice their tongue and jaw movements. The exchange, right behind me, of sugary fluid.

They stopped kissing. Undisturbed by the line of students around her, the girl continued, "Think about the prize!" A prize? "If I take this trip we can go anywhere in the world, for a whole year." A whole year?

I hung on their every word. I'd decided to tie the pullover around my waist but then changed my mind and dropped it over my shoulder. Finally, I just shoved the errant piece of clothing into my rucksack on the floor and pushed the old pack forward with my foot, to keep up with the moving line.

The girl had prepared a whole little speech. "We'll never get a chance like this again," she said to her boyfriend. "Never! If my funding has arrived, we're going straight to the travel agency. We ought to have colloquia on the beach and rub each other with sunscreen. All winter! Forget about finding a flat here in Oslo … Think about you and me on the beach. I've had it with the reading hall. Why am I in it? To prepare for the world, right? Life's nothing but preparation! I'm sick of preparation. Just so you know, you can't stop me. Just wait up for me by midnight tomorrow. I'll do this for us both."

The last syllable of her tirade, both, didn't come out quite right. And finally, the couple went quiet.

Indeed, the boy looked horrified when I turned to face them. "So tell me"—I was unable to hold myself back any longer—"what kind of prize are you two talking about?"

The girl gaped at me briefly before speaking. "You'd go with me, wouldn't you?" she asked in a whisper. The chewing gum lisp had vanished and the boy stared conspicuously at my crotch.

12

A SERPENTINE QUEUE of money-hungry students clogged the on-campus bank, too. To save a few minutes, I rushed next-door to the travel agency and drew a numbered ticket there as well, but that was a miscalculation. While I cashed my long-awaited student aid check at the bank, Kilroy Travels inside Café Frederik passed my number.

I held up my paper tag as proof and told the travel agent I needed to get on a plane right away. But the agent, possibly a student working part time, told me to remain in line.

"Let him sneak ahead of me … I can do this later," muttered the grown-up behind me, promptly marching off.

"Thank you," I said—still amazed to be carrying this much money—and devoted my full attention to the counterperson. "I'd like a High Five."

For a second he looked at me in disbelief and then he shouted after the mature-aged student to stop him from leaving. However, the coffee mill was grinding and the noise muffled his cry. Raising my hand for emphasis, I repeated my request.

"No way," the young man snapped. "You can't just leave and expect to be first in line whenever you decide to return. And then expect a High Five."

Could this whole thing be a cruel joke, or an utter misunderstanding? I looked around in despair, but for some reason the amorous couple from the administration building was not around. "It's a special offer," I pleaded. "I just heard about it. If you fly with five different airlines before midnight tomorrow, you get a trip with each company to anywhere in the world for free." A giveaway of that caliber had sounded a little too good to be true. My throat felt tight and ticklish.

"So tell me," he said disbelievingly, "are you planning five trips abroad?"

"He wants a Fly Five!"

The other staff member, an energetic young woman, not only knew what I wanted, she confirmed its existence. "It's the five-year anniversary offer from the Star Alliance Network, and it's hidden away on the websites of the participating airlines," she explained to my agent. "It was in the newspapers last week, while you were in Italy. Why don't we swap customers?"

Impressed, I moved over to the more knowledgeable travel agent. Although her next question—"so where do you want to go?"—took me by surprise, the answer became pretty obvious when I gave it some thought. I finally had my student funding in place, and apart from my art history exams in May of next year, I had no obligations at the university except to collect my next student aid check in January. I longed to spend as much time as possible in shorts on a beach with another boy.

I was prepared for anything to happen, for a full twelve months.

I wanted to make up for lost time.

I ached to get the most out of absolutely everything.

I fancied skipping fall and winter altogether and experiencing spring and summer all over again.

I craved to visit all the exotic places I was missing out on.

I desired to go as far as I could (this thought I voiced out loud).

I sought to get the maximum value for my limited money (this much I also divulged to the travel agent).

To sum things up, I wanted to canvass the entire world for perfect bliss.

At this point, I noticed that my hands were leaving sweat marks on the counter.

"I commend you," she answered swiftly. But today, she added, I probably wanted to make my trips as short as possible, since it was less expensive and I had only thirty-six hours to qualify for the promotion. Furthermore, I should pick my carriers carefully, for the ones I chose now affected where I could go later.

She had some experience in putting together the qualifying itinerary. I got only one trip with each airline I selected from the Star Alliance network. One-way tickets were permissible, and cheaper to students, but I couldn't just buy them and stay home; I needed to board every plane and save my boarding passes too.

Next, all travel had to be booked before October 1 and completed within the following twelve months. An extra ticket was included on the prize journeys—the couple was right, I could bring a friend!—although it had to be the same two travelers on all five award trips.

So, Ragnar, you were in for quite a surprise. I could hardly wait to see your reaction when you realized what you'd tangled yourself into by taking on my company.

We could travel between any destinations covered by the individual airlines and make stopovers too, one per direction. That amounted to a total of fifteen destinations around the globe for me and my lucky friend. We could be away for the entire year!

While the agent's fingers maneuvered me from one airport to the next over the next thirty-six hours, I stressed how important it was that I returned to Oslo as early as 6:00 p.m. tomorrow, because Röyksopp was playing at Rockefeller at 9:00 and you'd bought concert tickets and I'd probably need to shower first.

She laughed at my request. "That's really pushing it! Are you trying to break a record or something? Tell your friend to sell your ticket or give it to me—assuming I can arrange this for you at all."

Then, with an empathic look, she explained that I was about to dash to Asia or America—I'd never been outside of Europe and shivered with excitement. And she sent me off to a photo booth to get a picture for an international student ID; in the meantime, she'd set up my itinerary.

My first stop was Frankfurt—as a big hub, it was a logical starting point. From there, I'd travel on Air Canada to Toronto. She studied her screen and then glanced at the wall clock, which read 11:06 a.m. The Lufthansa flight was scheduled to leave Oslo airport at 1:05 p.m.

She instructed me to head straight for the gates with hand luggage only—and to be aware that if one flight were delayed, an unpleasant domino effect might ensue. I could then miss my later connections and get stuck somewhere in Europe or North America; it would be one close call after another. I wondered aloud if the Toronto flight would be a jumbo jet. She revealed that, yes indeed, there would be two of those.

Tonight, I was set up to travel from Toronto to Washington and Washington to London. Tomorrow, I'd fly from London to Amsterdam, Amsterdam to Copenhagen, and then finally, Copenhagen back to Oslo. The SAS flight would touch down on the Norwegian tarmac at 8:40 p.m. Quite an itinerary.

If I were able to argue that a delay was somehow an airline's fault, Star Alliance would probably let me qualify anyway. But if I failed to board my first flight from Oslo's airport, she doubted they'd feel obliged to help. Corporate entities weren't responsible for no-shows, she cautioned. Boarding would cease twenty minutes before takeoff; in other words, I had little more than an hour and fifteen minutes to get from the University of Oslo to the correct gate at Oslo Airport. I could hear Mum and Dad's list of objections with this one on top: I had absolutely no margins.

While the agent cut out a surprisingly nice-looking portrait and glued it to my ID card, a moment of second thoughts overcame me. Although the qualifying trip was cheaper than she'd anticipated, 14,998 kroner constituted the lion's share of my current installment—almost half of my fall funding—and I was flooded with an impulse to listen to my parents' concerns and stride off, despite the drudgery I'd just caused the helpful Kilroy representative. Picturing you and me naked in your tent, I braced myself and managed to pull out fifteen thousand-kroner bills from my jeans.

The representative wanted me to double-check the itinerary and compare arrival and departure times in case she had made mistakes, but I was unable to concentrate on anything except the wall clock behind her. She handed me my two kroner change. "You get right to the airport express train now," she ordered, smiling encouragingly. "Don't even think about saving money by taking the bus or the regional train. And *don't* forget your passport."

Fortunately, I'd been careful enough to bring the document with me to Oslo—my important papers were tucked inside Dad's Norwegian-English dictionary and the book lay buried somewhere in my room in Hafrsfjordgata.

13

AFTER IT STOPPED working, I no longer wore Dad's old watch. Yet I kept checking my wrist and cursed myself each time for doing so, because I needed to hold on to my jeans.

My original plan on Friday, September 13 had been to park my bike in the city center and take the free bus from Oslo Central Station to IKEA to buy office supplies. In the end, that arrangement would have to wait—because all opportunities come with deadlines. Mine would pass at midnight when Saturday, September 14, 2002 turned into Sunday, September 15, 2002. And so I jumped.

With my passport in place, and for the first time since I moved to the capital, I descended the stairs and ran down the sidewalk to catch the bus. Obviously I'd want to save the maximum money for my year of travel and stay away from Norwegian taxis. But where are they when you need them?

Bygdøy Allé was undergoing reconstruction, and the regular bus stop, near the Swiss Embassy, had been removed. A poster indicated a thirty-meter walk to a temporary stop, near the Polish Embassy in the opposite direction from the Central Station, but no replacement sign and no workers could be seen. A suit-clad elder, speaking in a refined Northern accent, wanted to know if I too was looking for the bus stop; he suspected the transit company had forgotten to put one up. Perhaps the arrow pointed in the wrong direction? An empty taxi, slowing for a red light, took off before I had a chance to come to my senses and flag it down.

Fetching my bike required a five-minute run, and my landlady, Eli, had warned that it would get stolen or ruined if left outdoors in the city center overnight. Other bus stops, of course, existed along the way, so I started jogging. But sure enough, as soon as I passed the Latvian Embassy, I recognized the unmistakable, prolonged squeaking of bus brakes behind me. 30 Nydalen let off a passenger at the regular, currently unmarked, location.

With my backpack bouncing up and down on my shoulders, I rushed into the street to block the driver's way. He gave me a dissatisfied look, but to my relief he opened the front entrance. He too may have been a student, a rather handsome one, I couldn't help but observe. I immediately asked if he drove past Oslo's Central Station. The answer was no. "So which bus stops there?"

He sighed. "This one does. In fact, they all do."

This driver made a point of speaking in puzzles. Now he demanded to know whether I was getting on or not. The older traveler was catching his breath on the stairs behind me and snapped, "You're stopping at the wrong location." However, the driver ignored him, and when I retrieved a clammy thousand-kroner bill from my pocket, he sighed with increased exasperation.

"You want a single ticket? I don't have change for a single ticket. A flexi-card with eight journeys is a much better buy," the quarrelsome one behind the wheel said to me.

I could hardly wait to tell you about today's events, Ragnar! I gave in, accepted his suggestion, and without removing my backpack, dropped into the first available seat. Next, the young driver scolded my fellow passenger, for he too held out a thousand-kroner bill. "Pay the exact fare, or leave the bus right away. Give me twenty kroner or get off! You're causing a delay."

Stupefied, the old man just stood there.

"Are you deaf or senile? Good God, how I hate these North-Norwegians … You can walk!"

"You're stopping at the wrong location," the senior repeated.

"The temporary bus stop's moved and impossible to find, and you're the rudest pup I've ever come across." Red in the face, he strode defiantly down the aisle, mumbling that he'd done enough for the country as it was and deserved a free ride for once.

Then, with a crackle, the driver's voice emerged from the loud-speaker. He declared that the bus wouldn't move until either the hanger-on left of his own free will or the police showed up. "I've experienced this before," one teenage boy said to another in front of me. "The bus might be stuck here for an hour."

The two teenagers got to their feet and disappeared outside. Again I considered scrambling for my bike. Instead—eager to help find a quick solution—I rose and stamped my brand new flexi-card one time extra. Busy speaking on the radio, the driver ignored me. So I tore the paper in two pieces and passed half to the older passenger, who to my surprise shoved my hand away and then obstinately stared out the window. On the positive side, I'd won the support of the only other passengers left on the bus. In the back, two middle-aged women sighed in disapproving unison.

"Please," I said to the man, about to bribe him with a curled-up thousand-kroner bill as well. "I'll miss my plane. And if I do, I might have to quit my studies. So please?"

Luckily, the old man gave in before it came to a money exchange. And the driver must have been watching in his mirror, for in the next instant, with the door still open, we accelerated away from the sidewalk.

A digital clock in the ceiling gave the time as 12:03 p.m.—but each timepiece in the city showed a different time. According to a clock occupying an entire wall, I'd already lost my 14,998-kroner investment and my chance at supreme adventure, so I got out my cell phone, which had turned itself off during my earlier stumble.

These were only the first of my troubles. Abruptly, as we waited for a stoplight to change along our route, the driver left his seat and marched down the aisle, shaking his index finger at the senior. "I just talked to central dispatch. They told me the stop hasn't been moved."

"Then why don't you go back and read the announcement?"

"You wouldn't dare to," one of the women butted in from the back. "Drive on if you care about your job at all!"

Yet the driver didn't seem to care. Cars were honking, the door remained open, and for a long second I was about to make a run for it. At last, with another big sigh, the uniformed transit employee returned to the front and closed the exit.

At the following stop, Frogner Church, a whole crowd of passengers waited to board. Two junkies on rollerblades, both incredibly tall and bony, plunged into the seats right behind me. The conflicting rhythms of their Walkmans proved impossible to block out, and I shifted restlessly. From my window seat, I noticed another teenage boy across the road, speaking on his phone and waving at the driver while impatiently looking for an opening in the traffic. Did he really expect us to sit tight for him? To my great approval the overly hopeful rider's appeal was ignored. Bustling with passengers, the bus gained velocity at last. Yet within seconds, someone yelled, "Stop the bus! Stop the bus!"

Evidently, we'd now skipped a stop. The driver scratched his finger and blew air onto his microphone. "Relax, everyone. We're on our way to Fredrikstad nonstop to visit my parents and my three sisters. Expected arrival time is in ninety minutes, traffic permitting."

His Fredrikstad dialect came through and by now he seemed to struggle with more than just anger issues. Sounding completely out of himself, he informed us that he had a message for a young passenger from Northern Norway.

"Larsen from Bodø … we won't stop until you show me your valid ticket and tell me you still love me."

I couldn't grasp what I was hearing. I still don't understand what went through my mind. It felt like I'd been gutted, like all my nasty secrets had spilled out of me, in front of all those strangers.

Waiting passengers jumped aside as we sped past a second bus stop. We were now approaching the Norwegian Nobel Institute, a small yellow building. One of the giant junkies dragged himself forward, shouting, "I'll talk to the driver!" to the other.

Holding on to the seat in front of me, I struggled to get things right. If the driver was really addressing me, how could he know my family name—and how could he love me?

That website, Gaysir.no. That was the only possibility I could think of—Gaysir. Had I chatted with him there sometime in the last year? Had he somehow spied on me and found out my name? A boy on Gaysir once warned me that I should be careful about meeting him because he thought he could fall in love with me. Was it he? The driver hit the brakes in a roundabout and effectively dispatched the junkie.

As the latter landed on the floor, I found myself staring at the bulging tendons of his lower arm, at his disturbingly flat ass, and completing his long-winded sentences, as the addict complained about the state of public transportation in Oslo. And then, after several long sobs, the driver went on: "Jonny—I love you."

Turning my head, I finally spotted my fellow Bodø boy. Jonny clutched a Coke bottle behind a man and a woman who were lifting up their fallen suitcases. He kept pressing the backdoor opener. He looked so much sharper and taller since the last time I'd seen him.

We'd come to a complete standstill, and the young man in the front seat added, "I've changed my mind. We won't move until you come forward and tell me that you love me too."

"Jonny Larsen from Bodø," shrieked the woman in the back. "Whoever you are, would you be so kind to save us from this mad-man?" The capital might be the shortest way out of the country and might be brimming over with opportunities, but it was starting to feel more than a little claustrophobic.

The fallen giant, barely back on his feet, brushed past me with an outright panicked expression on his face. We'd parked outside the American Embassy—a landmark building protected by wires, rein-forced concrete barriers, fences, security cameras, and sci-fi-look-ing communication equipment. Out of the dark, imposing building emerged several machine–gun toting guards. Jonny Larsen rushed forward as people began screaming. "Lars, here's my ticket … but I don't love you!"

"No, listen—I just want you to love me back. Okay?"

"It doesn't work that way…. Lars, please, open the door."

I could barely hear the two of them over the din. An apprehen-sive security guard knocked on our front door.

Further commotion unfolded in the back. A passenger had suc-cessfully pried open the rear exit, and now Jonny broke loose. Lars, the driver, at long last released the front entrance as the lead guard shouted, "Go! This bus can't stand here."

Jonny Larsen climbed over the cement wall and took off on the sidewalk—within seconds, we'd overtaken him with open doors, but he avoided looking in our direction. The old man and I, the sole passengers left on board 30 Nydalen, were also the only ones to hear Lars's frantic call, "Jonny … don't leave me like this."

14

WHEN I RETURNED from the bathroom, I found you guarding two plastic cups of white wine at the bar, much less than I'd asked for. Confusion bordering on unhappiness engulfed your face when you handed me the change from my thousand-kroner bill—they didn't sell it by the bottle.

I knew it would sound rushed, but I had to get to my question—plant my seed—while I still had the courage. I wanted you drunk and easily convincible, and there wasn't much time.

"The wine's trembling," I said. "Let's fix that." And we toasted. "I think you should obliterate my debt, treat me to this concert, and give me another 4,500 kroner." With only one warm-up band, Röyksopp would arrive on stage any second. Distracted by the smell of my armpits, and your not offering any easy-to-read responses, I pulled out the crumpled ticket and laid it on the counter between us, pointing at all the different destinations on my itinerary. "Look … I've been getting around since yesterday—Frankfurt, Toronto, Washington, London, Amsterdam, and Copenhagen. What have you been up to?"

Yah, I was still brimming with confidence.

You'd been so good to me, and in return, I'd offer you a ticket to the world, my world, for full a year. Crossing the Atlantic twice in twenty-four hours changes everything, I thought.

I was prepared to cross all sorts of boundaries with you.

I wanted you to be my sounding board in all matters of intimacy.

I ached to tell you exactly how I felt.

Above all, I wanted to be sincere with you.

You wanted to know if I was involved in some kind of trafficking. "Yadda, yadda. Go ahead and think that way about me if you want to." When you remarked, coolly, that the price, including taxes, was 14,998 kroner, I snapped, "It's a Fly Five ticket. It's really cheap." But the moment you moved your foot in between my legs, to rest it on my stool, my mild irritation subsided, and I pictured you in a pair of shorts on a deserted beach in Australia.

I wondered if you tanned easily and gestured at your glass. Bushed, I signaled to the bartender that I wanted four more such glasses and, taking a cue from other customers, two cups of chili nuts. Whenever I closed them, my eyes vacillated beneath their lids. I'd hardly slept since my departure.

I assured you that I could pay back everything I owed and asked if you'd heard of Fly Five. No? Neither had the Canadian immigration officers—they'd even taken me aside in a back room and demanded to know why I was entering their country with hand baggage only. I'd quickly been established as "another one of those Norwegians, what the hell is going on?"

I'd thought carefully over the proposal. If we slept in your tent, we'd save lots of money. And so I walked you through my plan. Did you think it would be possible to camp directly on the beach? You wondered, quite correctly, if I were trying to make you drunk. And I wondered—almost heard myself asking—if you had muscular thighs. You seemed to in those cargo pants.

Could you read my mind? The colorful spotlights on stage tracked across my field of vision, leaving me nauseated. Even your jaws shifted in a curious way. The expression subtly changed the shape of your temples and the way your crewcut reflected the light. I asked you to go heavy on the chili nuts, like me, demonstrating by throwing them down by the handful. In anticipation of the headliners, we took a glass in each hand and tried to make it through the crowd. "I'm sorry," I said, "but tell me if I stink. I haven't had a chance to shower since yesterday morning."

Suddenly you shouted in my ear, "Do you feel it swaying? If everyone jumped at the same time, we'd plummet through the floor."

"What do you mean?"

"It's the wooden lid of an old swimming pool. Either we drown, or it will simply be a hard fall to the bottom."

I wasn't through convincing you, though. "Hey, we'll save heaps of money by going away. I mean, at least it'll be a much more exciting way to spend the same amount of money."

"Can you still afford your room at Frogner?" you shouted back above the din.

"No. I really can't. Everything's too damned expensive here in Oslo." To this you didn't reply, so I yapped on. "Admit to me that you're the adventurous type. You want to cover territory, fill in all the white spots on the map."

"The adventurous type? Well, you seem like the restless kind." Could you please show a little excitement about the prize?

"Well, that's because we have to decide quickly. You see, we need to order all our tickets before October 1. Then we could study on the beach. Rub each other with sunscreen. I bet you can't reach every part of your body with your own hands …"

"What? You can't be serious …"

Okay, so I'd gone too far, but fortunately, we were also out of time. The band entered the stage and we were thrust forward by the mass of bodies. Losing a cup, I grabbed the waist of a girl and finished the other wine as fast as I could, standing wide-legged for balance. I certainly didn't want us to crash through the floor. The next wave forced us rearward—and a boy with an enviably straight back suddenly appeared in front of me. Determined to stay put, I grasped hold of his thigh for support.

Perhaps I was just a part of the crowded pack engulfing him. Perhaps he didn't care, but each surge from the mob brought my fingers closer to his crotch.

He was certainly more responsive than you at the moment. It was impossible, however, to tell whether he was developing an erection. Given the thickness of his jeans, I'd have to squeeze pretty hard to find out more. Was he really grinding his butt against me? I wasn't going to move one centimeter. You were engrossed with the show, by the looks of it, and also the only one who knew me there—I felt, for the moment, completely anonymous. You finally said something in my ear. Then I heard you. "Your pants are down."

Mortified, I yanked them back up. "These trousers drive me crazy!" To my luck, my cell phone and airplane ticket remained in my pocket.

You didn't seem amused. "What's going on?" you whispered with moist lips into my ear. "Your boxers looked like a tent."

"Oh, come on, I just love this music so much." I gave you a feral look. "Let me be your tent pole in Australia."

"Kurt! Stop it!"

You seemed preoccupied, distant, and pale. Your jaws moved even when you weren't talking. And you were suddenly spilling wine all over us.

And unless I gathered all my strength, you'd drag me to the floor with you. The second your face changed color—it seemed to be going dark blue—I panicked. I'd never been so terrified—I'd made you faint, I'd poisoned you. Your body jerked, you struggled to inhale, and as I held on to you, something warm seeped through your pants.

Yet no one seemed to pay attention. Other people kept bumping us with their movements. Eventually an older guy took notice and helped me transport you to the wall, away from the wild crowd.

I really thought you needed medical attention. Your body was still jerking—an alarming sight—and the stranger didn't seem to hear anything I shouted to him. Everything was a struggle—I wasn't prepared to leave you on the floor to get help. My phone had turned itself off again and took forever to restart, and I struggled to recall my access code. I finally pushed 9-1-1 but was unable to find the send button. Then I realized it was the wrong emergency number anyway—I'd watched too much American TV. Deleting the erroneous digits also proved a challenge. All I could think to type was 1-8-0, directory assistance. Each time I looked down at your wincing face, you looked so vulnerable and troubled, yet so beautiful.

There was a hold in the music and I managed to ask the stranger for directions, but again he gave me a bewildered look. From his sailboat at sea, he said the emergency number was 1-2-0, but he didn't know about cell phones. It might be 1-1-2 or something. When I tried to call directory assistance, the line was dead. He asked if I was dialing the correct number.

"Yah, 1-8-0."

"No, that's not the right number any longer. They changed it. There are several options now. One of them is a year beginning with eighteen … Let me find security. It's probably easier."

It was obviously a good idea, and he took off toward the exit. I hunkered down next to you and was trying to calm myself when your touch on my hip startled me. You grabbed my hand and practically pulled me down with you. "Ragnar, you're awake! Some guy went to get assistance," I pleaded. "We're trying to get you an ambulance. By the way, do you know the number for medical emergencies?"

You needed to get away from the stage lights, and there wasn't an easy way to break loose from your grip. Although it was a surprisingly discreet maneuver in the drunken crowd, I'd never felt so self-conscious. You'd grabbed my hand and wouldn't let go until we'd reached the coat check … I swear it's the longest time that someone's ever held my hand in all my adult life. And then you asked if I'd follow you home.

I'd do almost anything to make you say yah, and I was quick to reclaim my backpack with my passport, notebook, and toiletries. On our way out, it was easier to talk, and you said, "Kurt! Aren't you the son of a doctor? That number you're looking for is 1-1-3, but you're not calling."

15

I FOLLOWED YOU past the government complex toward Sank-thanshaugen, where you lived. I begged you to walk slower, but you wouldn't listen. Adjusting my backpack, I inquired if you wanted to take a taxi.

You finally threw me a quick glance. "That's a bit extravagant, don't you think?"

When I tried to walk closer, you threw me another skeptical look. A gang of Somali-Norwegian boys approached us on the sidewalk, shoving each other into the street, in front of oncoming traffic. Their behavior alarmed me, but you couldn't be distracted—your eyes hardly strayed from the ground as we hurried on.

I asked if you remembered at all what had happened, if you remembered that my pants fell down, that I wanted to be your tent pole.

Evidently, there was nothing more to say about that matter. After a moment's silence you said, "Have you read *Death in Venice*, the novella by Thomas Mann?"

"No," I answered. "But I think I've heard about it."

Although it was difficult to follow your thoughts, each sentence you uttered rang precise and sounded somehow impressive. "The book might interest you," you went on. "I read the Norwegian translation last year, when I studied comparative literature. The German original was published in 1912. I think the Norwegian translation came out in 1963 and has been re-issued many times since. It's about this aging writer, Gustav von Aschenbach. He succumbs to an acute sense of wanderlust at a graveyard in Munich, after he spots someone there wearing a straw hat. So he travels to Venice, presumably for rest and inspiration."

"Okay, what happens next?"

"He dies from a local outbreak of plague. And it's only because he takes too much interest in a young boy at the hotel, Tadzio. Anyway, that's not the point. Listen to this. The bathing attendant is a bareheaded old man in linen trousers, a sailor's jacket, and a straw hat. He shows Achenbach to his cabin and sets up the awning. The sun rises to its zenith, to a terrible power ... Hey, didn't you notice something funny?"

"Something funny?"

"Kurt! A bareheaded old man with a straw hat? Is he holding it in his hand, maybe?"

"Maybe it's lying in the sand."

"Basically I have misplaced a-ha moments. Guess what? It handicaps my studies."

I thought your talk often sounded a bit pretentious, but kept my tongue and let you continue.

"I know a seizure's underway when I feel like I'm on the brink of a breakthrough. It's like I'm on the verge of grasping something vital. And then, when I regain consciousness, the revelation's gone. Listen—the straw hat's a leitmotif reappearing throughout the story. Basically the only bareheaded person outdoors is Tadzio! When the boy smiles at Aschenbach, the writer's so shaken he flees to his room. He breaks down all trembling and shuddering."

"Wow. That sounds a lot like you."

"*Very* funny. Anyway, I bicycled to the university to look up the German original. On my way, I barely had time to pull the bicycle up on the sidewalk before I had an epileptic fit. This was just before the library closed, but I made it. I skimmed through the text as fast as I could—it was so nerve-wracking. The poor old man isn't bare*headed*, he's bare*footed*. The error's been in print for forty years!"

"You had a fit over that?"

"Yah. There's a lot of hiding from the sun in that novella. In Chapter 4, the Norwegian translation got it right. The barefooted bathing attendant escorts Aschenbach to his cabin. Kurt! Hello! So I have epilepsy. So what? I'm back on my feet in less than a minute."

A passing taxi produced giddy phantom images in my field of vision. I asked, "Did you have an a-ha moment at Rockefeller?" But you didn't answer.

Instead you told me that whenever you went into details, people got overly nice or scared away. People always worried that they might trigger something. Therefore, you must be treated with the utmost care. Next, they'd worry that you're too much work, that you're clingy. You exclaimed, "If only they'd just stop worrying!" Because you had surgery in junior high and that killed the attacks for the most part. They removed the top of your skull and then they stuck it back on. "The important thing's to hold me," you said. "I'll tell you when."

You wouldn't notice while the seizure's going on, and so I should stop you from knocking your head and from biting off your tongue. It's a problem if you swallow the severed appendage. Apparently if you keep it in your mouth, a tongue can be sewed back on … Finally, I couldn't help but change the topic.

"That's a nice park," I muttered, looking through the metal fence alongside the narrow sidewalk.

"Watch out," you said. "It's a graveyard. The Cemetery of Our Savior." Acting on some whim of your own, you grabbed my hand again—and led me through a gated entrance.

For a moment, my heart raced with anticipation, slowing down in the lush semi-darkness only when you let it go. "You know," you said, "we shouldn't be in here. Although they never lock the gates, the cemetery's closed after dark."

Then you told me a story about your sister Anniken. She'd bicycled through here in the spring, on her way home from a night of drinking, and ended up falling, head first, into a deep hole in the path. There had been no barrier and she figured it was a grave. And then she felt someone under her, moaning. Some man had been down there for a while—he was so drunk he couldn't get up on his own. When she helped him out, he became quite enamored with her; he thought they were meant to be but was too drunk to chase after her bicycle. Even after she'd moved to Denmark to study psychology, Anniken regretted that she hadn't let down her guard and taken down his contact information.

Was there a lesson in there? I struggled to discern your facial expression as we kept walking. "So," I said, "you like that story, *Death in Venice*? About succumbing to wanderlust and ... adoration?"

"Yah, very much."

I hesitated, trying to think of what to say next. "Those fits of yours. Are they dangerous?"

"Well, as I said, the important thing's to hold me..."

"I'd be more than willing to hold you..."

"Then follow me. I need to take a leak."

We took a few steps off the path and unzipped between the trees.

"You said *yah* to me at Rockefeller. You're coming with me."

"No, I did not..."

"Ragnar, you're supposed to yield to acute wanderlust right now." I couldn't help my words.

"Please, be kind! We haven't seen a man with a straw hat yet."

"We should do *something* together."

"Like what?" you asked keenly.

And there, treasuring the moist residuals of your wine and urine on my thigh, I came up with a new proposition. "We should open a contemporary art gallery!" By the white flash of your teeth, I knew you were grinning and I contemplated moving closer. "But first we must travel the world and see some world-class art." My voice trailed off.

As our streams of pee splashed into the invisible grass, sending mist into the clear air, a strange sight distracted me, though. A furry animal was closing in on us from the path. It was fairly big, but not a dog. "Hey, watch ... Oh shit, it's coming right at us!" I warned.

"That was a badger," you exclaimed. "So much for the nonexistence of wildlife in Oslo." The creature thought better of it—tottering away among the crypts and headstones.

You wanted to show me some painters' tombs, Edvard Munch's bust in particular, but had forgotten where they were located and said we should come back some other time. Rather disappointed, I trailed you through another gate. And finally we stood outside your apartment building, where you lived with your parents. Like most Oslo streets, yours was packed with cars. Lit by streetlights, along both sides a massive row of tall, century-old brick structures in pale colors rose like frosted cakes.

As we stood there, measuring everything—the street, and the sidewalk, and all the parked vehicles—I exclaimed, sentimentally, that there was no street like this in Bodø. "The wooden houses in my hometown were bombed asunder in 1940 by Thomas Mann's countrymen…"

I didn't know why I was talking. I knew one thing, though: we were two spectacularly awkward students. At that thought I smiled.

"No more fits tonight?"

"No more fits tonight!"

You promised to have your answer ready by our 8:15 a.m. seminar on Monday. You were being difficult now—difficult and shy.

16

"ALL RIGHT," DAD had chastised on the phone, "if you need to learn absolutely everything by trial and error, by all means do. And if your student loan hasn't arrived by December, why don't you dig yourself a nice little snow cave to live in?"

Everyone had told me so back then: Mum and Dad, the student welfare foundation, the State Educational Loan Fund—even you at Café Frederik. No, I didn't have to be under financial pressure. No, I didn't absolutely have to be penniless and, until recently, ipso facto homeless.

If I'd applied for student funding in time, my check would have been waiting at the beginning of the fall term. If I hadn't gone to London to watch football three times in one year with my brother Kåre, I would've had some savings. If I'd filled out and submitted my student housing application in time, I would've had an inexpensive flat too, probably in the student village at the edge of the city, near that tenting boy in the newspaper. If I stopped taking for granted the last-minute mercy of other people and made better plans, everything would have been taken care of before I headed south.

I was hurt. "In principle, it's possible to be proud of me," I'd replied to Dad, after some thinking.

"Of course we're proud of you."

Yet he wanted to know why I had, the moment the term started, all of a sudden swapped from informatics—the study of computer systems—to art history. He didn't so much mind the actual choice. But to his taste, it sounded a little too impulsive.

Instead of letting him in on my budding gallery plans, I answered, unwisely I realized, that art history was something I desired to explore while I worked out what I truly wanted to get my hands on—which probably wasn't computer science in the first place. Dad reminded me that wasting another year not knowing what to make of oneself was much cheaper in Bodø.

Feeling defensive, I didn't get myself to mention that Kåre and I, more or less by chance, had come across a cluster of gallery openings in North London. Although the artworks much invigorated my spirits and had made me feel alive and completely present, I was willing to admit that the effect had had a little to do with the overall atmosphere of the neighborhood hangouts. There were free drinks and well-dressed youngsters and Kåre, about to study architecture, seemed to get along.

Oh, how I envied my little brother who'd made up his mind and made all the arrangements. Meeting new people, he was about, at least in my eyes, to live the high life in the big city—London, a place chockfull of promise, of exciting encounters! If only he'd let me move into his tiny student flat permanently, I'd jump at the opportunity.

All I had to show for over the last year was my part-time work at the printer, my writings for the handball club match-day program (unpaid), and my successful studying for, and passing, my preparatory exams for the university. Since the events in 1999, I'd slid to a standstill, to a state of moratorium.

It was duly noted that Kurt Larsen didn't have a girlfriend. There was nothing more to say. When Otto pressed me, I told him that my private life was an open book with mostly blank pages. All right, so I did have a secret Gaysir account. It was cheaper and faster than a mailbox. But it was all talk, no real attraction, unless I was prepared to travel.

Mum mumbled a few things to Dad in the background—I heard her. In a vigorous showing of support, she thought some time in the Norwegian capital sounded wise; besides, she and I could go to art exhibitions together whenever they came to visit me in Oslo. Thank you, Mum.

"You tell me I can make my own decisions now," I reminded Dad. "But then they all seem to worry you, or puzzle you. That's not very consistent. I'm not in, or causing, any serious trouble. I'm not exactly a delinquent, or a junkie. So please stop always second-guessing me."

"All right then," Dad answered, "as soon as you stop burning money and relying on everyone's mercy all the time."

After hanging up, I mulled over his words. I'd brought my bike, the hybrid Dad had put together with old parts from the trash heap up north, and wasn't relying on public transport. That was saving money.

Everything was more beautiful from a bicycle seat anyway, especially in Oslo. You didn't notice details like cigarette butts and dog shit and the chewing-gum-smeared sidewalks, so everything looked fresh, and interesting too—at night I peeked into people's well-lit apartments.

Ragnar, I remember our first talk at Café Frederik, about our different childhoods, and relived my sting of envying yours.

You'd grown up near every institution one learned about on television—the Crown Prince and his girlfriend resided only a few blocks away. When you were seven years of age, you'd moved to Oslo with your American mum and Norwegian dad. Since then you had lived in the nation's capital, right there in the urban center at Sankthanshaugen. And since age seventeen, you'd made money working part time across the street from the parliament, as a waiter at Peppe's Pizza. Your bank account must've been chockfull, because you still lived with your parents for free.

But Oslo, I'd countered, wasn't a nice place for children. Here they'd be deprived of any closeness to nature and wilderness: real qualities, real elements. They'd play on concrete and get run over by cars. Or be carried away in one of them by a kidnapper. Or, as winter tires churned up the asphalt, develop asthma from the street dust—that is, if they didn't already have the condition from spending too much time indoors.

You looked at me in bewilderment. "But there's the Oslofjord … It's great for swimming and kayaking."

"It's polluted, a filthy foam bath."

"And there are all the small fishing lakes in Nordmarka. They're crystal clear."

You kept jabbering about tenting in Nordmarka, the city woods, and about how much you liked bicycling and fishing. You had your pocketknife, your fishing rod, your sleeping bag, and your tent. You weren't going to starve, freeze, or get wet. You felt independent, safe. You stressed that your childhood summers were longer than mine above the Arctic Circle, some 1,280 km north—you had checked these facts on the Internet. Naturally, I retaliated by claiming that you hadn't experienced real, lasting snow, and then you couldn't believe how shocked I was to learn that Oslo, at the inner end of a fjord, was much colder than my coastal hometown in winter.

You even told me about the time King Olav, the late monarch, reprimanded your father deep in the forest.

"Can you imagine the king's voice?"

You and your sister were pre-school age and the previous king, then in his eighties, was the first cross-country skier you'd come across all afternoon. From the opposite track, with his distinctive, high-pitched voice, the monarch had shouted, "That's irresponsible! Those kids are improperly dressed to be this far into the forest." By the time your father slid out of the slope, the monarch had disappeared behind you.

That particular morning, the temperature had registered at minus eighteen degrees Celsius down in the city and even colder up beyond Sognsvann. The three of you had taken the subway to the final station, put on your skis, and spent hours out there. You hadn't developed pneumonia, or asthma for that matter. You'd managed fine. Growing up in Oslo hadn't exactly been to your disadvantage.

Before you lent me money, my belongings, which included an old CD player and my eight favorite Burt Bacharach compilations, were temporarily stored in a series of campus lockers. I'd had a heated argument with the student representative who managed the select few available. I tried to make him understand that I was desperate and that he was being unreasonable, for the five lockers meant only momentary relief—now at least I wouldn't need to fret about my possessions getting stolen.

During this time, I slept on the floor of the old university gymnasium, sharing my nights with an increasingly eccentric clique of undergraduates, who, several weeks into the semester, were still without proper accommodations. One of these evenings someone had left a copy of *Aftenposten Aften* in my spot on the floor and the newspaper instantly grabbed my attention. From the front cover, peeking out of his tent with sleepy eyes and a rosy face, another first year, a twenty-year-old from Northern Norway, stared back at me. I lay down and started reading the article about this resourceful person. While the weather remained mild and comfortable, the young student was saving on rent by camping in the forest by Sognsvann, the lake near the student village. As I lay there on my mattress reading the article, I texted you on my cell phone and asked directly, "Ragnar, can I borrow your tent?"

Ragnar—it was only natural that I should ask to borrow your tent. Perhaps you'd go camping with me, teach me a thing or two about inland fishing, and then maybe some ice fishing. That way, I'd also save money on food. But I immediately discovered that the idea of loaning out your parents' equipment held little appeal to you. You decided to lend me several thousand kroner instead. With your help, I rented an apartment room in Hafrsfjordgata at Frogner, a thirteen-minute bicycle ride from campus.

I'd been longing for a space with an unmonitored entrance in a bigger city, and I enjoyed the privacy of my room. It afforded me a window view of the American ambassador's residence. It was like facing a park—albeit a highly fenced one—and I kept the window wide open. Reclined in bed, I imagined myself sleeping outdoors with another person next to me.

A single mother, Eli worked as a part-time interior designer. I'd found her telephone number on a university notice board. She hadn't wanted a security deposit and didn't even ask for a written contract. Upon hearing the news that I'd achieved one of my initial goals, Mum's response wasn't one of excitement. Instead, she'd stressed how important it was to make proper provisions. Otherwise, she warned, I might find myself locked out one day, with no place to sleep.

One particular thought would haunt me even more, though. If I didn't get my hands on more money, my plan to exchange Oslo for greater cities as soon as possible would be put on hold indefinitely. Then I might have to go home to Bodø and work part-time at the local printer for another year.

I managed to talk Eli into signing a note specifying a room of my own, conditional on my contribution of 4,000 kroner each month toward our common living expenses. The agreement could be terminated with one month's notice, but if anyone asked, she emphasized, I wasn't a tenant; I was her ex-husband's cousin from Bodø. Admitting that she wasn't really allowed to sublet, she explained she needed the money and was willing to live under the risk of the occasional inquisitive neighbor. To compensate for the circumstances, she promised me a discount of 100 kroner for each hour I baby-sat her two girls, a task I was welcome to carry out while completing my homework.

Unfortunately for my financial situation, I guess it takes a while to develop the necessary trust needed to make good on such an offer, because so far she hadn't asked me to do any baby-sitting.

17

SLUMPING OVER ON the toilet bowl, I couldn't decide whether my pains originated in my stomach or in my back. I tried to empty my mind of thoughts about anything but the porcelain goose on the bathtub—with the most blissful expression. Eyes shut in sheer joy, it stretched its long neck and beak toward me. From the garden of the American ambassador, birds pestered me with their incessant cries.

Then I was distracted by light knocking on the door and a girl's voice meekly stressing that she needed to pee. I told her to wait for her turn. After a brief moment she replied, "I can't wait any longer!"

"Well ... then you should learn how to contain yourself."

The amplified buzz from my cell phone on the tile floor startled me. Other than drinking lots of water and fruit juice, you had no good suggestions for how to cure alcohol poisoning. I wrote you another message, asking you to just give in and go with me.

"Kurt, will you be done soon? Gry needs to use the bathroom."

Hearing my landlady's voice, I jumped to my feet, held down the plastic button, and flushed for a long time until all the water in the tank had gurgled down the drain. I apologized profusely as I made my way past Eli and the longhaired little girl who waited impatiently outside the bathroom door.

Before I had a chance to answer her knock, Eli walked into my and wanted to know if I had a fever, if I'd thrown up. She brought with her a plastic bucket and a large glass of something blue. Her eyes darted around my private chamber as she sat down beside me. It was the first time she'd entered since I'd moved in. My phone beeped on the wooden floor—we both looked at it. And then, without warning, she put her tiny hand on my forehead.

"Oh, my! Your skin's so moist…. Here, sit up and have some blueberry juice. It's good for your stomach. Did you drink too much last night?"

Catching buses, traversing airport terminals, and crisscrossing the Atlantic Ocean had taken its toll. Eli stared at me intently, weighing her words, and I was getting rather nervous.

"I see some cash on your table. Did you get your student funding on Friday?"

I nodded.

"It's a little embarrassing," she said," but I'm running short this month. Do you mind paying the rent now?"

I swallowed. "Now?"

"Wouldn't it be nice to get it over with? Then you won't have to worry about it later. I wanted to ask you before but you've hardly been around this weekend."

I struggled with the glass and constantly forgot to avoid the drenched parts of my bed. Each time I moved, the cold sweat that had soaked into my sheets overnight startled me.

"Mummy! Is he sick?" Gry peered through the door and Eli placed her hand back on my forehead.

"Yah, he has a fever."

The girl disappeared from the door and Eli was back on her feet—she considered herself rather kind not to ask for a deposit. And her chili nuts were missing. They were supposed to be for a cozy snack last night. And some of my food must have gone bad in the kitchen—there was a peculiar stench. Carrying a book with both hands, the other twin daughter, Eva, stepped back into my room with her twin sister in tow. "Can we read him fairytales?"

"No, he needs to rest and think," their mother said softly. "We'd better leave him alone."

She hesitated as the girls left my room. Then she asked, "I can trust you, right? You seem like a quiet and responsible and fairly innocent boy."

Cutting through the uncomfortable silence, she added that she needed to explain something. She was taking the girls with her, to her ex-husband's country house, tomorrow. They'd stay out there until the end of the month. During that time I'd have the entire apartment to myself. I could use the living room as much as I liked. Would I promise to take good care of her place? But of course!

She demanded only that I bring in the mail and the paper and let the phone ring so people could record their own messages—she'd call to check them periodically. In case of emergencies, she'd leave the number to the country house in the hallway for me.

She was eager to make her point. "I'm taking a calculated risk here, leaving the house. You know, since there's no security deposit," she said. "I'd feel so much better if you paid October's rent before we went away."

It was all the money I had until next month—and it wouldn't even cover my debt to you and my parents. Plus rent wasn't due for another two weeks. Eli just looked at me with wide, questioning eyes.

I couldn't understand why, but my room smelled intensely of mint. Bothered by the distinct scent, and impatient to close the subject, I said I'd think about it. But my landlady laughed shrilly. "What's there to think about? Don't you get most of your funding in one go? It's not safe, all this money floating around."

18

MY LANDLADY HAD left her contact number by the phone. "Just remember," her Post-it read, "you're my ex-husband's cousin from Bodø. Do not, under any circumstances, mention to anyone in the building that you pay rent." I removed the note before you noticed.

Arriving at my door in Hafrsfjordgata late Monday afternoon to call on the sick, you wore the same green T-shirt you had on when we first met, three weeks ago, at our first 8:15 a.m. seminar in the wooden barracks on the campus lawn—a temporary setup, as summer renovations had drawn out.

That seminar had taken ages to start; it never would. From the very beginning the Monday morning seminar was the least popular one. Each week the number of enrolled students dropped further. Most of the desks sat empty yet you and your green T-shirt had settled next to me at one end of the horseshoe-shaped seating arrangement.

I must have been tired, or plain lazy, but gazing at your fingers and staring at your temples through that close-cropped haircut kept me going.

The room reeked of your coffee, and while you drank it, you scribbled something in your notebook. An elderly woman from the front office came by to inform us that the department had, unfortunately, forgotten to spread the news to the new students that our original seminar leader was away all week, and class was canceled. After she left a guy suggested, mischievously, that we should all go for breakfast at the student pub.

Only a few joined him.

I had no money and nothing better to do—no books to read, no class until 2:15 p.m.—so I decided to ride home.

You'd obviously noticed my looks and, perhaps to diffuse any tension, talked to me. "You want to grab some coffee?" You clearly liked that drink. Leaving the little barracks building together, you offered me your hand and introduced yourself.

I withdrew the smallest amount of money the ATM would dispense, which turned out to be the last hundred-kroner bill in my bank account. Then you introduced me to Café Frederik as well.

In spite of passing its big windows several times, I'd never entered—besides being a waste of money, cafés made my clothes reek of cigarette smoke. Yet to my surprise, this was a smoke-free coffee shop. Kilroy Travels, in the corner, hadn't yet opened for the day. I drank my tea, the cheapest item on the menu, and took in the posters from around the world. I even remember saying, "This place makes me want to travel."

Painful as it was to sit so completely still, I enjoyed the feeling of your foot on mine. We discussed, to the point of brief exhaustion, the dissimilarities between growing up in Bodø and Oslo and whose background gave an advantage in terms of health or worldliness. I guess you won, because you were four hundred pages into *Gardner's Art Through the Ages*, our primary textbook, which I had yet to buy. In case you hadn't realized it already, I didn't want you to know that your brown leather shoe rested on living ground.

The people walking past in the corridor mechanically drew my gaze. Your eyes, following mine, were unnerving. So I stifled my habit altogether and concentrated on your coffee cup instead, and then at every feature of your handsome face. I gave an excuse for my slow progress with the class reading—complained that I relied exclusively on my lecture notes and couldn't do any serious reading until I could afford to buy the books. So you took me to the main library and showed me the shelves where all the curriculum text-books were stored.

The next day I returned on my own. I recognized several students from class. You called my name from the desk where you were working and didn't seem to pay attention to the fact that your gesture annoyed all your neighbors. As you rotated your swivel chair, your knee brushed my leg persistently but ever so lightly, and I couldn't decide whether this was the act of someone keen on friendship or a refined method of flirtation. In any case, a connection now existed between us that seemed to separate us from other students. Since then, I've measured the passage of time with memories of your touch.

We were seated at the same table during a student party. I didn't know the girl who sat opposite me, but you chose the spot next to her. For most of the meal, the three of us talked while I tried to determine whose foot lay on top of mine under the table. It didn't become clear until she left for the bathroom: I kept serving as your footrest.

Perhaps we delicately agreed you weren't supposed to know, that neither of us was supposed to pay attention. You'd probably have to remove your foot permanently, out of courtesy, if I made clear where it rested. Struggling to control my own bladder, I decided the shared moment was worth any discomfort I suffered.

What did we talk about? I can't remember. What was going on? I didn't know then; in Hafsfjordsgata I still didn't.

Our glasses emptied and we didn't refill them. I told myself that if anything happened, at any stage, it could only be spur of the moment. More visible effort would kill the tantalizing ambiguity. It would make rejection, I imagined, so much more likely. And harder to bear.

It was your first and only visit when I lived in Eli's apartment, and you only knew half the story back then. You'd brought the notes from today's seminar, and to lighten up my spirit you'd also brought a newspaper—the latest edition of *Aftenposten Aften:* "Lovesick bus driver triggers U.S. terror alert." You seemed amused. What an impression Jonny Larsen must have made on that bus driver—those were your words. At that point I hadn't yet told you that I knew him—that was still long into the future.

I had only one office chair in my room, and since no one else was around, I thought it would look weird to keep you confined to my bedroom. I was opening a potato chip bag in the kitchen when I remembered the two pieces of dried cod on my food shelf—departure gifts from Dad—and dared you to fence with me. Whoever won the stockfish duel would get to choose what the other did for the next twelve months.

You declined the challenge and implored me to keep those dead, smelly things out of your face.

Leaving Eli's apartment to rent a movie—*Funny Bones*—that was your idea. And what followed happened so quickly. You wanted to start the film as soon as we got back. No one was around to watch us, yet in the living room we sat down on opposite sides of the couch. You devoured potato chips and put your feet up, resting them over the armrest at times, away from me. Whatever happened to your restless legs, furtively searching for contact with another? All I needed to do was leave for the bathroom and sit closer when I returned—or initiate a mock fight, some submissive wrestling to end these games once and for all. I resisted the urge, however, since I suspected it would create one eerie state of affairs.

Tearing off threads of stockfish flesh and popping them into my mouth, I cursed my inability to win you over and kept asking you the same questions: "Hey, you. Why do you need more time? Why can't you just say yah?"

All this pestering was giving you a headache, you replied. I, on the other hand, was through with inhibited cowards. They represented human beings of the most discouraging kind. I let go of the dried cod and it hit the coffee table with a loud bang. I paused the movie, declared that I wouldn't turn it back on until you had made up your mind. We should follow your sister's and my brother's and your mum's example—travel while we were young and healthy, and supple and fit and bouncy, and while we had all the time in the world! We had to get our act together and our asses out of Norway! We could go to Las Vegas or Blackpool and search for those places in the film if you wanted to.

You countered that following my lead would cause you to miss too many lectures. That sounded almost like a no.

But why?

For God's sake, why were so many so vested in the idea of making so many in this world stay put, why's it so valuable that most people stay right where they are? Ragnar, tell me or just say "yah."

You didn't need to attend the lectures; they weren't mandatory. You could just bring your books on our trip. And beware, an educational reform was about to take place, one where class attendance would, in fact, become mandatory. I'd read all about it in the student paper. Roll calls and sign-in lists would soon constrain us. You should learn the meaning of that word, mandatory. It would be impossible to get away after that.

I pleaded with you: Second chances don't exist! Later in life there'd be work, family, and the twenty-four-hour job of raising children. One year from now, you'd never see sunshine again!

Besides, people undervalued the importance of their surroundings. Didn't you want to find, as soon as possible, the one place in the world that best fit your particular talents and temperament? Did you really think you'd be the same person doing exactly the same things no matter where you lived? Didn't you ever consider conducting a little more research before you concluded so categorically that your life elsewhere wouldn't be as full as it was in Oslo?

I maintained that you hadn't explained yourself very well. Yah, you hadn't yet given me a valid reason to stay home. So I expected you to say yah, or explain yourself promptly.

People never ask for explanations, you claimed, as long as you did exactly what you were expected to do. If you had said yah, as I was begging you to do, I wouldn't have nagged you with the why, why, why. But you were dead wrong there too, and I begged you to test me—just test me! I promised to question your yah...

You barked, "I'm afraid what you're suggesting will be costlier than you make it sound. You like to walk through life on razor-thin margins, don't you?"

You had, as a matter of fact, talked to your parents. They estimated that each of us would need a minimum of 500 kroner a day for food, accommodations, transportation, and any activities. Ten weeks of travel would drain each of us of 35,000 kroner, and that figure didn't even include the cost of airfare. Staying away for the whole year would come to a total of 190,000 kroner. Each.

You and your family must demand lots of luxury, I thought. Staying here would be costly too. My parents had argued that living in the capital equaled wasting money on rent—wasn't Oslo one of the most expensive cities in the world? By that logic, we ought to sleep in your tent anywhere food was cheap. And we could simply choose to travel when there were no lectures to miss—during fall break, Christmas break, winter break, Easter break, and summer break. Your parents would save a fortune on food and electricity if you spent some time abroad—factor that into your calculations. For Christ's sake, if you were living with your parents and studying in your home city only because you were afraid of taking out a student loan, at least apply for the stipend to live on your own. It was free money—spend it on travel. If you didn't have the energy to open a book in hot weather, we should take our sleeping bags to Alaska or Greenland, New Zealand or Northern Japan.

There, I'd answered all your concerns. Did you want to see the world's art museums with me or did you want to stay put in that self-built prison cell of yours? Dreams, I declared, could be split into whims and true goals. The difference is easy to spot because only true goals bore any lasting influence on one's choices.

Yet you continued to protest. In order to qualify for the stipend, you'd need to put down an address other than your parents' residence. I suggested using my address in Hafrsfjordgata. "That's *swindling!*" you said.

"Then move in for real. At least until I give notice! I'm sure Eli would take only a small fee to hold our mail."

Investigating the whole world before deciding where to live— you deemed the idea silly. No one had time to do that much research. You planned to turn your savings into a down payment on your own apartment someday. Besides, I was just being a pest.

"I find it unfair," I said, "that you're forcing your parents to subsidize the educational system and pay for your lifestyle."

With that, I turned the movie back on. The clock approached midnight as the credits rolled. I should have brought up the rent issue with you, asked for your advice, reminded you how imperative it was that I moved out quickly, before I wasted my funds. But I didn't want to raise any more alarm.

You remained on top of my list of candidates for sexual perfection and I implored you to stay the night, since you hated traveling without money in your pockets. You didn't think my single bed was wide enough for the two of us. And you worried that your bicycle would get stolen. You could always bring it upstairs, and there was Eli's double bed—we could talk there all night. No, you needed to store your contact lenses in saline solution. Yah, sure. Everything became so difficult when no one was watching, when I had the whole apartment to myself.

Maybe it wasn't your fault though. Maybe I should've blamed my nagging or the damned cod.

RAGNAR—HOW COULD you say no to me?

After you left, I fought hard to fall asleep. I relived my struggle to qualify for the prize journeys and my difficulties in persuading you to join my sojourn.

By Pascal Confectionery, a few blocks away from the American Embassy, Lars had turned off the bus engine and run off, in his driver's uniform, to chase his love interest. As the old man and I exited the abandoned bus, I kept a tab on him and Jonny Larsen—*I just want you to love me back. Okay?* The oncoming 30 Bygdøy barely avoided them as they scurried across the street. The line came to a brief halt by the Royal Palace Park. When the bus drove off, Lars and Jonny were gone.

I was able to hail a taxi at the nearby tram station and begged the driver to take me straight to the airport express train as fast as he could. He pointed across the road and said the closest station was right down the staircase, by the Foreign Ministry, just a minute's walk away. I couldn't spot any of those things and was close to losing my grip. Sensing my panic, he gave me a 200-meter ride to the National Theatre station and didn't even want any money.

Somehow I made that first connection; I was the last passenger to enter the 1:05 p.m. flight at Oslo Airport. A crewmember quietly announced "boarding completed" before I had time to find my seat in the back. After the mobile loading ramp pulled away, the Lufthansa aircraft lurched a couple of times then returned to the gate. A problem with the landing gear had arisen, the pilot informed us in a heavy German accent. And before I had fully regained my breath, everyone was told to disembark. We were to be taken to a different part of the airport where another plane was being made available.

When it finally arrived, the transit bus packed quickly. I had nowhere to sit, nothing to cling to, and the doors kept closing and opening until someone explained that I needed to get my backpack away from the sensor and move further inside. "You're welcome to grab me a little tighter," one boy said to another while I tried not to step on anyone's feet. I had a lot to learn. Those two boys seemed so comfortable in each other's space.

I was the first to exit onto the tarmac. Other travelers, the utterly impatient ones, squeezed past me up the flight's staircase then took their time getting out of the aisle. Obviously boarding a shorter plane, I was unable to locate my seat and I couldn't find any cabin personnel to confer with in the rear of the jet. Maneuvering back past entering passengers wasn't really an option. Soon others found themselves in the same predicament, and there was nowhere to stand. I made room for a married couple as they settled into their seats and stepped aside for a businessman lifting his briefcase into his overhead compartment.

An elbow jabbed into my back. There it came again, intentionally thrust, no doubt. When I turned fully to face the seated husband, he glared into his newspaper and pretended not to see me. He wouldn't accept my apology for invading his space. Even his wife in the window seat lifted her newspaper to block me from view. For a moment, I wondered if they were German, but they were utterly engrossed with their Norwegian newspapers. "I really don't want to be in your way," I ventured apologetically. "I just wish I had my own seat." I didn't know why I continued my jabbering. Why couldn't I be a little more overbearing? By that point, I felt excluded, lonely, exhausted.

The Lufthansa personnel finally offered me a double seat right in front. My stomach rumbled, the strong air conditioning coupled with my sweat-soaked T-shirt robbed me of body heat. Glancing absentmindedly out the window, I noticed a fox—a big-eyed pup sat in the grass near the runway, its fluffy red ears twitching back and forth vigilantly. The engines roared to life and the puppy fled. Not quite in the appropriate direction, however, so we chased the scarlet animal while a crewmember on the loudspeaker thanked us for our attention and patience—that was all I registered of her message.

The aircraft fought against centrifugal force and the pull of gravity. Lights and shadows slithered along the cabin's synthetic surfaces; the sun blinded me. Every time I squeezed my eyelids together to block out its rays, my field of vision exploded in sharp colors. I flicked restlessly through an onboard magazine. I was too worn out to get out my lecture notes, yet too alert to fall asleep. A male flight attendant placed two bottles of white wine in front of me. He then clenched my shoulder and urged me to enjoy them. Free alcohol. It reminded me of the gallery openings in London.

How could you turn me down, just like that, Ragnar? After breakfast that Tuesday morning, I bicycled to the university while I carried on arguing with you in my thoughts. You be the rational, responsible one; keep Oslo to yourself, leave the rest of the world to me!

Taking my seat in the computer lab, I peered around to make sure I didn't have anyone's undivided attention. Then I pushed enter and kept my head close to the screen. No one in the room was actually working, as far as I could tell—students were scrolling newspaper sites, typing emails. One obnoxious boy spoke loudly to a friend on his cell phone: "Is Guro coming? Can you make her come? She has to come! No, I'm not going if she's not coming."

Ragnar—think about the boys in Frankfurt, Toronto, Washington, London, Amsterdam, and Copenhagen who had no idea who I was. More than ever, people needed to collect and filter the appropriate background data to make smarter, more informed choices. I didn't want to get stuck with someone simply because we'd somehow fallen into the same hole in the ground and never bothered to look for a way out. Surely you couldn't leave life choices like that to chance, to outer circumstances like geography? Theoretically speaking at least, how many would have shown up at the airport last weekend to take a closer look if only they'd known about me and seen my new photo ID?

I understood that boys had to learn about me in order to desire me. I needed to meet all the relevant candidates—for a travel companion, a life partner, etc. I was willing to canvass my entire population of peers to find out. The more undisguised the slobbering, the clearer my options, yet I suspected that the most desirable boys were the least detectable ones.

Behind me, the latest person to arrive in line stomped her boot heels against the floor to let everyone know she was there. Struggling to ignore her impatience, I put together my new Gaysir profile. First there is hope, the impulse to check who's on. Hope—my most reliable friend—showed up at the oddest hours to tell me so.

COMEWITHME20

Let's leave the country together on October 1. If you can pay half of 14,998 kroner, we can travel to any 15 destinations we agree on, worldwide. Just remember to be fit, handsome, and masculine plus of a similar age (20 years).

I delayed lunch until hardly any energy remained in me. Gaysir boasted thousands of profiles and my inbox quickly filled up, mostly with emails from unacceptable candidates who grunted a minimalist dialogue of half-sentences:

"Hey …"

"Are you rich?"

"When?"

"Are you a prostitute?"

"Looking?"

"Where?"

"Into?"

"??"

Soon, answering each one with a polite rejection held the potential of turning into a full-time job. Hardly enough time existed to delete them as they steadily arrived, but I needed to erase some responses in order to receive newer messages.

The same people wrote again almost immediately. One person in particular reacted extremely badly when I disregarded his mail. "Yah, just ignore me, you slimy hypocrite. The fact that you don't show your picture proves that you're ugly as hell. How can you expect to have a decent conversation with anyone here when you're that stuck up? I know what you want and you'll never get it. Grow up or die!"

I was happy to accept his challenge quietly, but he kept on:

"Are you there??"

"Hello???"

"????"

And finally: "I hate superficial conversations on the Internet. Why don't we just meet in person instead?"

To take care of the issue, I added to my profile: "Don't bother to write if you want sex now and are older than twenty-three, fat, or ugly." He was twenty-four and should feel disqualified.

The solution became so self-evident now that it finally hit me. I'd conduct an extensive profile search—I wanted to find Jonny, Lars, or almost anyone. If, as a side effect, I happened to smoke you out, so much the better.

I began to look for boys under twenty-three who had a picture of themselves and defined their body type as *slim, normal, some muscles, rather muscular, muscular,* or *mouth-watering.* Thus, I weeded out those who lacked a photo and described themselves as *thin, some stomach, buxom, well-rounded, round,* and *bear.* I still had 941 results.

Happily, I possessed a gift for multitasking. To the more interesting-looking ones, I copied in the text field, "I'm afraid I don't have a photo, but you look good—so do I. Do you want to travel with me?" while I read my other messages. After studying some 180 profiles, I had another stroke of insight. There was, of course, directory assistance. It was invigorating to feel such purpose and determination. There was no Jonny Larsen registered in Bodø, but my Internet search produced eleven hits in Oslo, eight of them listed with cell phones only. Those were my boys—migrating students were unlikely to own landline phones. I fetched my own device and forwarded the eight promising finalists the mass message: "Hey, Jonny Boy, you're from Bodø, right? How are ya t'day?"

Within seconds, my cell phone started beeping. Turning off the sound, I flicked through a few more of my original 941 results until I could no longer hold myself back. I grabbed the device.

"Huh?" read the first text.

"What makes you think so?"

"Wrong number."

"Who are you?"

"No!"

I sent my three medalists—everyone except 'Wrong number' and 'No!'—a second mass message packed with typing errors: "Do you like coy dun? A handsome dun boy is ready to meet yot now. I have an entire apartmnt to mytelf!!"

The mobile device glowed in my hand.

"Get away from me, you illiterate lunatic!"

"I'm not from Bodø, but I'm splendid. I just caught a mackerel on the fjord."

Then I got what I was waiting for: "Kurt from Bodø? Do you want to meet me now outside the main gate of Oslo University College? Do you know where that is?"

This, I decided, was so much more than a silly whim. I'd just wasted three days pushing you, Ragnar. I needed to find a more suitable travel partner before October 1 and I was steaming with impatience to make up for lost time. Jonny didn't know it yet, but I was about to lock eyes with my new lucky prizewinner.

ACT III (Still 2002)

OUTSIDE THE OLD redbrick brewery, several students loitered, smoking. As I raced down the sidewalk, the phone started ringing inside my backpack. I squeezed the brakes and was almost thrown over the handlebars. The oily teeth of the bicycle sprockets dug painfully into my leg. Rolling my bike into the large courtyard, I realized Jonny wasn't there yet, but according to the information board, this was the main gate.

Now that I scrambled for it the device chimed again. I picked up at once. "Hi, Kurt! You sound out of breath."

I recognized Eli's voice and cursed myself for failing to check caller ID. Some students were scrutinizing me from afar. Did I really look so out of place? She wanted to know what I was up to, and I didn't know what to say. How strange—today everything was happening in staccato.

"Is everything okay?"

"Yah!"

"Do you remember to bring in the papers and the mail?"

"Yah!"

"Do you remember to lock before you go out?"

"Yah!"

"No one has stopped you in the stairway to inquire who you are, have they?"

"No…"

The phone vibrated, indicating a text message, but Eli kept talking and I could feel her anxiety brewing. I knew what was coming.

I told her yah, I'd given her proposal some thought since our last conversation. I said the answer was no. I'd pay by the end of the month, as we'd originally agreed. I couldn't part with my money right now. Rubbing my sore leg and absentmindedly inspecting my clothes, I managed to smear chain oil on my T-shirt as well.

What if Jonny was waiting around the corner and getting impatient? What if I'd gone to the wrong entrance?

Eli sounded hurt. But she assured me that it was only a question, not a demand. She'd work things out differently. Moments later I discovered that she'd phoned from an unregistered number. I resolved to become more careful before I picked up additional calls. I moved on to check my latest messages, noticing that they'd all come from another number that belonged to a different, more impatient Jonny Larsen. It stung, what appeared, in reverse chronological order, on the small screen.

"I know your address, you sleazy pervert. My army friends will hunt you down and rape you with broken beer bottles." "It's really rude of you not to finish what you've started. My girlfriend thinks so too. Go to hell!" "Are you there? Answer me! What the fuck is coy dun?" "What's coy dun? Is it good? Are you offering it?"

It occurred to me that I might've been set up. It also dawned on me that I should call the person who'd invited me here—and see if he happened to be the right Jonny. Yet when I dialed the number, partly to check his dialect, I reached an automated message: "The cell phone is turned off or in an area outside of coverage."

Why had he turned off his phone?

"Where are you?" I texted him, forlorn and brimming with questions.

Had he gotten cold feet yet again? Or had friends noticed a nervous Bodø Boy by the gate and invited him with them? According to the information board, Jonny Larsen studied here to become a businessman, a nurse, a journalist, a librarian, a physiotherapist, an information scientist, or a public administrator. That was, if he was studying here at all. The phone vibrated in my hands—this time it was a message from you, Ragnar.

"Kurt, don't hate me or ignore me. Thank you for asking me first. It's such a great offer. I'm so sorry I can't say yah. I'm absolutely sure you'll find another travel companion. You won't have to repay me anything before you do. Lots of people dream of hopping around the world. P.S. The Röyksopp ticket's on me."

I couldn't help thinking about the unidentified guy who ground his ass against my groin (or was it the other way around?) at the Röyksopp concert. He was probably a student, too. I wondered if there were any chance I'd run into him again or find him on Gaysir. Yah, Ragnar, why did I continue to waste my time on the Bodø boy, or you? By turning me down, I decided, you'd basically said no to seeing me over the next year. Indeed, I had several hundred Gaysir profiles to peruse and probably piles and piles of messages to answer or delete.

In the meantime, I intended to practice on boy love in Hafrsfjordgata and to clear my head in the process. My thoughts drifted toward the porcelain goose on the bathtub—blissfully stretching its long neck and beak toward me. Furthermore, I needed to remove my oil stains if I were to return to the computer lab looking hot and presentable.

Half an hour later, standing in Eli's bathtub, I applied skin lotion all over the head of the goose, smearing its features with the thick cream; then I rubbed my butt against its slippery surface and next, holding it with one hand and supporting myself on the windowsill with the other, I let the beak, head, and long, slick neck slowly slide inside me.

"Testing, testing," I muttered to myself and I smirked into the fogged mirror as my phone vibrated inside my shorts on the floor. Could it be you, finally giving in? Could it be Jonny, apologizing? Did I care? Very carefully, I maneuvered to read my newest text message.

"Are you still around? I have a fifteen-minute recess now. Let's meet."

No, I had no patience for this sort of conversation! Jonny hadn't mentioned a class; had he already returned to it? To speed things along, I dialed his number with my free hand and this time his mobile was ringing, but he simply wouldn't pick up. Instead, I got another text message: "Did you show up? I waited for you by the gate but had to run. I forgot about a lecture."

Why should I believe him? Obviously he didn't like speaking directly, so I typed my reply. "Yah, I showed up. Then I went home. Now I'm taking a bath."

The lecture was boring, Jonny Larsen admitted. And he was deciding whether to go back for the second part. I wasn't so sure how do deal with someone who seemed unreliable, someone who seemed to take my interest for granted. When he asked for my advice on what to do, I didn't respond. I just stood there with my hands full.

And then suddenly he wanted my address. I made a leap of faith—concluding that I'd little to lose by giving him my location, I sent it to him. "We're practically neighbors," he wrote back. "I live in Odins Gate! Keep the water hot and steamy! I'm on my way!"

I let the goose propel into the sink. How quickly things could change. This somewhat more mature version of Bodø Boy was efficient when he set his mind to it. The doorbell rang relentlessly even before I was done in the bathroom.

Thinking that Jonny must've been home in Odins Gate all along, I pulled a towel around my waist and hurried across the black floorboards, feeling dirt and dust collecting on my damp feet.

21

TWO HANDYMEN WITH a toolkit stood on the landing outside Eli's door. One of them was my age and quite handsome. How they'd already made it into the building, I had no idea.

"May I help you?" I asked.

"We'd like to speak with Eli Løvik," they answered.

"She's away," I said, "but I'm happy to take a message."

They both glimpsed at my towel and I stared back at them, very troubled. The older handyman cleared his throat and asked who I was. "I'm Kurt, a relative."

The talking one now revealed that they were from the Legal Enforcement Office. When I asked if Eli had sent for them, he said the judge did. I nervously clutched my towel. "The judge?"

"Indeed."

As his younger, silent partner looked past me, down the hallway, I made clear that I didn't understand what this was about and repeated that I'd take a message. I then learned that they happened to have a message for *me*. I was to leave the apartment at once. "What? I live here. I have all my things here."

They had a court order to seal the door; no one was allowed to enter until the eviction case had been settled. They'd let me put on clothes, but then I must leave everything else behind.

What eviction case? Was my life in fact unraveling? Things were undoubtedly moving too quickly.

I could hardly keep myself together at the thought of losing my belongings and becoming homeless again. "We're just doing our job," the man said. "If you need more details, call the Enforcement Office."

"You can't kick me out on the street! I'm a student! I'll talk to the papers! I don't even know what kind of office you keep referring to…"

"Well, I'm sure the woman you're living with does…. There are always plenty of warnings."

"Stay right where you are," I insisted. "I have to make a couple of phone calls."

"We'd prefer to come inside, if you don't mind."

I did mind, but they didn't listen—so much for trusting me to return to the door.

I was in desperate need of parental advice. Besides, I couldn't find the note with the country house number in the hallway—until I remembered hiding it in my dictionary with my money yesterday when you came over. And then for some reason Eli wouldn't pick up.

"Some men from the Legal Enforcement Office are here," I stammered into her answering machine. "They're evicting me from the apartment, this very minute. They're locking me out and holding my property."

A loud, metallic shriek at the other end assaulted my eardrums. At long last Eli's voice materialized, strikingly calm. "Hello Kurt, I don't get it. My lawyer promised to take care of this weeks ago. Let me talk to them."

The older handyman picked up while I stepped back to the kitchen door and tried not to shiver. His younger colleague flashed me an embarrassed look, as he brought out a roll of thick, distinctive-looking tape. I should've been gathering all my things and demanding to take them with me instead of just standing there. I turned away, miserable. The talker pulled a pen and notepad from his front pocket and asked Eli too who I was. Finished writing, he handed me the receiver and looked at me with sympathy.

"We're done here for today," he said, to my relief. "She's still on the line. She wants to speak with you now."

22

AS THE TWO handymen closed the door behind them with surprising politeness, I could hear Eli's kids in the background. I said hello into the receiver. Eli started talking at once.

"Did they leave? Did you tell them you're my ex-husband's cousin? It's all a mistake. But it's all so very complicated. I didn't want to bother you with this. But I guess I have no choice." My hands shook as she explained her ongoing fight with her landlord.

Some awful real estate shark had bought the apartment last year, and now he was trying to more than triple the rent. But he had no right to, she said. The apartment was rent-controlled for another six years. The only problem was that her lawyer didn't do his work. The lease was in her ex-husband's name. Since he'd moved out, the owner claimed that he was illegally subletting her the apartment. That, according to Eli, was *bullshit*—she had settlement documents showing that the contract had been transferred to her when they divorced. "But the lawyer just says yah, yah and then forgets everything. He's my ex-husband's lawyer actually. They're old drinking buddies. I'm calling him right away." The second the doorbell buzzed—different-sounding this time—Eli's voice reached an uncomfortably high pitch. "Are they back? Can you check?"

From the street, someone mumbled softly into the intercom with a strong North Norwegian accent, "Hello … it's me."

Jonny.

I hesitated. How could I put on a bright face, or even a calm face, when I introduced Bodø Boy into this household?

23

IN HIS STRIPED Rugby shirt, Bodø Boy came across as thoroughly groomed. Kneeling on the floorboards by my own stinking sneakers, he removed his fancy Nike running shoes. Then, jumping to his feet, he murmured, "Hello, you hairless handball player."

He stood so close I could feel the warmth generated by his body. "Hi there, dark-haired marching band boy."

My voice cracked momentarily. I couldn't help it. And then he thrust his chest into mine. I stiffened my legs so as not to fall backward and shuddered—his hand had entered inside my towel. Okay then! I struggled with his clothes. We tripped on the hall carpet. And Eli's phone started ringing. Oh no.

I had no idea how to turn down the volume. Loud and clear, Eli's voice emerged on the answering machine, and she started gabbing. "Kurt, are you there? Kurt, please answer. *Oh God*, don't tell me they came back..." And then: "*Please*, let me know when you get this message. No one's allowed to seal off the apartment until further notice. My lawyer's taking care of everything with the Enforcement Office right now." I was able to hold Jonny's attention—I don't think he even blinked. She hung up. No more interruption, no further delays, please!

Everything in the entire world was on hold but *this*.

Still wearing his long-sleeved Rugby shirt, Bodø Boy moved his finger slowly along the length of my neck. He took pleasure in giving me goosebumps. Intertwined, soaking in sweat, I wiped some pebbles off my sticky shoulder.

"Yum," he said, "that was quick. You do this a lot?"

"That was the first time ever."

"Yah, whatever." He shrugged. "Sending out text messages and seducing boys with your towel. You seem rather experienced at it."

24

MY EXPRESSION MUST have unsettled him. Now Bodø Boy looked me over more closely. "The first time ever, huh? All right, maybe not that experienced then. On second thought, you performed with a complete lack of skill. Happy now?" He grinned. Entirely hypnotized by his hand stroking my balls, I hardly heard him.

We were lying right next to all the shoes. Our sperm clung to our bellies in milky drops, and my cell phone lay vibrating on the bathroom tiles. I assumed it was Eli. Today I was much in demand.

"All right then, you're a natural," Jonny went on, eyeing me for a reaction. "I have to admit your dialect disturbs me quite a bit though. It feels awkwardly incestuous. I've never had sex with another Bodø boy before. I can't decide whether it's a turn-off or a tremendous turn-on. Now, what's this thing about the Enforcement Office?"

I explained what had happened and he almost shouted back at me, "I'd move out today if I were you. Kurt, how old are you?"

"Twenty."

Self-consciously, I discovered that I still had oil on the back of my leg.

"You were born in 1982?"

"Yah."

"Oh."

Jonny looked confused and wanted me to explain exactly what I meant by first time ever. I gave him an offended look. "Come on, stop this questioning."

"No! Kurt, was this the first time with a marching band boy, or simply the first time with me?"

"First time for everything. Period."

"Everything? As in with a boy?"

"Everything … as in any other person! End of discussion. You can choose to believe me or not."

"You should have said something earlier … I'd have taken more care. Wow. Twenty years. That's old for a first timer. Did you really not hook up with *anyone* after we met? Were you that traumatized by me? Is it really true?" Jonny glanced at me teasingly as the milky substance on my stomach turned transparent and ran down my side.

"So how old are you?" I ventured. "Twenty-one?"

"I'm seventeen."

But that didn't make any sense. "Huh, you're still a teenager?"

"Yah, born in 1984."

I looked him over. "Didn't you send me a picture from your confirmation? That should have made you at least fourteen when you wrote that letter."

"Oh, I remember that—I did it on purpose. Those pictures were taken for my big sister's confirmation. The whole family went to the photographer."

"You could have turned me into a criminal."

He laughed. "Only if we'd had sex. I used to think you were a lunatic with only one thought on your mind. And I was right—you just proved it! And just so you know I turn eighteen no later than *Friday*. First thing in the morning, I'm going to the wine monopoly to buy a small bottle of vodka."

I made out that Jonny must still be in high school. I wondered why he lived in Oslo and asked, "Do your parents live here too?" No, Jonny Larsen wasn't in high school, he'd just started journalism studies at Oslo University College. I couldn't understand how it was at all possible. He was way too young to be a student. He'd clearly thought about the issue and gave me a condescending look.

"The average Norwegian loses so much time," he said. "Here, students finish high school a year later than in many other countries. On top of that, if you're a boy, you're expected to serve in the army for another nine months. Nine months! I'd leave the country tomorrow if I had to do that. You can't be drafted if you're abroad. I want to make my own decisions *now*, not when I retire."

That sounded eerily familiar.

Filling me in, Jonny explained that he had an international baccalaureate degree. All instruction had been conducted in English, none in Norwegian; a perfect foundation, he maintained, for studying abroad. A secondary education in two years instead of the customary three—he'd started off in Wales and completed the second year in Oslo.

Still worked up, he disentangled my towel and cleaned himself off along with the bottom of his Rugby shirt. He even wiped my stomach and ordered me to apply for a student flat immediately. He wouldn't listen to my objections—the waiting list existed only at the beginning of the term.

Then, muttering something about a mandatory seminar, he grabbed his jeans. "You look a bit depressed," he said, as an afterthought. "But that's quite normal for a beginner, after your first orgasm."

"It's not my first *orgasm*."

"You said your first *everything*."

"With another person."

Jonny laughed mischievously and moved to put on his bright white shoes. He blushed when I got up and grabbed him. "You're obviously in a post-orgasm funk," he maintained. "You're questioning your values. It's common when you're new to it all."

"I'm only sad because you're leaving... Didn't you want to take a bath? I'll wash off that cum so it doesn't start smelling suspiciously during your seminar."

Plunking his shoe down, Bodø Boy reluctantly followed me down the hallway and observed with his hand that the tub water had gone cold. Of course I tried to stop him, before he even lifted the porcelain goose from the sink and rubbed the figure affectionately against his cheek. He grimaced, noting its stickiness.

I let out an exclamation—the goose's eyes were missing.

How could I explain away its expressionless face with any conviction? I was constantly running short of readily acceptable justification.

25

UNDER THE KITCHEN table, Bodø Boy put his hand inside my shorts and asked if I had condoms—I didn't. After I'd served him gravy stew and thin wafer crisp bread, he wanted to take advantage of Eli's oven for dessert, for he didn't have a full stove to use in his own flat. As it turned out, the mandatory seminar wasn't until next morning.

I asked if he liked Burt Bacharach.

"Who's he?"

"I'll put him on when we get back from the supermarket."

But first we had to wait until Jonny removed his hand from inside my shorts under the kitchen table.

I was visibly nervous when we strolled down Hafrsfjordgata. He mocked me for it, wondered if I were afraid to be seen with him in public. No, I agreed that it was only natural that two students from Bodø were gleefully walking together in Oslo.

I should've brought the mountain backpack, just in case the enforcement people sealed off the apartment while we were out. Jonny wouldn't stop grinning at me. "Your looking around's stressing me out," he laughed. "Do you really think they're lurking about, waiting for a chance to break in?" Then he let pass that if I promised to apply for a student flat tomorrow, I could stay with him in the meantime. "Would that make you more relaxed somehow?"

At this point, Ragnar, it mightn't come as a total surprise that I wasn't quite ready to trust Jonny to keep his offer. I glanced warily at him.

"It's an old maid's room with a double bed," he added, as if to make his proposition less daunting. "It was big enough for me and my ex."

"You mean … you and that bus driver?" I shivered at the thought.

"Yah. He moved out a few weeks ago."

Lars was a student too—but he and Jonny didn't talk anymore. Jonny said we should ask for some leftover cardboard boxes at the store while we were at it. "Relax now, Kurt. I'll be your watchdog."

My own, private watchdog! I liked the sound of that yet wondered if there was something to his post-orgasm depression theory after all. He moved away slightly each time I bumped into his side, and I took it rather personally. I constantly craved physical contact but tried not to walk too close, as I'd done with you.

Once we were done shopping, we hid the condoms among the groceries and split the cost evenly. And when we got back with our bags and cardboard boxes, the apartment, thankfully, hadn't been sealed.

To collect myself, and set the general mood for the afternoon, I headed straight to Eli's stereo and turned on my favorite Bacharach album.

"It's so slick," I said. "It's even called 'Make It Easy on Yourself.' The music just gets to me. It's sad and uplifting at the same time." Sitting down next to me on the floor by the sofa, Jonny wondered how I'd come across such an elderly singer. I'd found an old record at home in Bodø, I explained. It was my mum's. I'd had nothing better to do sometimes than flick through her old collection. I'd never seen her buy or put on any music except for around Christmastime, so I was intrigued by the songs she owned. This album was from 1969. I used to listen to it over and over. When there was no one else at the house to stop me, I'd play the same song again and again. My favorite track used to be "Pacific Coast Highway"—the part with the flute—and as I listened to it, I went over all the things I wanted to do.

I grew quiet. But yah, Ragnar, I could've continued. All the wind instruments had taken on new meaning when I learned that Jonny played the euphonium.

"The things you wanted to do? When?"

"When I grew up."

"So then we should put it on repeat! It's easier with a CD anyway. Come on, we need to hear it."

Jonny had an idea about a secret ingredient for the pastry dough: shooting our loads into the middle as a filling. And during the rising, he wanted to deflower me in every way, and in every place, conceivable.

"We'll make a mess of ourselves unless we use those," he said, pointing at Gry and Eva's mini aprons hanging by the oven. They barely covered our genitals. When pressed, I muttered that I'd always dreamed of having someone next to me in a double bed. This boy could get anything out of me; it didn't take Jonny long to figure out which door led into Eli's room.

He dragged me past a mirror and I caught sight of a distressing hickey on my neck. You were likely to notice in class.

26

I TREATED BODØ BOY to a second soak in the tub, borrowing some bath salt. Leading me on with a lazy, seductive look while his toe made its way in between my butt cheeks, he confessed that he had discovered my ad after a marching band rally. In Eli's bathroom, the pieces of what had happened in Bodø finally came together.

He'd bought the porn magazine at a railway station together with three older musicians, and since he'd put down the money, it was his to keep. And he'd been setting the dinner table when, in the kitchen, his father had called out his mother's name. After a long silence, his mum had called out Jonny's name. Gray in the face, they both stared at him from different corners of the kitchen. She spoke first: "Do you know a man named Kurt?"

Standing there in the narrow room between them, he'd answered *no*, at once. Shockwaves coursed through our bathwater. "Your parents opened your mail? That's a serious breach of trust." His admission shocked and upset me. How could they do this to my Jonny Boy?

Yet his mum wouldn't relent. "You don't know *anyone* called Kurt—someone who'd send you letters?"

Should Jonny confess that he did know a *boy* called Kurt?

Yet before he had time to consider, his dad had asked the underlying question: "Do you like boys?"

"Huh? No!"

At this point his mum shot his dad a dissatisfied look.

"Are you sure?" his dad asked.

"Why … yah. Of course!"

Dad pointed at a handwritten envelope on the kitchen bench. "Would you care to read this letter then?"

"Not really … not anymore."

His mum interjected, "He doesn't have to."

But Jonny had grabbed the letter and it began something like 'Dear Ronny…'

I screamed, "That's not possible."

Bodø Boy splattered some water back at me. "Your letter went like, 'Dear Ronny, I want to tear off your band uniform while you practice the trumpet.' Just so you know, I never played the trumpet," he corrected me. "That was an extremely popular instrument. By the time it was my turn to pick at our first practice, they were all gone. I struggled to bring this huge euphonium home. I was only eight and Mum thought it was a tuba. Although you were considerate enough to write 'From Kurt' on the back of the envelope. Oh well, I guess you meant that as a sign so I'd open the letter in privacy. So much for privacy."

What was this business about meeting at the regular place? His dad had demanded an answer. He wanted Jonny to explain why someone would send him such a letter in the first place. Frantic at the thought of irrevocable evidence, Jonny had answered, "But the letter's for you, Dad."

"Jonny," I interrupted. "This is crazy."

"That's why Mum gave him the letter in the first place. Dad's name is Dag Ronny."

His dad had actually blushed. "Why, I don't play any instrument. And this is probably a kid's handwriting. Jonny, please explain. What have you been up to?"

There was only one reply to all of this. "Nothing!"

His parents concluded, on his insistence, that some offensive little pep band lunatic was playing a horrible, utterly sick joke on them—because like mine, Jonny's sex life was an open book of empty pages, and by the way, dinner was overcooking.

His mum looked at his dad. "Should we keep the letter? In case there's more harassment?"

"No," Jonny demanded. "Tear it up and throw it away!"

As Bodø Boy stormed out of the small kitchen, his sister glanced up from the sofa. "Dinner's served," he snorted, taking his seat at the table.

Without further mention of my suggestions, or any other topic for that matter, they devoured the food—cuttlefish balls in white sauce with new potatoes. It was a muted affair, yet a meal never to be forgotten.

And from that day on, Jonny diligently brought in the mail himself.

Yet in spite of his effort, during her lunch break one day, his mum discovered one more letter addressed to Ronny Larsen—same handwriting, same envelope, postmarked from the same town. She obviously hadn't decided what to do right away nor shown the letter to his dad. Instead, she showed up in his room in the evening—and watched him, stunned, as he tore up the sealed envelope without reading its content.

The very next day, there was a phone call. Jonny heard it ringing long before his mum knocked on his bedroom door. Hoping to avoid more awkward questions, he declined to pick up. Several minutes later she returned with the phone number. She sat down on the edge of his bed.

She said that she wouldn't be surprised if many people developed a liking for her son—both girls and a few boys—because he was turning into a good-looking young man.

I agreed with her observation. Although this particular boy—she meant *me*—was a bit on the sordid side. She seemed relieved, though, that I sounded so *young* on the phone. She offered to speak to me about *ending* my correspondence. Jonny told her to go ahead. How could he?

"I hated you," he explained, splashing water at me. "And still, here I am."

We let the moment sink in. In Eli's living room, Bacharach had long finished singing. And all of a sudden Jonny lowered his voice. "Could that be the Enforcement Office?"

"What?"

Now, outside in the staircase, the twin girls Gry and Eva could clearly be heard giggling, calling for their mum. Those were sounds I was ill prepared for. "Hurry," I said, "take a towel. Run and hide in my room."

27

I RACED INTO the kitchen to pull on my shorts, hang up the aprons, and remove all our clothes from the floor. Next, I hurried into Eli's bedroom to fix the covers.

The entrance door was unlocked and I could hear the three of them meander into the hallway. And then she materialized. Upon opening her very own bedroom door, my landlady froze in her tracks. Startled, I dropped a sock—one of Jonny's—on my way to the bedroom's other exit.

"Oh hi, Eli," I managed to say. "You're back."

"May I ask what's going on?"

She plunked her bag on the still disheveled comforter. Clasping my armful of garments, I picked up the sock.

"I was in the bathtub and … then I heard someone at the door and I panicked and wanted to hide. I just … I thought it was the Enforcement Office. I didn't know you'd be back so soon."

"Why didn't you return my calls?"

She gave me a mistrustful look and said she'd left a message on the answering machine and two on my cell phone. I claimed I hadn't paid any attention to the phone—which was almost true.

"Everything's sorted out with the Enforcement Office," she

said. "There's nothing more to worry about." She was just home to take care of some other business because she'd received an unexpected commission from a potential client. They were heading straight back to the country house before the weekend. "Gee, the place's such a mess. You've splattered water everywhere, even in here."

Then I remembered Jonny's white shoes in the hallway. I burst out, "Yah, I'm sorry. You're probably wondering what I'm doing in your bedroom. My brother's visiting from Bodø. I was just moving his clothes."

"Really? Has he slept in here? Where's he now?"

"In my room, I guess."

"Oh."

"We've been making cinnamon buns…"

Eli began to tear off her bed sheets and I decided to leave her in peace. Impatiently waiting behind my door, Jonny wanted his underwear back at once and told me he was leaving. That wasn't an option, I replied, at least until tomorrow. He wanted to know why they'd come back early. He wasn't laughing when I said that he was needed for moral support and pretend brotherhood.

"She mentioned something about a commission," I said. "She's a part-time interior designer."

"Yeah, right. You've seriously got to get yourself out of here before you lose everything…"

We hid my cardboard boxes and her roll of trash bags behind my door, and to conceal the bluish hickey on my neck, he lent me his Rugby shirt and turned up the collar. I'd forgotten and started to panic, but he assured me that since it was on the back, there was a good chance she hadn't noticed.

Unexpectedly, he seemed to fancy the old, faded T-shirt I offered in return. Guardedly, he followed me back into the kitchen. The leftover dough that he had shaped into a phallus on the kitchen table had, fortunately, grown into an indistinct mass. He lifted the first tray into the oven as I began, rather forlorn, to clean the counters.

Gry and Eva were talking quietly with their mum in their room. After a few moments, Eli entered with a cheer. "It smells so good in here… and the girls are so hungry after the drive. Do you think they could try one bun each?" I stared blankly at Jonny—clearly we were both at loss. A moment of complete awkwardness hung between us, as if we were too mean to share the treats, until he collected himself.

"By all means," he replied sheepishly. "I love to bake. Have as many as you like."

"Oh thanks, that's really generous. So you're Kurt's brother?"

My 'brother' blushed as he and Eli shook hands, and she declared that we looked strikingly similar—we could in fact have been twins, although on second thought, perhaps not identical ones like her own.

"I've got an inflatable beach mattress that you can borrow," she informed us, her demeanor now exceptionally welcoming. She made blackcurrant cordials for everyone and, bringing in an extra chair, set the kitchen table for five. "Oh, they're so good and moist," she exclaimed between mouthfuls. "Isn't that right, girls? These are the best buns I've ever had. Jonny, you have to give us the recipe."

"Readymade bun mix straight from the box," he muttered at once. "And maybe one or two secret ingredients."

"How exciting. What secret ingredients?"

"No, that was just a joke," I interrupted, worrying that a blood vessel in Jonny's forehead might burst. Eli probably intuited that ingredients were forbidden territory, for she proceeded to ask him all kinds of questions about his journalistic studies in Bodø. I watched him squirm during the interrogation and noticed that the girls seemed even more shy than usual.

Never mind that though. I had to agree with Eli—the cinnamon buns were marvelous.

28

WE ALLOWED OUR streams of urine to cross as they cascad-ed into the toilet bowl—I even let Bodø Boy borrow my tooth-brush. My lips were sore. And my groin ached remarkably. And my sleepover guest didn't have time to shower, because we'd let our-selves sleep in.

For a moment we gazed at the hind of the now-blind goose, which was facing the corner on the tub. I said I could read the por-celain bird's mind. Having traveled far and wide, the goose obviously felt too ashamed and mortified to face us ever again.

Jonny grinned and blushed. There, standing on the cold bath-room tile, our heads lightly touching, I hugged him goodbye, before anyone else awoke.

A stayover—Eli's beach mattress had remained unused on my floor. Going through the strangest emotions, I dropped back into bed with a thump. Seconds later, Eli knocked on my door. Needless to say, I grew worried. Had she heard Jonny leave? Had she over-heard us in the bathroom, or even worse, noticed sounds during the night? She murmured my name and wouldn't leave.

I pulled on my new Welsh Rugby shirt. On closer reflection I tugged the hooded pullover on top of it. Then I unlocked the door, bracing myself to hear her out. Eli was standing there in her robe, and she looked nervous. "Did your brother take off? Is he coming back? But … have you been crying? Did you fight?"

I rubbed my eyes and tried to chuckle. "No, this is how I look in the morning." I added that Jonny'd gone to sit in on an early seminar at the University College on his way to the airport.

She said it was a shame he wasn't staying longer. His baking was certainly something worth trying again, and if she had known he'd be leaving so early, she would've said goodbye properly last night. To calm things down a bit, I told her that she might yet get the chance to taste his buns again, for he planned to change schools and move down here pretty soon.

Then, without warning, Eli asked if I'd seen her roll of trash bags. The bag in the kitchen was filling, she explained, and the garbage truck would be coming any moment.

Dumbfounded, I gazed at her naked feet, unsure of what to say. She was certainly very attentive to what went on in her home. Finally, she gave the impression of remembering why she was standing there in her robe in the first place.

"Yah, Kurt, there's one more thing. I need you to pay the October rent at once. Because I've got to cover some unexpected expenses arising from my commission and I'd really like to get back to the country house tonight. If this is an issue for you, I'll need to ask for a month's advance instead. As security. Because I really can't start work without some cash."

"But that's not in our contract!"

I'd lost my temper and now she lost hers, too. "We'll rewrite the contract. You've been using my whole apartment including my bedroom. I'll need one month's security in case something gets damaged."

Trying to be reasonable, I asked my landlady to wait a second and got the black roll from behind my door. I certainly made sure with my hand it didn't swing open so she'd eye my cardboard boxes. Seeing her surprised look at the roll, I explained that I'd panicked when the enforcement people came by and wanted to gather my personal effects. I added that there was one thing I'd actually been meaning to tell her since yesterday.

"What?"

"I'm moving."

"You're moving?"

"Yah."

I'd have to take my chances with Jonny's offer. Eli asked if this had anything to do with those guys from the Enforcement Office. She stressed that they'd acted in error.

"It has nothing to do with that…"

"Then what's this all about?"

She demanded an answer but I was at a loss. The fear of being locked out, along with sudden renegotiations, sounded like a perfectly valid excuse for releasing myself from her contract. But my words came out so fast I denied myself the use of my best card … and for what, to avoid an argument, to avoid hurting her feelings? All I said was "I got an offer for a student flat this week. It's just cheaper that way. I'll save a lot of money."

She blinked. "And when's this move happening?"

"Quite soon."

"How soon?"

"In a few weeks."

My offer to put up "For Rent" flyers at the university was entirely ignored. She too was close to tears. "You're putting me in a very difficult position," she said. "You know that. It's not good for my kids to have people moving in and out."

I said I completely understood, because I totally did!

Clutching her trash bag roll, she crossed her arms. "You said you planned to stay for the full academic year. That was my one condition. Yah, you fooled me. How am I supposed to find a new tenant now? You realize that most students have found a place to live by now?"

Again I was lost for words.

"But fortunately, we have a written agreement," she continued. "There's a clause specifying one month's notice in advance of moving out. Since I can't trust you anymore, I expect the October payment before you leave the house today."

"Excuse me, you can't just make demands like this," I mustered. "I owe you nothing right now. I'm only willing to pay through October 18th, one month from today. I'll pay you at the end of the month." Why didn't I just demand a cancellation of our agreement? Everyone'd tell me later it was a fair demand.

I'd managed to make Eli angrier than Jonny's mum had ever been. "Oh, *I can*, and I do have the right! You use my yeast, and my oven, and my electricity. And you made no effort whatsoever to replace my chili nuts. Just get your stash of money and your calculator out here and pay now, so we're done with it. And if I lose this commission, I'm billing you for time lost. I'll stand here in front of your door if I have to. Neither of us leaves my apartment until this is settled. Kurt, be warned—if I fear any more delay tactics and false play from you, I might need to put on the deadlock on the apartment door. For that, there's only one key."

She left my door ajar.

I got up and locked it.

EVERY TWENTY MINUTES or so, my landlady knocked on my door and demanded her money. Once she even yelled that I had to start behaving like an adult.

To escape my jailor, Jonny suggested that I drop everything out the window and pretend I was going to the bank to fetch her money. I had to remind him that I lived on the third floor and owned a CD player. My stomach growled as the text messages darted between my bedroom and Jonny's seminar, and my arms trembled from packing.

This boy had really learned how to just say yah now that he had his own place with no parent interference. "You're moving in with me *today*?" Bodø Boy responded to my desperate question. "That's fast. But I like it."

If worse came to worst, I'd call Mum and Dad and tell them my landlady was keeping me hostage and ask if they could call the police. That should take care of things promptly, but it might also cause some concern.

So I decided to stay put in my room until Eli had left for her ex-husband's vacation house. Although the buns and the rest of my food were in the kitchen, I didn't want to leave my bunker to check if she'd made good on her threat until I had someone to protect me.

Then I'd have to tell her she'd made my brother cancel his return flight and bill her for that. Because there was nowhere to pee but in two empty teacups, my room took on a disconcerting tang of urine and ginger in addition to the mint.

"Just threaten to make it known that she's in the illegal sublet-ting business," Jonny wrote back. "By the way, I really don't think it's illegal unless she's renting the whole apartment instead of a single room. But never mind, let her fry. I'm coming over as soon as I'm done at the seminar."

For more than an hour, I heard nothing from Eli. When Jonny finally texted that he was waiting outside the building, I unlocked my door noiselessly and looked into the living room.

One of the armchairs had been turned to face my door and in it a spectacled, wavy-haired man—who must have been well past sixty—looked up from his copy of Ernest Hemingway's *For Whom the Bell Tolls*. Eli's father, perhaps? We nodded to each other and he demanded to know where I was heading.

"To let in a friend," I replied, securing my door in embarrass-ment. "If it's still possible in this household."

"You need to lock your room to do that?"

Without answering him, I rushed to the front door to buzz Jon-ny into the building. The deadlock wasn't on and I left the entrance unlocked. Then I ran to empty my food from the cabinet and fridge into a trash bag. Eli and the kids were nowhere to be found, but she'd confiscated each and every bun from the breadbox—very well, she could keep our baked sperm samples.

After gulping down cold water from the kitchen tap, I dragged the food out on the landing, where Bodø Boy stood waiting in my T-shirt and looking amazed at the quick changes of atmosphere in Hafrsfjordgata. I whispered that some old man was guarding my room entrance.

When we returned to the living room, however, the guard had vanished. Only the book rested, spine up, in his armchair. Had he gone to the bathroom? Obviously, there was no time to get my toi-letries or clean or remove the teacups, which, together with the buns and the missing goose eyes, made my getaway feel more awkward than I'd have liked.

I put on my mountain backpack; Jonny took the smaller backpack and the cardboard boxes. To confuse the guard, I locked my door quietly. Then we tiptoed through the living room and down the creaking hallway. As I grabbed my food bag at the landing, I got the creepy feeling that something wasn't quite right—the flight was going too smoothly and we didn't seem to be carrying much with us. "Hey, we must have forgotten one thing or another," I whispered.

Expecting Eli's guard to show up from the bathroom any instant, Jonny insisted that we get down the stairs at once, but I begged him to hold on. "There's nothing left," he sighed outside Eli's front door. "I looked around."

Counting my belongings, I made an unpleasant discovery: The box with my CD player and half my Burt Bacharach collection was missing. While I stood there immobilized, Jonny gave me the sweetest look. "Are you sure that stuff isn't inside my box? It's rather heavy. Hey, how about this? Let's bring everything we've got into a taxi. Then you can decide what to do."

No taxi could be seen out on the street. "Let's hide everything near the wall," I said, "so the guard won't see us from the window."

"Does it matter? He probably knows we're down here by now."

My trousers fell down when I tried to call for a taxi. Fuming, I told my co-conspirator to make the call, and keep an eye on everything, because I was going back upstairs. Jonny looked alarmed. "Are you sure it's worth the risk?"

"Why, of course! If it comes to fight, I'll beat him."

Preparing for battle, I changed into the basketball shorts I'd wadded up in my mountain backpack. Then I whiffed that suspicious and utterly irritating mint scent again, it really clung to my nose. Tracking it to the inside of my jeans—yuck—I discovered a green smear of chewing gum. I never chewed green gum. Those jeans had turned into garbage collectors.

All I needed was a better pair of jeans; maybe Jonny could help me pick one. As soon as I ran into Eli's living room, the guard stood up from his armchair, clearly expecting me. "Did you steal something?" I yelled.

"You mean did I take out a security deposit?"

"Yah, ha! That's break-in and theft. I'll report you to the police.

I'll nail Eli for burglary *and* illegal subletting."

"The keys and 2,400 kroner, please."

Since I'd promised Jonny that I wouldn't get into any grim physical fighting, I threw the keys on the floor then ran off. I could always blackmail Eli later—if the man wasn't coming after me. My savior Jonny waited downstairs in the backseat of a taxi with the door open. I unlocked my bicycle and chased the car to his building in Odins Gate. Exhausted, I spat on the curb to clean my mouth so I could kiss him and thank him.

"Hey, don't do that," my new roommate scolded. "And you owe me eighty-five kroner for the taxi ride."

30

THE GATE'S LOCK and doorstopper were broken. Its swinging panel slammed behind us. As I slipped the chain lock through the spokes in my back wheel, I was unsettled by some rather obnoxious knocking above me. In a window, an ancient, gray-haired woman happened to be staring at me, murderously.

Still bent at the waist with a mountain backpack swaying over my head, I decided to take another look at the wooden fence and the unsecured bike rack, even though the only anchored piece of metal I could find in the backyard was the pole of an empty clothesline.

The moment Jonny moved toward her window though, the woman's angry visage disappeared behind a curtain. "Oh, so she doesn't want a discussion," he said resolutely. "Just leave the bike where it is. There's no room for it upstairs."

"You don't think I'll be asking for trouble?"

"Not at all. I've never seen her using the drying stand. She probably worries that someone would steal her clothes, but who'd want them?"

Cigarette butts lay scattered on the steps and Jonny apologized for the rotten smell. He sat down on the two boxes, caught his breath, and adjusted his erection. Relieved and impatient, we lingered on his landing, our lower bodies rubbing against each other.

"Oh, Kurt," he whispered, egging me on with his hands, "you're so cute in those shorts. Your legs have great definition after all that handball playing. And your thighs are so easy to reach." He wanted me on his lap and I keenly obeyed.

The other tenants in the building had larger living quarters and entrances on the street proper. Only Jonny used the back door, so it was basically private, he assured me, although the people in the flat share above him never bothered to close the back door when they went outside for smokes. It upset him that they were too lazy to carry out their own trash even. They left it on their landing, using it as their private dump.

That explained the smell.

"And they've got this big, fat cat... They just open their door and it finds its own way out. I always close the back door when I see it open, but once the cat got trapped in the stairwell and peed on my mat."

"Oh no, how gross."

Jonny wondered how I'd handled my stuff from Bodø without a suitcase. I really didn't think it was that much—I'd caught the train and Mum mailed some of it. I'd planned to bring my cross-country skis after Christmas. Just wait until I bought my textbooks tomorrow.

"You know," he added abruptly, "last summer there was this one muscular guy who always sunbathed in the grass, stroking his stomach. Slowly. Like this. Between his navel and Speedos."

I didn't quite follow his thought. So he leaned back to give me a demonstration. His ex hadn't been sure what to make of it, and to be honest I couldn't make much of it either. "Maybe he was testing you," I suggested. "Or maybe you filled him with desire."

Jonny considered the idea and then told me that Lars had wanted to put on a competition—mirroring the neighbor's every movement. In preparation, a few weeks in advance of his eighteenth birthday, he'd given Jonny a new pair of swimming trunks. They never dared to attempt the trick though. Instead, Jonny had worn his gift indoors.

Bodø Boy finally seemed to understand that I didn't particularly enjoy this kind of talk. Instead, he wanted to know the value of my CD player. It was six years old, bought with the money I'd gotten after my church confirmation, and couldn't be worth much, maybe 500 kroner. That nutty couple in Hafrsfjordgata could just forget about their 2,400 kroner demand. I'd spend that money on new stereo equipment.

31

"SAVE YOUR MONEY," Jonny said. "I own an excellent player." He got on his feet. "Welcome to the old maid's room," he announced as he unlocked his door, making it sound like an afterthought. According to him it really used to be a maid's room—although he hadn't had the chance to do any maid's work this week.

The double bed, made up in clean, white covers, took up almost half the space. The door jammed behind the bedstead, he explained, led to the section of the apartment where his landlord lived. On a small, collapsible table, a bowl of cornflakes soaked in sweet-smelling milk.

"Today's breakfast?"

"I'll tidy up in a moment. I'm sorry to admit it's from yesterday." Jonny quickly fixed me a glass of orange juice. "There you go. Breakfast at last. Yah, that's the bathroom," he said, seeing my guarded expression as I took in the door plastered with a picture of three bare-chested men carrying thick car tires.

"That's quite a poster," I admitted.

He wanted me to inspect the one taped to the fridge next. There wasn't much left to the imagination. It depicted a black man in tiny white shorts lifting a large free-weight; his back muscles were reflected in a huge mirror. Jonny looked me over teasingly. "Now, what do you think of *that*?"

"I don't know. Those guys aren't even attractive—they're just old! Even as works of art, they're pretty bland. I'd rather look at you."

"Don't worry, they belong to Lars."

I couldn't help my alarm. "Huh, he left them behind?"

In his early twenties, Lars had moved back in with his parents and probably didn't want the suggestive images hanging in his room. Although the pay wasn't that great, Jonny's ex-boyfriend commuted by train, all the way from Fredrikstad, every day to drive the bus. Jonny guessed that when he decided to relocate, he hadn't planned on moving out permanently, but in fact he had. I asked how long they'd been a couple.

"Ten months. Impressive, huh? You know that Internet site, Gaysir? I met him there."

I admitted that I knew about the website. After refilling my glass, he handed me half a pack of oatmeal biscuits, and I felt his hands glide up my thighs. Although it made me quite uncomfortable, I held on to his every word—he was a talker. "I gave up Wales to be with him," he said. "Mum and Dad had no idea why I'd swap schools like that. They didn't find it rational. Gee, I'm finally my own man."

With Lars he had come to believe that he had less freedom, less privacy, than as a kid back in Bodø, for Lars was always breaking up with Jonny. It seemed like there was a new emotional crisis to deal with every week. One day, Lars wanted them to stay together forever and become registered partners; the next he didn't want to see Jonny ever again. The mood swings proved exhausting, and Jonny rarely got enough sleep. Lars told him that he was a silly child in need of a proper upbringing, in spite of Jonny's much better grades. So the last time Lars broke up with him, less than a month ago in late August, Jonny decided to learn, grow up, and accept his resignation as final.

From now on, they were flatmates who happened to share a bed. Yet Lars strolled around the flat in his underwear and touched himself like the swimmer in the backyard. Every time Jonny walked past, which was often in their small living quarters, Lars rubbed against him ever so slightly. Jonny begged him to stop.

The moment they had casual sex, Lars assumed they were back together. Hence, Jonny decided to prove that they were not.

And so a slightly younger boy, a skinhead, came in to the city by rail to meet Jonny following a chat on Gaysir. They talked at Café de Stijl all evening, and when the out-of-towner missed his train and started freaking out, Jonny took him home. "I wasn't planning to have sex with him," he said. "But he misunderstood and we got started on the stairs, just like you and I did except that he started it. The whole time, Lars was yelling through the door, 'This is unbearable, just unbearable!' and threatened to move out the next morning."

Jonny claimed he'd intended only to provide the boy with some space in the double bed—that was all. However, Lars barricaded the entrance and offered them two options: either they got themselves a sweet little hotel room, or they paid for his. He had no intention of sharing quarters with a stranger, not even for one night.

Jonny took the sixteen-year-old to a student union bar, but it was closed for the night so they roamed the streets instead. They climbed a fence into a kindergarten playground and sought shelter inside a children's playhouse. For hours they talked, until they ended up naked and shooting their loads onto the wooden boards. So in the early hours, when parents began to arrive with their kids, they fled—the boy straight to the railway station, Jonny to the University College.

No, Jonny didn't go easy on the details. That day he ate at the cafeteria and attended all of his lectures, and when he returned to Odins Gate, he found Lars's keys in the mailbox. The bus driver had taken his things with him, including their shared condoms, and had left a note on his pillow instructing Jonny to check his bank account balance.

For a second, Jonny panicked—he thought Lars had emptied his account. On the contrary, he returned to the computer lab and found out that his ten-month boyfriend had honored their housing arrangement and transferred three full months of rent. "Surely he wanted me to feel bad, to think that I was taking advantage of his kindness," he said to me. "He must've hoped I'd beg him to come back."

For now more than three weeks, Jonny had ignored Lars's calls and messages. And he'd never take Bus 30 into the city center again. After changing his work schedule, Lars—this I already knew—was now driving the damn thing. And the broken gate lock and the un-locked back door proved a real problem, because one night he stood in the stairway howling that Jonny had to return his Britney Spears CD, the ID card he had borrowed, and his Speedo bathing suit—the premature birthday gift. Jonny had put on the CD and ignored him and had since purchased earplugs, in case his ex returned.

The mention of Britney reminded me of my own CD collec-tion, and I wanted to open my cardboard boxes and find out which albums were missing. Suddenly, Jonny demanded to know if I was able to do a West Norwegian accent. "If Lars does come back, I'd like you to shout through the door that you're that muscular swim-mer guy. Can you do an older voice?"

Then he told me to remember what I'd told Eli—that I was sort of his big brother from Bodø and his protector, nothing more.

Okay then.

32

LARS HAD LEFT behind several public transportation maps of
Oslo, all showing a fairly large lake, Maridalsvannet, to be the source
of Akerselva, a river that wound through the city and released fresh
water into the Oslofjord. My parents had walked along it on roman-
tic strolls in their youth, before they married. They'd dropped this
fact without further ado when we discussed my move to Oslo. The
idea clung, triggering my imagination.

While Jonny cleaned the small table and prepared dinner—Tik-
ka Masala with ground beef and rice—I made myself comfortable
in his double bed. Jonny let me play my own music at a low volume.

Maridalsvannet was clearly the biggest body of water within
the metropolitan area, and so wide it should be impossible to miss.
Lying somewhere beyond the last tram stop, the lake seemed even
more isolated than those near the student village. I wouldn't mind
seeing it with my own eyes.

Hopefully Maridalsvannet would be mostly deserted so late in
the fall. A surprise dip in his never-used-outdoors swim trunks before the water got too cold—that would be my one-day-early birthday present to Jonny.

I wrote you a text message for the first time since Monday,

asking gently if you'd be so kind and lend me your tent, a sleeping bag, two pads, and your bike. Because if so, I could go on a little expedition with this girl I'd met at school, Conny.

"Conny?" you wrote. "That's an unusual name. I rather like it." Indeed, you promised to bring everything except the bike to our lecture the following day. So it would have to be a hike then.

Jonny spontaneously agreed to a surprise trip out of the apartment the following day after classes. He even agreed to wear a Speedo underneath his tight jeans. "Where are you taking me?" my confused love interest asked.

"Somewhere wild and wet."

In truth, this guy didn't deny me very much at all at the moment. With no other passengers on the last stretch of the forty-minute tram ride, we held hands in the rear seat. The trip almost put us both to sleep, and we yawned our way past apple tree gardens and followed a tiny gravel trail into a perfumed pine forest full of birds, bright light, and shadow. I carried our provisions in my mountain backpack and couldn't stop peeking at the lanky boy just to my side, his legs in particular. Clad in his rolled-up jeans and skater shoes, he was undoubtedly the most fashionable boy in this forest. He seized my hand and wouldn't let go. Apart from us, not a soul existed. "You're just one big smile," Jonny said. "And yet you act so serious, so secretive."

"Remember, it's your birthday present. You're in for a surprise." Today, there was no rush and we were constantly making unscheduled stops to touch. Smiling sweetly, he revealed to me that he hadn't camped since junior high school.

A mountain biker—the first person to appear among the pine trees—rushed past us, ringing his bell. Distracted, Jonny followed me off the gravel trail, through the scrub, downhill.

"Come on, Kurt. Where are you leading me?"

"Somewhere private. I'll take you to a place where we can be outdoors and still do whatever we like..."

Under a huge spruce tree, he grasped me by the hips and slammed my groin against his, offering me so much tongue it was difficult to keep my balance. After brushing a few conifer needles from my head, rather painfully, he kissed me again, more tentatively.

I grabbed his ass with both hands, grinding him toward me like he did me.

A little farther on, we crossed an old railway line I didn't recall seeing on the map. We decided it was closed down, for it looked rusty, and wildflowers bloomed far and wide along the track.

Seagulls glided away, eyeing us suspiciously as we closed in on the sharp blue splash of color that lay visible through the foliage. Relieving me of my backpack, Jonny shoved me up against a rock. "Your skin looks so pale," he said, timidly. "This might be your last chance this year to get some color. You'd better undress completely."

"You mean unless we go somewhere."

"Yah, let's go to Spain at fall break."

Bodø Boy thrust his hand inside my shorts, careful to remove them and the boxers underneath at the same time. He let me keep my sneakers on, though, for traction. On the opposite bank people in bright colors were cutting down a tree with an axe. Their voices carried distinctly across the glittering surface of the lake and their presence was making me rather tense. Jonny's watch stopped sliding up and down his bare forearm.

"Relax, they're too far away," he remarked with a smirk. "They won't catch the particulars." He folded back his swimming suit, putting his sexual arousal in plain view. "Well, if you insist," he added, "I'll cover you so no one but me can examine your body."

I reminded him to stop making marks on the back of my neck, but he wouldn't hear of it. As he climbed on top of me, the rock dug painfully into my back. "Now I won't get any sun," I grumbled.

"Oh shit," he said. "My balls are getting squashed by these swim trunks." Struggling to maintain his balance, he pulled them over his Nikes. As he did so, I finally spotted a sign by the lake's edge: Drinking water, Oslo's principal supply—bathing prohibited. Jonny remained nonplussed. "I'll lick you clean before we jump in." Yet suddenly he winced, and his curious expression captivated me. His penis impressively erect, he stood completely motionless. "A fly just landed behind my balls," he explained. "It's moving so tenderly toward my asshole and it tickles. It must feel attracted."

I laughed. Taking in the sensation, he heard something and stared up the hill—he had seriously good hearing and now I noticed it too. I struggled to decipher the weird, hissing reverberation I detected in the distance, but before I could, a baffling whoosh of air engulfed us.

There was a deafening whistle, followed by the unmistakable sound of metal gnashing against metal. And then, traveling at a rather leisurely speed, a passenger train materialized. Inside its red cars, miniature heads took in the view.

Bodø Boy concealed me as best he could and chewed on my ear for comfort until the last car disappeared behind the pines. When he got back to his feet, another green fly landed on the slit of his erection. This determined insect remained in place even when he jumped up and down and waved his hand. Jonny snapped his fingers at it, bemoaned the mistake, and dashed off into the sparkling water with the persistent bug still on his shaft.

He returned grinning—with goosebumps all over his skin. "We need to take more care," he chuckled. "Even I hate attracting this kind of attention."

33

SHORTLY BEFORE NIGHTFALL, everything alive seemed to have gone into a frenzy of activity—we heard birds calling from the branches above and fish jumping from the water nearby. The pine trees glowed in the setting sunlight; their long, naked trunks cast lengthy shadows as the closest star bathed the hill across the valley in its deep orange rays.

We'd followed a tractor trail away from the pebbled path into a clearing that was covered in fresh sawdust. There, on the softwood shavings, we resourcefully set up your green tunnel tent.

Jonny crawled inside, bare-chested. After taking a leak somewhere in the lush vegetation, he seemed a bit out of himself, as if something had disturbed him, but he'd just let his imagination run wild. "Kurt, what if some murderer tears through the fabric with a knife? What if we get shot through the canvas?" I ignored his alarmist concerns, brushed away old spruce sprigs from the floor and rolled out our sleeping pads, and said there were two things I wanted to ask him, since his birthday was coming up at midnight. "But I feel vulnerable," he continued, before I could utter a word. "We can't see who's approaching. What if someone rolls over us with a tractor?"

"Gee, we'll fight off any predators! I'm your protector. And you're my watchdog. At least out here we're safe from bus drivers."

How could I make him listen? I moved closer, but Jonny wouldn't stop with his erratic talk. Indeed, he'd read about some scouts who'd died from suffocation because snow had covered their tent overnight and then froze into an icy shell, melted by their body heat. "Jonny, what are you saying—snow, at this time of the year?"

"Ouch, your stubble's razor sharp! You make my whole face sore." I'd tried to kiss him. "There are a few stray hairs sticking out of a mole on your back," he went on. "Do you want me to pluck them for you?" I told him to wait until we got back to the city and had a razor blade handy. But no, he didn't seem to hear me. While I spoke, he shoved his hand inside his jeans, rubbed his hairy balls, and sniffed his fingers; he placed them under my nose so I could inhale their scent myself. "I'm addicted to that smell," he confessed. "Have you ever tasted that fruit physalis?"

"No, I haven't even heard of it…"

"It's small and yellow. Perfectly ripe, it tastes like butt sweat. Really. I'm your dog, remember. Dogs lick their own asses! Let me show you!"

Stripping naked, he seemed to have no recollection of the possible dangers outside. "Now, look," he said, surprisingly coy. "Are you ready?"

"Sure," I said, rather intrigued. "Can't wait."

"I have to bend quite a bit, so you must watch my back. First tie me up though. Use my belt."

That was a new first; after closing the tent zipper, I diligently strapped his hands together behind his back. His toes hit the roof forcefully as he raised his ass in the air. Then, slowly, his feet descended past his shoulders. There was a dribble of spit sliding off his lips. His whole modernistic figure looked rather wobbly, yet after a little rocking back and forth, he relaxed into the position he clearly was aiming for. In the tent, however, I was lost for words.

This guy had some flexible muscles. I'd never seen someone's entire body change color before, either; he was flushed sweaty and struggling to breathe. Moist around the eyes, he released his penis from its current entanglement and parked it on his chin, so that it appeared as if he'd been devouring a live, throbbing lollipop.

"Sometimes I dream at night that my dick grows so long I only need to bend my head to work on it," he said, gasping for air. "Do you ever have dreams like that?" Breathing heavily, I couldn't really remember. On either side of his darkened red forehead, his pulse pounded alarmingly. Now he rested his dick suggestively against his lips. "Hmm, Kurt. There's something I'd like to ask you." He had questions, too? He groaned in anticipation. "Can you lick my butt, please? It should be clean after a swim."

I laughed. "So you can't really lick your own ass then?"

"Unfortunately, no."

"How did you come up with this concept? Regrettably, I've never thought of it myself."

Jonny gave me a sweet look. "It doesn't require much fantasy, does it? Shit, the blood's disappearing from my dick." His feet came down and he curled up against me, hands still firmly bound behind him. He was panting. "This used to be the closest I could get to having my dick sucked. I decided I liked actually sucking it myself. You might call it a Eureka moment. But you need an exceptionally flexible spine and I get so little of it inside my mouth though. Sometimes when I'm out of practice I can only lick it with my tongue. I wish I had a much longer tongue. Now Kurt, why don't you tell me to shut up or you'll stuff a dirty sock in my mouth? Lars always told me to shut up. He was very manly that way. I know I talk too much."

"That ex of yours doesn't sound well put together."

Jonny giggled. "You should tell him so in a West Norwegian dialect. I'll get my cellphone. Tell him to leave your precious puppy alone. But first, let me be your naughty penguin."

"My naughty penguin?"

While I did all the work, I let him be my naughty penguin. Still tied up, he placed himself over my stomach, awaiting the warmth of my tongue on his organ. Masterfully, I drove him to spurt on my chest and shoulders. Turning around to grasp hold of my cock, he managed to send my own waves of ecstasy into his palms and up his back. We knew our ways swimmingly when it was time for some serious Boy Fun.

Then, massaging his arms, he said, "Hey, didn't you want to ask me something?"

So he'd paid attention after all.

"Yah... two things in fact. First things first … Jonny … are you quite sure that you don't want to be?"

Fervently, he grabbed my hands. "Be …?"

"Yah …"

"Your penguin? I already told you I wanted to be your penguin." He gauged my embarrassed expression before he helped me through my first question. "Kurt? Do you really, truthfully fantasize about being Jonny's boyfriend?"

"Yah! That's it. You're a mind reader." That was actually more than I'd planned to admit tonight. If he'd go steady, see where it took us—that's what I'd prepared to ask. Shy me.

"But *why*?"

I laughed uneasily. "But *why*?"

"Yah, isn't it a bit soon?" Jonny chuckled. "You're acting fast. We met properly only two days ago. And you moved in with me yesterday."

"I want you to myself."

"Clearly you do. You're so mean and selfish!"

"You get me in return."

He considered for a moment. "Lars and I moved too quickly," he then said. "And why? To save on rent. We were so shortsighted."

He went on to tell me that relationships are difficult. That he knew from first-hand experience. That it's so much more fun just being horny. I said that I disagreed, but he didn't fully listen. "Ouch." He slapped the side of his face. "What are those? I can't hear them! They make no sound!"

At first I had no idea what he was on about. It had turned rather dark inside the tent. Then something bit my shoulder too. I smacked it and discovered what he was on about—midges.

Acting resolutely, I wrapped my sleeping bag around us and told him to press his body against mine, in the hopes of massacring as many of the abhorrent insects as possible. But the attacks wouldn't end, so using the dim blue light of his cell phone, I located a rip in a corner of the tent by the floor. Damn you, Ragnar! You could have at least warned us!

Resourcefully, Jonny and I plugged the hole with T-shirts. And to foil any midnight assaults, we slid into separate sacks, zipped up, cinched the elastic bands tight, and concealed our heads on the inside. "Good night, cocooned treasure," he said through the fabric. "You know you're incredibly cute when you're being purposeful like that." Then he added, "My face's getting wet. What if we suffocate inside our sleeping bags?" And finally I heard what I wanted to hear: "So we're boyfriends now? That's what this trip's about?"

For a moment, I suggested snuggling my way into his bag, but he wouldn't hear of it. "It already feels like I'm sleeping in a condom," he whimpered. "It's not really a good place for two people." He chuckled to himself then exclaimed loudly, "God, those bloodsuckers are still coming inside my bag! Please, Kurt, I want to evacuate."

34

SINCE THIS TRIP had been my idea, I remained in charge of the mountain backpack, while Jonny used the small light from his phone to look for trail markings on tree trunks.

If we hurried, and didn't get lost, we could catch the last subway train back into the city from Sognsvann, so there was little time for kissing. We held hands for most of the night walk, partly to prevent ourselves from scratching our midge bites. We spoke little but he knew something more weighed on my mind. After pushing the issue and getting nowhere, he claimed he was no longer interested in my second question.

Of course I was hurt, and a bit unhappy that our first trip came to such a fast conclusion, but he kept eyeing me, warming me up until I was tempted to go ahead and ask that second question.

Remembering your response, however, I didn't want to rush it. I wanted to wait for the perfect—the ripest and most persuasive— moment. Only it had to happen soon.

We'd reached the edge of the city.

As the gravel of a huge, deserted parking lot crunched underneath our feet, we were blinded by a set of high beams somewhere in front of us. Steadily, yet ever so gradually, the beams came closer.

Jonny let go of my hand, sounding a little alarmed. "Welcome back to civilization. The station's on the far side of the lot, behind the scary car."

"Jonny, why is he rolling toward us like that? Is the driver toying with us?"

"Hey, stand still."

Jonny got in front of me, grabbed both my hands, and made me grope him from behind. More car lights flashed from several directions. What kind of bizarre car game was going on?

In the distance, out on the road, another set of beams approached. My reaction was to let go of Jonny and run off in terror, wanting to reach the subway station.

Backpack bumping up and down on my shoulders, I shouted for Jonny to follow, hoping a chase wouldn't ensue. There were four cars altogether on the parking lot, engines rumbling. My boyfriend yelled after me, urging me to slow down. When he caught up, he embraced me firmly and wouldn't let go.

He looked stern. "Don't be a wimp. Those guys can't hurt us. Let's tease them some more."

"Tease them some more?" I stared at him in disbelief. "No way. I don't want to."

"Cutie, don't be so tense. We're just exploring."

"Exploring? I don't want to, not in public."

He laughed at me. "I thought *you* were the brave one outdoors. They only flashed their lights to let us know they're here. They come up here because they're horny. We just made their week."

He let me in on the fact that there's a little birdcage, packed with condoms, in the bushes, and if the drivers saw us snooping around over there, they'd go insane with lust. Didn't I want to stock up on free condoms? He told me that I was delicious in basketball shorts. "Look at all those lovely little midge bites on your legs."

Sure enough, the artificial light revealed dozens of tiny black spots of dried blood. The car farthest away caught up with the others, sending pebbles flying in all directions. "We've been exploring all day," Jonny whispered in my ear. "It's not over yet. The last train leaves in half an hour. It's after midnight and officially *my* birthday."

I pushed him away from me.

"All right, all right," he said. "Just ask me the second question. And then we'll leave. I promise."

"No, not here. I've had enough of this place. You can stay if that's what you want."

Almost tripping in a pothole, I ran until I reached the illuminated platform and the waiting train across the lot. By that point, I was freaking out. When I boarded the empty car, I couldn't find the ticket-validating machine. "The machine's outside," Jonny said nonchalantly, strolling past me.

A young man in a runner's outfit and reflective colors stepped inside. His presence made me feel a little safer. As he surveyed us, we both turned quiet. And then, before I had time to validate my ticket, a voice over the loudspeaker declared that the doors were closing.

Nervously, I sat down next to Jonny, who discreetly grabbed my hand and whispered in my ear, "You little criminal. Watch out for ticket controllers entering at one of the stations down the line. By the way, did you notice how that guy fancied you?"

He sat a mere two seats away. Although the runner wore a headset, I worried his music was off and that he could hear us. "We're behaving strangely," I replied. "No wonder he stared. I don't like this kind of talk."

Jonny snorted. "Everyone has their excuse for being up here. But who goes running at midnight?"

Angrily, I told him he was making unreasonable assumptions. Either that or he knew the goings-on of Sognsvann's visitors disturbingly well. Looking hurt, my boyfriend apologized, but only half-heartedly. He said he only wanted to open my eyes, but obviously I preferred to keep them shut.

"No, please," I protested, urging him to go ahead and explain how he knew these things so well. Now it was his turn to look gloomy.

He said that Lars had read about it. That the two of them came up here to barbeque and collect free condoms all summer. Nothing happened apart from that. "Hey, no shuddering."

At the next station, Kringsjå student village, a crowd of international students waited and Jonny withdrew his hand as they boarded.

"Kurt," he mumbled a little further from my ear, "let's go to London." Fortunately, that marked the end of the fight. His hot breath on my neck excited me almost as much as the suggestion.

"London? When? Maybe we could stay with my brother."

"London Pub, silly. Down in the city. They've got free condoms there too, in their restroom. Hell, I'm eighteen! I'll buy you a beer to cheer you up!"

35

MY EIGHTEEN-YEAR-OLD boyfriend was counting my visible midge bites, tapping each one with his index finger, and our knees touched lightly under the bar table. "You have twenty-seven bites on your face and neck. And I must have one on my ass. I keep trying to scratch it on my stool."

"Have you heard of Fly High?"

"Oh, you mean Fly Five?" Jonny beamed at me and grabbed my thighs. "Hey, did you qualify?"

"Hey …"

"It's five journeys across the world," he went on. "To places of your own choosing. Yah, I know all about it. I actually thought about entering it but couldn't get my act together."

He said that his mum and dad might take him and his sister to Thailand over Christmas but thought it would probably just turn out to be talk.

"I could take you to Thailand tomorrow." As I spoke those words, a warm sensation took hold of me. "Although I think we need to repair Ragnar's tent first, if he'll let us take it along."

To stop me from scratching myself, Birthday Boy seized my hands. "You could? Well, that's my mum's idea. I'm not so keen on

Asia. It sounds so sticky and scented there. I'd rather go to South-ern California, or Hawaii, and become a surfer. Or maybe Australia, since it's full of beaches and extremely different and so far away."

As I thought about the two of us on an Australian beach, my shorts suddenly became tighter around my crotch and I prayed that the older couple by the bar wasn't watching. Crying out with joy at the thought of exploring the major, most bustling cross-roads of the world, together with some of its most scenic, exotic, and heav-enly backwaters, well before he turned nineteen, my boyfriend want-ed to head straight back to the maid's room. He wished to be fresh in the morning, ready to make arrangements before the best Fly Five seats were taken, for he had a whole list of places he wanted to see.

Which was all okay with me. Because of his hyperactive hands caressing my legs, however, we had to wait several minutes before I was ready to leave. "To think we nearly missed our chance because of your crazy ex," I mumbled, leaning over to nuzzle his soft hair. In the meantime, we finished our beer, which allowed Jonny to con-ceive another idea.

"My rent's 7,000 kroner a month and I have two more months until I've spent the rest of Lars's advance. Why don't you stay for free during that period, and then in addition, I'll give you 500 kro-ner? That way, you won't feel so broke."

500 kroner? According to your parents, that would last me a full day abroad. I wanted to get out of the country on the first possible plane with Jonny by my side. I certainly didn't want to waste two full months in Oslo. He'd need some convincing.

We half-emptied the rack in the restroom—the top compart-ment of my backpack was now packed with condoms and small lube pellets. When a man with a mustache wondered aloud whether we were going on a sex trip, Jonny replied frankly that we were just re-turning from one and needed to re-supply. We found the back door ajar when we finally got home—tango music and foul odors filled the air. "Those goddamn awful neighbors," Jonny yelled, sounding quite drunk. Then a fat rat scurried up the stairs ahead of us.

We followed the scoundrel to the third floor. Once there, it seemed uncertain about whether to keep going up the stairs or hide in the pile of trash resting on the landing. It chose the latter, apparently unfazed by the overpowering scent of cat shit. It wasn't alone, though. At least two bags of garbage rustled and changed shapes. Staying clear of them all, Jonny rang the bell repeatedly until a muscular boy in his underwear opened the door. He was stroking his tattooed neck, and he too appeared a little drunk. There was hardly any hair in his armpits. "Hi there, Swimmer Boy," Jonny said, startlingly merry. "Can I borrow your cat?"

"Huh?" Two longhaired girls, both dressed, appeared behind him, curious to see what was going on. "No," he said, "you can't have the cat."

"One more question then. Is this your trash? I mean, I'm assuming since it's outside your door?"

"What does it matter to you?"

"I'm supposed to clean the stairs this week."

"Well, why don't you clean it up then?" His tone shocked me. Then a bag turned over. Everyone noticed, even the girls beyond the doorway. The boy wanted to shut the door.

"No, wait," Jonny said. "I'll clean up right away." His face had grown deep red again—I could see the veins bulging in his neck.

"Just hold the door open," he added, "so I can toss everything back inside your apartment."

Emboldened, he was really emptying his heart. "And keep the back door closed! And stop dropping cigarette butts all over the stairs! And stop masturbating in the backyard! And if you don't have enough keys for your entire harem, copy some more!"

As Swimmer Boy struggled with the door handle, Jonny threw the bag at him and kicked another one inside. "You scumbag," the West Norwegian yelled back at him. "Get that filthy thing out of here immediately." Clumsily, he picked up the plastic bag with only two fingers and seemed intent at hurling it at us. A small vermin fell out. Landing on his naked foot, it let out broken shrieks and tailed off, scurrying past the astonished girls. I couldn't stop staring at Jonny's ecstatic expression as he shut the door.

We headed back downstairs, where Jonny led me into the maid's room by the genitals. He wanted more Boy Fun and whispered, "You. Me. With spit, so we're even." Even to the tones of Röyksopp, it was hard to ignore the busy footsteps above us. My eighteen-year-old boyfriend cum soon-to-be travel companion and co-adventurer drifted off to sleep first, his midge-bitten body convulsing next to mine.

PART TWO | *Drains*

ACT IV (2002–2003)

36

DO YOU REMEMBER my United Nations postcard?

When Jonny and I gaped at the mural that soared above the roundtable seating in the Security Council Chamber, I remembered, from my art history textbook, that tapestries formed a principal part of the splendor expected of any powerful ruler. The drapery showed strong men and women, in the process, evidently, of rising to higher standards.

It was called the Norwegian room. Since the organization often found itself unable to respond resolutely to a crisis, the fifteen members of the Security Council must be present at the UN headquarters at all times, so they could convene at any moment. It didn't occur to me at the time that each country might have more than one representative who rotated at the task. I thought it sounded like a prison.

You could have been here with me, I reminded you, in the international territory between First Avenue and the East River.

That night, Jonny and I shared a cramped dormitory with Israeli soldiers on leave, hardly daring to kiss goodnight and too shy to share a shower in the morning. I wouldn't admit so, but it had been a blessing in disguise that Jonny had talked me into making our journey to New York a short trip. Since I couldn't find any camping sites near Manhattan, we spent far too much on youth hostels. After days of asking at the reception desk, we eventually got one of the few double rooms at a YMCA near Central Park, only to realize once we locked ourselves in that, like the others, it came with a bunk bed.

Each night we started off together, optimistically, in the lower section, with one of our black condoms that look like mini trash bags.

As usual, my boyfriend cum travel companion and co-adventurer drifted off to sleep first, his still midge-bitten body convulsing next to mine. But every time I changed position, he woke up, and every time he made a stir, I awoke; worn out, I'd eventually climb into the upper section for the remainder of the night.

We roused before 6:00 a.m. each day. Because my boyfriend, with his slower metabolism and more selective taste, rejected every café I suggested for breakfast, I was constantly hungry. As a result, my hands shook from what I believed to be undernourishment. And we hardly stopped walking. Additionally, it proved difficult to take photos of the two of us together.

Stretching out my slightly trembling arm and pointing my pocket camera back at our faces, I'd usually miss one or both of us. Either that, or I'd end up with a result in which we appeared contorted, red-eyed, pale white, or out of focus. And I remained too shy to ask strangers for help. So while Jonny soaked in the atmosphere of New York University, I paid a crazed-looking street artist to draw our joint portrait in Washington Square Park. From the result, I wasn't convinced whether he was, in fact, what his cardboard note stated.

Jonny wanted to inspect the different university campuses at least once, so he could select the ideal place for future study, the surroundings that would bring out our full potential. One afternoon, at an Internet café chosen by Jonny, I was working on my fourth bagel with cream cheese—the cheapest thing on the menu—and knew at once that something was up when he returned to the table. He looked awfully agitated after reading his email.

Jonny, at least, had told his parents about Fly Five. Unfortunately, they also thought he was traveling with a fellow student from Oslo. Explaining that Kurt Larsen had landed in his lap in the capital had proved an unbearable notion. Regrettably, he'd even decided against admitting that his fellow nomad came from Bodø, out of fear that it would raise too much parental interest.

"Guess what? Mum and Dad are coming to Oslo."

"Really, when?"

"On the day we get back."

We looked nervously at each other, for I could read his thoughts. I offered him the rest of my bagel and asked the inescapable question: "Are they sleeping over at our place?" His parents had thought he lived alone ever since he moved to Oslo.

"I don't know yet. They plan to wait for me at the airport," my boyfriend said glumly. "They're flying to Greece the following day."

As of this moment, there were several things he needed to sort out. First of all, there was the issue of my Bodø accent. Secondly, even if I happened to be willing to fake a West Norwegian or East Norwegian dialect, we needed to win time so I could scramble together my stuff and hide it somewhere. To simplify things, he'd have to talk his parents out of waiting at Oslo's airport. To be on the safe side, he wanted me to stay at your place, at least for the night.

He should have known by now that my feelings were delicate. I agreed that we needed a cover-up, but I resented his bossiness and disliked the idea of having to ask you for more favors. "You'd ask the same of me," he patronized me. "And what if your own parents decide to make a last-minute visit and you're not where they think you are? You should tell them about Fly Five. I'm sure they'd understand."

This, I felt, was pushing it. Explaining to Jonny that you'd probably ask why Conny was kicking me out for the night, and that you lived with your parents, and that there was a whole family involved, I begged him to find out where his folks intended to spend their one night in Oslo.

Maybe one day next year I'd introduce my Jonny Boy to you and, if that worked out well, to my parents. That was my thinking at the time, but for now there were too many things up in the air to even try to explain the series of events to just about anyone. I thought, one thing at a time, because I wasn't ready for any second-guessing until I had all the answers worked out.

Finishing my bagel at our Internet café, I felt certain that Jonny's parents' imminent visit would put a damper on the rest of our first overseas journey together. I was wrong. Our feelings turned more intense. Jonny worked overtime to make up for any grudges on my part.

On our last day in New York, following a 7:00 a.m. second excursion to Columbia University, we ate sandwiches in Riverside Park. Watching the sailboats parked on the Hudson River, we fantasized about owning our own. I suggested, jokingly, to take it for our honeymoon. Whimsically, Jonny put away his half-eaten sandwich, grabbed my hand, and proposed, using my rolled-up caricature drawing as our engagement picture.

He added that we should order the necessary papers for registering our relationship upon return to the old country.

Was he being serious?

I blinked at him. He held my hand with the look of a dog begging for food. For a long time we looked at each other, and somewhere in there, I said yah.

He was just too cute to turn down. And then, for once utterly unmindful of people around us, we kissed a long time. Distracted by my constantly sagging pants, he even went about and bought me a new belt and dubbed it our joint body-sized engagement ring. There, Ragnar—I'd found my co-adventurer for life, only no one knew.

But just as I'd thought: One thing at a time.

37

OUR FIRST TRIP was supposed to be a nonstop journey. Yet our morning flight from Oslo to New York had been overbooked. Intrigued by the incentive, we volunteered to stay behind and fly the extra distance via Copenhagen instead, and in exchange we received $800 in travel vouchers and a lunch coupon each.

The flight from Copenhagen turned out to also be overbooked. So in addition to being awarded another set of vouchers and food coupons, we got a free night at a five-star Hilton hotel by the airport.

Despite the security camera monitored by the night receptionist, and because we hadn't brought with us swimmers, we dipped naked into the indoor swimming pool. Our international adventure had begun. And if the peculiar business practices of the airlines continued, your argument about our travel fund needs would become obsolete.

After a detour to Washington, D.C. and a third round of compensation, we made it to New York City and set out to make up for lost time, but by then our backpacks were gone. The Scandinavian Airlines representative blamed us for bringing mountain backpacks that had loose straps and belts, claiming they weren't built for travel, but she gave us cash to spend on toiletries and new clothing nonetheless. The next morning, the backpacks waited for us at the hostel reception—the airline had had them delivered—so we ended up spending the money on food.

Unfortunately, SAS didn't need volunteers to stay behind in the Big Apple, despite our asking. However, within the next year, the complimentary vouchers we'd accumulated thus far, totaling $4,800, could be exchanged for tickets or cashed out for half their value at any SAS ticket office. It would make for an extravagant honeymoon, which would come in handy, for Oslo proved to have turned remarkably colder.

Following our one night in Copenhagen and eight days in New York, we learned that the mail, too, had accumulated in Odins Gate. Apparently, Star Alliance had grossly underestimated the popularity of their offer and was losing big money. For in a letter, SAS promised a cross-continental business trip for four people if we were willing to surrender our remaining Five Fly tickets.

There were also two letters from the student welfare office—we'd each been granted a furnished flat in the housing complex at Grünerløkka across the city. Studying the print more carefully, Jonny realized that the offers had expired two days ago. He swore at the short deadline and said he'd try to talk the landlord into extending our rental term in Odins Gate. He then opened another envelope and screamed, twirled me around in the air, and said it came a little sooner than he'd expected, but *Aftenposten*, his favorite newspaper, had offered him an internship. He finally saw my confusion.

Journalism students, he explained, had to intern with different media companies and so he'd probably need to work throughout the Christmas break and would only make it to Bodø for the holiday itself.

I didn't answer at first. Getting student flats in Oslo was one more concession to Jonny—he'd argued that they'd be easy to sublet when we left the country. Our itinerary for December and January involved escaping winter to work on our tans in Los Angeles, Honolulu, and Rio de Janeiro—also his ideas, including the fact that each trip lasted only two weeks.

I just said I was happy for him—my dream year of travel had just been crushed further to pieces.

"Hey, Kurt, don't act so surprised. We just got home from our trial honeymoon." He grinned at this thought. "Any way you look at it, this Fly Five thing's a great deal."

"Particularly for you, who only paid 500 kroner then earned $2,400."

He chuckled uneasily. "We'll work something out. Maybe we could just cancel the winter trips. Or you could go without me. Please, we need to ready up before my parents arrive. We'd better hurry." He saw no point in further discussion. Outrageously cheerful, he said that if you're serious with your studies, as he happened to be, you don't just turn down opportunities like the one he'd just been handed. Tracing his steps, I couldn't get out another word.

A pile of trash bags, occupying most of the landing, barricaded our door. "This is war," my self-appointed protector pledged as I helped him bring our neighbor's garbage back upstairs, eleven bags in all. Only I'd just been utterly defeated, or so I was starting to feel as I locked myself in the bathroom.

After nine days of disuse, our toilet bowl was remarkably stained. I pushed the lid down, took a seat, and watched the door handle wiggle. "Hey, hug bug, don't be a crybaby," my fiancé's voice whimpered from the other side. "Please open up, sweetie. I already miss you. When the prize stud's unhappy, Jonny Boy's miserable too."

38

OUT THERE MAKING mental calculations, my fiancé argued that we'd be apart for a maximum of thirty-three days, split into two periods, with Christmas in between. "It's nothing if you put it in perspective," he said. "A month out of our life, that's all." The really good thing, Jonny thought, was that when we started to miss each other, we'd learn to appreciate what we had together and look even better after it. So it would be a really good test of the quality of the relationship.

"And you'll get a ridiculously dark tan, which I'll envy you for," he went on. "Plus the upshot is that I'll be able to afford a much higher budget on our trips to Sydney and Vancouver next year. We should hold on to the vouchers for as long as possible—see if the dollar goes back up. Then we'll sell them to students for seventy-five percent of their value. Am I not smart?"

Besides, after all the sitting on planes and sleeping on top of each other in narrow beds, he felt utterly out of shape, he explained. The poster boys on the bathroom door reminded him that if he didn't exercise, he'd turn into a quivering lump of jelly.

"Listen, Jonny. I'll give you all the exercise you need," I barked. I knew that I had plenty of good arguments up my sleeve. We could fight the surf and run on the sand and wrestle in your tent, Ragnar.

"You're not very good at being nice," I maintained. "A single trip to New York's been a great deal for you. Yet you knew all along that I didn't just want to go away for nine days." I didn't want to be jetlagged the whole time during five short, expensive vacations. I'd wanted an entire year of supreme adventure together with my Jonny Boy. I wouldn't enjoy traveling alone all winter. I'd miss him.

As I moped on the toilet bowl, my inconsiderate fiancé turned silent. Did he, at long last, feel bad? Had I made my point well enough? After a moment, he pushed one of his travel checks under the door. He begged me to cash it in, saying it should cover my Christmas rent at Odins Gate and some text messaging too. He still sounded despicably hopeful as he continued to pull on the door handle. "Kurt, please, why won't you let me watch you pee?"

A quarter of an hour later, when I emerged from my confinement, he'd removed the muscular boys from the bathroom door and had hung our engagement portrait in their place. To clear him and his treasured parents of the least suggestion of my living there, I thought it wise to leave the premises the moment I'd grabbed *Gardner's Art Through the Ages*. I wasn't ready to give him my stamp of approval this time, so I left him to hide my belongings, including our engagement portrait, from his parents' view on his own.

And so, with fresh tears in my eyes and the unfolded letter in my hand, I showed up at student welfare to explain, in person, that I'd been away and come back only this morning to find my housing offer expired. I told them that, terrified, I'd rushed straight to their office without even showering, because I didn't know what to do, in the winter, without a proper roof over my head. Yah, it may have been a little too much information, but was somewhat even the truth, and the trick worked.

Sympathetic to my predicament, they extended their offer and told me that I was now free to go home and freshen up. I was relieved to accept, and sign off, at once. Jonny and I'd at least be able to cut costs in half by secretly sharing—or subletting—my single room.

Of course, I still hoped that he'd change his mind. But if he seriously planned to stay on in Oslo alone all winter, he'd certainly have to take care of the whole rent. Thus energized, I hurried to the computer lab and used my new student loan disbursement to make the first payment. I then conducted an Internet search on how to become registered partners, downloading and printing out the necessary forms from the Office of Public Registrar.

I didn't feel like bothering you at Peppe's Pizza—I couldn't handle more talk about Conny—and so, jetlagged and struggling to keep myself awake, I ate at Burger King, without much appetite. Flicking through my textbook, I waited there until 10:45 p.m., when Jonny sent the all-clear text message deeming the apartment safe and parent free.

"You Mister Fix-it, you," Jonny saluted me upon my victorious return to the maid's room. His dad sounded a lot like mine—he'd found the apartment overpriced and tiny even for one person, and he had wondered if the student flat was any larger, although Jonny had lied and said he paid only half as much. Yet the student flat would be cheaper, he'd added, and that seemed to have appeased his parents for they'd then taken him out for Indian food near their hotel.

That night my fiancé rejected all my painstaking suggestions when I begged him to delay his internship and, for the time being, become a travel writer or overseas correspondent. The domestic partnership application paper, however, was quickly signed. We needed more signatures, from a witness each, though. There were always Lars and you, we thought. We also considered faking them but assumed that would be fraud. Not the sort of crime we'd want to commit.

Jonny, too, had used his hours resourcefully that Monday. He'd not only packed away our engagement drawing, my shoes, and books, but he had also returned them to their places. He'd made a second call in one afternoon to his landlord too, offering to help the man come up with new tenants if only he'd free us from the lease without any notice period—it worked. He'd even been busy talking a boy from journalism class into taking over the small flat with his girlfriend the very next day.

Jonny looked exhausted as well, but after another kiss, I convinced him that in order to get over my lonesome misery tonight, I deserved some late-night American ice cream for dessert. Yawning his way into his thick autumn jacket, he took his sweet-natured self out in the chilly night to 7-Eleven for the benefit of my sweet tooth.

Upon returning, he gave me a long hug. He wasn't very proud of lying to his parents about his living situation, and so now he needed that squeeze. Feeling how warm and sweaty he had gotten from our fight, and enjoying his many kisses, I felt slightly better about our return to Oslo and also more optimistic.

39

OF COURSE WE overslept—it would be our last night in a double bed. As I rushed to tidy the bathroom in my underwear, Jonny made a disturbing exclamation so I ran back to him to see. He'd removed his sheets from the bed. "Look," he said with a shudder, "our greatest hits ... quite literally."

Not only the mattress but, upon closer inspection, even the bedstead and the door to the landlord's flat were stained with dried and discolored semen. His, mine, Lars's, he explained. Jonny asked me to use my hot water and an old towel to scrub it away but I politely refused. Since the lease was in his name, the mess belonged to him.

And after four tram trips back and forth with our things in trash bags and backpacks, it was finally Jonny's turn to move into my place. The two last items on our to-do list were to carry the actual trash to the neighbors upstairs and to tape Lars's old posters to their door. Yah, it was all rather childish, we agreed, but for the most part so is the human need to get the final word.

For the first time, I had the key to my own flat. And despite taking on a fixed Oslo cost, I liked the feeling. Twelve square meters in all, my circular space on the seventh floor came with curved

furniture as well as a luxurious view of the Cemetery of Our Savior
and the yellowed treetops of your neighborhood, Sankthanshaugen.
A former grain storage tower and mill, it held nineteen floors of student housing. The student silo at Grünerløkka was, by far, the tallest building in the neighborhood. And Akerselva, the stream from
Maridalsvannet, flowed directly below the structure.

The kitchen and bathroom we shared with our next-door
neighbor. If he asked directly, my brother Jonny lived with me temporarily due to a housing emergency. So far, however, we hadn't
even met him. We'd only heard him return at night and leave early
in the morning.

We knew he was a man, because he'd spread his toiletries all
over the bathroom and his smelly shoes outside his door. Jonny
marveled at how crammed the space was. "It's going to be difficult
to concentrate when we're both here. We'll distract each other from
work. I'll just want to cuddle."

He seemed quite concerned about this possibility, so I promised to do most of my reading at the university. In any case, for
thirty-three days he'd have the flat to himself. That should give him
plenty of time to catch up on his studies and his journalistic writing.
In return, he'd handle the December and January rent himself.

Our living arrangement—two people sharing a flat meant for
one—violated the student welfare rules. Hence, we decided on our
own rules: no unnecessary visitors and continued nonstop discretion.

In the meantime, we bought a collapsible camp bed at IKEA
and made continued use of your sleeping bag. Following a transitory
period of slumbering head to toe and partly on top of one another,
one of us would crawl into the collapsible bed during the course
of the night and we'd hold hands across the gap, until overtaken by
sleep. The mysterious disappearance of the papers from the Office
of Public Registrar into our heaps of gathered belongings, we concluded, didn't matter for now.

On December 3, despite the request for volunteers to stay behind, I boarded another overbooked plane from Oslo, lest I lose
my United Airlines connection to Los Angeles—my third jumbo jet
flight. The airlines were taking fewer and fewer chances on flying
with empty seats.

40

COMPUTER USAGE WAS always free, but at this hour there wasn't ever a line. At what turned into the regular hour—somewhat before 4:50 a.m. Hawaii-Aleutian time—I logged on to Gaysir from the youth hostel. My fiancé, waiting in the Oslo University College computer lab, offered his usual hugs and kisses. So, what had I been up to? Whom had I talked to?

It was almost 4:00 p.m. Norwegian time, and we carried on numerous conversations with each other at the same time. To explain to outsiders that each of us was taken, that we were using the service solely to communicate with each other, we'd created Gaysir profiles with clear links between them, explaining that we were taken and not interested in others.

I wrote: "Takeiteasy,sweetheart.Ihavenodesiretoexplorecrappy-Hawaiiangaybarswithoutyouatmysidetoprotectme."

And so in spite of the greasy keyboard, and the ineffective space bar, and an Internet connection so slow that I could hardly sit still, I remained bent over the screen, disregarding my back pain.

I typed that I'd bought earplugs to deal with the traffic in and out of the dorm room. I fell asleep just after sunset, with an image of my fiancé in my head. Then he appeared in my dreams, and guess what? When I woke up, he was the first thing on my mind. When the rising sun glared in the hostel window, it grew difficult to read through the reflections on the monitor.

I wrote: "Theoceanhere'sbeautifullybluishgreen.Yourhead-wouldhavelookedlovelyinit."

Although, I continued typing, I constantly worried about being bitten by sharks or stung by poisonous rays. So I often lost energy, fell asleep on my towel, and woke up both dehydrated and desperate for a pee. I shouldn't complain. At least I was on a beach and wearing shorts. But when I stood up, my bowels went crazy. I'd been wearing his Speedos underneath—Jonny was unbelievably generous to let me borrow them. They were so nice, those swim trunks. Every time I put them on, or took them off, I thought about my fiancé's touch. Obviously, I couldn't have nice things because I ruined them. I told him I was awfully sorry—it had all happened so quickly and there had been no time to get to the beach toilet.

Afterward, I'd had to return to the hostel carrying them inside a plastic bag. I soaked them in the shower, but they still smelled. I was so disgusting! But I told him not to worry, I was taking them to a laundryman today. In the meantime, I'd have to swim in my old, loose shorts, with the risk of the waves stealing them.

I split up my message into shorter ones so Jonny could read them faster, but there were no fresh answers. In fact, I'd been writing without hearing from him for a few minutes. To soften the blow, I asked him to forgive me that thing with the Speedos.

I typed:

"Isitincafés,drinkicedtea,andthinkofmyBodøBoy.AndwheneverIthinkofMyBodøBoy,Ithinkofcomputers.Idonothingbutdrink-teaandlookforcomputers."

I kept him up to date on the details of my fantasizing about him. Yesterday morning, in the shower, I'd put on a condom. Then I'd pulled the-day-before-yesterday's sock on top. I'd used my hairbrush handle as a stand-in for my fiancé and pretended that my sneaker was his tiny asshole. While I thrust back and forth inside my shower stall I'd had to bite my shoulder to stop myself from crying out with pleasure. I'd dreamed that he and I would be interconnected this way forever, during daytime and while we slept.

Yet the brush had had sharp edges that made my anus bleed afterward. A little scratch remained that, for different reasons, never quite seemed to heal. Whenever I plunked back into my shoes, however, my feet and I'd developed a stronger connection. I felt a stronger grasp of what they sensed down there. For the first time in a while, Jonny wrote back to my latest message. "I'm quite disturbed. You said you didn't bring any condoms. You said you wouldn't need any."

Indeed, I'd tried to go without, but to save my footwear and my fragile foreskin, I thought protection was in order and had bought a three-pack. I assured him that I'd rather have him than any old sneaker or hard brush in the entire world.

I then received inexplicably dark answers to much older messages: "Are you an illusion, a trick of my mind? How do I know that you're real? When you're not around, it's like we're a fiction, one that's too good to be true." For some reason, Jonny was suffering from a sudden mood swing.

"Ofcoursewe'retogetherforreal," I wrote, a little frustrated. "HowcanIforgetyou?"

"I hate secrets," he suddenly wrote.

It was important that we shared every detail, however bad or embarrassing, because he couldn't stand keeping any information private between us—yah, however private the information. "I need to feel honest with at least one person. That person should be you. Because no one knows of us—no one except for you. That makes you very special, sweet, tasty hug bug."

And then he wrote, "Sweet, muscular Kurt, who looks so good in my Speedos. I'd like you to keep them, because I love you so much." We were finally back on the same page then suddenly he was ahead of me. "By the way, something weird happened right now."

I immediately refreshed my screen, asked him what had happened, and typed again: What happened? Hello? You're not telling me what just happened over there. "Oh, well," Jonny finally answered. "I just got an incredible offer. Right here on Gaysir."

I thought we'd agreed to ignore messages from strangers and told him so. By shortening our correspondence down to the bare minimum, and by taking the time to wait for replies, we'd finally whittled down to a single conversation. According to Jonny, this really old guy had been exceedingly persistent. He'd kept asking my fiancé if he'd been at Sognsvann last summer.

At Sognsvann? At that awful cruising place? Was he in one of those cars? How would he know it was Jonny? I kept my questions brief and expected immediate answers. We'd posted no photos with our profiles. In short, the stranger knew nothing about us. I typed that this was one hell of a fishy fishing expedition.

Jonny filled me in on the specifics.

To make Old Man stop nagging, my fiancé had asked when— and the man had said August, in a hard rain during a storm. Jonny had explained that when he was there, it had neither been a storm nor raining. In fact, he hadn't even been alone but rather had been with his boyfriend. "But now he wants to meet in person so I can prove him wrong. He offered me dinner."

"You'renotgoing!"

"Relax! There's a picture on his profile and I swear I'm not attracted. He's almost twice our age. He's got a receding hairline. His name's Truls Snøfugl and he lives on Marselis Gate, right across the street from the student silo. He's our neighbor. He's got a pile of Swedish meatballs. He wants to serve them with gravy, potatoes, and homemade mountain cranberry sauce. He claims that he always prepares too much food and hates to eat all by himself."

At this point my stomach rumbled. Normally, only when Jonny left the computer lab to make a lone dinner at the flat would I drift outside the youth hostel to grab a sandwich and a huge bottle of water on my own. Our intruder, *Snowbird*, appeared among my list of visitors—he'd already inspected my profile three times. I denied him the pleasure of suggesting any interest by looking at his profile in return and not making any contact, yet suddenly I received a message from him.

He asked for permission to 'borrow' my boyfriend for dinner. There would be meatballs but 'it didn't need to come to more than that,' for he respected other people's relationships and wanted only a clothes-on type of friendship. I had to read the sentences several times over.

It sounded hurried, illogical, crazy, what came next. "The bottom line is: he wants us to move in with him," Jonny wrote. "If we agree to be home for dinner on a daily basis, we can have his guest room for free. It's almost three times the size of your student flat. We'd get our own keys. He has a five-room apartment."

Moving, yet again, at the spur of the moment? Jonny continued, "Seriously, think about it. He has a television, even a dishwasher. We won't have to pay rent."

When I tried to explain that no normal person would make that kind of offer to someone he hadn't met, he wrote back, "You're always telling me how you hate to waste money in Oslo. We'll save a fortune on food and housing. Meaning: there will be more money for travel. The room's fully furnished—and I do miss a double bed. I'll text you as soon as I've eaten with him and checked out the place. Oh, and I'll forward his address and phone number in case he's a sadistic murderer and I go missing."

Appealing to his common sense, I asked my fiancé to hold on and consider how many boys the old man had approached with the same question.

"You're one skeptical, guarding lover boy, and that makes me feel very exclusive," he replied. "This Truls Snøfugl person insists the idea popped into his head right now. Students are poor and he feels lonely. He wants a family to support and a little more life around the house. He says he's impressed that we've found each other at such a young age. Perhaps we'll inspire him to find a boyfriend of his own. Listen, Kurt—even if he's trying to play us, we're big boys who can stand our ground. Let him be our sugar daddy if it turns him on."

Jonny copied one of Snøfugl's messages to give me his address and phone number. "The information matches his listing in the Internet phone directory perfectly," he wrote. "Smack on your neck and bye for now. Much more later!"

My fingers had never moved faster. "Hey, don't go!"

Too late. The little green dot by his name had already disappeared from my screen.

41

JONNY TAPPED ON the closest wall. "He sleeps right behind here."

"Oh no, he'll hear everything!"

"We're supposed to inspire him, remember? We're living proof that hope exists."

Our engagement drawing was taped next to the door on a huge IKEA cabinet. My fiancé removed my backpack, grabbed me from behind, and slowly escorted me into our new double bed on Marselis Gate.

Somewhere along the way my pants went missing.

A key had been placed in the keyhole inside of our door, so we could lock it for privacy. A rather sympathetic gesture on the part of our new landlord, I thought.

Since he needed to head for the newspaper, Jonny declared our double bed open for business and proceeded to pull down his favorite gray fleece pants. Divulging that we occupied the best bed in the household, and that our landlord wouldn't be home until 5:00 p.m., he claimed it time for our bi-monthly feisty fuck week. "But Jonny," I muttered, "I don't want to be all alone when Truls comes home."

"Don't be afraid. He's not that strange. In any case you can lock the door." Jonny explained that Truls had no sex life, only a Murphy bed—I wasn't sure what that was, exactly. Smirking at me, he suggested I take a look for myself later. Worn out from thirty-three hours of flying, I decided to postpone judgment. "Oh God," my fiancé suddenly exclaimed. "It's so nice to rest against a naked boy again." I'd have to discuss his malleable masculinity with him later on. He'd never spoken with such an effeminate intonation before. Was I witnessing some disturbing influence from our new landlord?

He pointed at the other wall. Truls Snøfugl had dubbed his daughter's room the girls' room. His, the adults' room. And ours had recently become the boys' room. "We got ourselves a little sister."

Truls evidently had a fifteen-year-old daughter who lived with her mother but occasionally visited. "All he does is lie in his Murphy bed and play chess with his daughter. On his cell phone, that is. They make their moves with text messages. There's no board. Only the positions of the chessmen in their minds. A single game can go on for days."

"He plays chess? And he has a daughter?"

"Yah, we've got the middle bedroom—we're right between the two of them."

Recycling auto parts, Truls Snøfugl ran an old-fashioned junk-yard somewhere nearby. He drove a crane truck and an old, un-washed van—I should notice his dirty fingernails. But I was paying little attention to Jonny's briefing, for a brand-new laptop comput-er, half hidden under a disarray of underwear and papers, stared up at me from the small cabinet desk in the boys' room. "Huh, you bought a computer?" I interrupted. "We could have gotten one much cheaper abroad."

"No, it belongs to Truls. We can use it as much as we like, but we don't have an Internet connection. Truls worries he'd spend too much of his spare time at Gaysir."

Jonny covered me with brief, wet kisses and promised to call in four hours to wake me up. There was bread and cornflakes in the kitchen, so I wouldn't be hungry. However, the moment he left I locked the door after him and placed the pillow that smelled the strongest of him between my thighs. I then curled up and fell into a deep, deep slumber.

Before my fiancé's wake-up call and at a time when, under less bizarre circumstances, I should have been at a lecture with you, I woke up with an overloaded bladder. Putting on Jonny's fleece pants, I found my way to the old, but spacious bathroom with its pleasantly heated tiles. Relieved, and curious to determine whether our landlord was respectable, I began snooping around, ready to explore every single part of our new home.

A hand-painted ceramic sign surely revealed Siri's chamber. I quickly closed her door though, because inside her room the heat had been completely turned off. On the fridge, laminated in plastic, magnets secured old childish drawings. The S in the young artist's name pointed consistently in the wrong direction. They must have been hanging there for years.

Occupying a bowl hazardously placed between the stove and the water boiler in the kitchen, an orange blob of a goldfish seemed unable to make up its mind when I pretended to feed it with my fingers. Unsure about whether I represented a meal or danger, the little creature raced to the surface then darted into the pebbles in panic, causing a stir among the threads of feces that drifted about its closed-off environment.

A balcony facing the student silo and my old home was loaded with snow, and the windowed door leading out to it proved the source of a wavering draft. So I decided to turn up every electric heater I came across. Above the sofa in the wallpapered living room hung a single-framed photo of father and daughter barbequing in the backyard. Siri was stunningly good-looking, I observed. The complete opposite of Truls.

Finding the door to the adults' room ajar, I discovered Truls's Murphy bed unfolded, yet meticulously made. I marveled at the thought of him sleeping with his head inside a closet, when his guest bed so clearly was the more attractive option. A drying stand, jam-packed with tired-looking briefs and dingy white T-shirts, took up most of his bedroom floor space. It must be humid in there at night, I observed. On his bedside table, a stack of suspense novels teetered dangerously close to falling over. I walked in and yanked open his bedside drawer, discovering it packed with interior design magazines all the way to the bottom. No dirty secrets, apparently.

It was time for a snack. Back in the kitchen, I chose the mug that read "King of the house," fixed a hot toddy, and made myself a bowl of cornflakes. The goldfish hadn't much adjusted to my presence so I brought my lunch back to the boys' room, feeling surprisingly comfortable in my new Oslo home. To make space on the work desk, I pushed aside the computer and some papers.

All I wanted was to look at my fiancé's writing, but when, out of habit, I pressed the icon for the Internet browser, Gaysir appeared on the screen. A little delayed in my thinking, I closed it, but when I reopened the browser the website again blinked into view, signaling a rather effective Internet connection to me.

I took a seat on the wooden chair, keyed in my login information, and pushed enter. My inbox immediately materialized; there was even a little green dot by Jonny's messages, signaling his presence.

Flustered, I logged out of my account at once. Evidently Truls and Jonny didn't know much about computers or someone was mixing things up—or right out lying.

As my toddy went cold, I created a brand new Gaysir profile, identifying myself as a twenty-year-old muscle boy who sought instant action. Strangers immediately bombarded me with messages, but I heard nothing from Jonny, even though I sent him several tempting proposals.

Next, following up on some dark, shadowy thoughts, I threw out another bait: "Come on, you handsome boy from the North. You liked me the last time. We should meet again. Are you available before 5:00 p.m.?" But my fiancé was no longer logged on. Had he seen my green dot just earlier, or was he one easily sidetracked, lively, and sociable yet trustworthy darling?

Instead, I received a message from Truls Snøfugl. His tired face, his thick glasses, and his receding hairline in the picture next to his message startled me. "Hi," he wrote. "Do you remember when I saved you at Sognsvann in the hard rain? The one with the punctured bicycle tire... that's you?"

I lied, feeling sick to the stomach. "But of course." If it ever did, my presence in this room no longer felt entirely real.

42

"YOU STUDY ART history, don't you?"

Having poured himself a glass from his bottle of white wine, Truls Snøfugl looked at me rather intently. I sat upright and warily faced our landlord cum flat mate in his armchair. Slowly peeling the tag off my beer bottle, I nodded.

"So then you probably know Tim Høiby."

"Is he another student?"

"No, he's a well-known artist."

Resting against my shoulder, my fiancé wouldn't stop examin-ing *Aftenposten Aften*, the local evening edition that contained his first published contribution. The only drawback, in his opinion, was that he hadn't written the article himself. Enchanted by today's achieve-ment, he finally tossed the paper aside, glanced at me, and gulped down the rest of his beer. He then dragged the laptop closer, to refresh the *Aftenposten* website, and read the latest reader comments below the article. "It's the most-read item on Aftenposten's web-site," Jonny announced with a grin. "I hope they won't hold back any more of my writing."

"Except you didn't write it," I said.

He looked so unhappy when I mentioned that part that I regretted my comment at once. "Except I didn't write it…" He hadn't even said, "And whose fault is that?"

If only Truls or I'd complied, he could have written the whole thing himself. Truls—shy to the bone—didn't want his face in the paper, period. And despite his begging, I too had refused to participate.

All I needed to do, he'd persisted, was pose under a false name, so his parents in Bodø wouldn't get the wrong idea when he mailed them the article. The scheme was simply out of the question—what if friends of my own parents came across the paper. Would they really believe I had a doppelganger in Oslo? I reminded him that you, my friend Ragnar, presently believed he, Jonny, was my little brother. How could an actual little brother, someone so intent on becoming a serious reporter, mix up my name? Blame the news desk, my fiancé said.

Earlier in the day, I, his first and foremost source, had read both the print and web version with unmistakable sparkles of pride. 'Is your computer unsecured?' the newspaper's Internet headline asked. No, the boy in the sofa with the mystifying laptop computer in front of him was the feature of the story rather than its author. Even though he didn't have a modem or an Internet subscription, he somehow had, according to the paper, free Internet access at home.

"My classmates thought I was kidding when I told them," he was quoted in the interview. "So I brought my computer to college to prove them wrong. When it wouldn't work, I felt insane." Yet back home on Marselis Gate in Grünerløkka, the young journalism student had access to the Internet, a printer, and, whenever it was turned on, the computer hard drive of an unknowing third party. Unintentionally, Jonny Larsen had walked through the wide-open virtual back door of this unsuspecting neighbor, the article read. You may think of this as yesterday's news, Ragnar, but don't forget this was 2002.

It took Jonny a night and half a day to forgive me, but in the end, he got both teamwork and his news story. The girl who currently sublet my student flat, another fellow journalism student of his, got the byline.

Since they were such good friends, Jonny didn't want it to appear as if he and I shared a double bed. And I didn't particularly want to pretend to live in the girls' room, so I'd left the apartment before the girl crossed the street with a photographer and a computer science major, other friends of her and Jonny, in tow. I knew that you were at work so I'd gone to the movies alone—to watch *My Big Fat Greek Wedding* from the last row.

When the journalist brought along a computer expert, the story continued, Jonny was amazed to learn that his laptop could connect with the unsecured wireless network of that unidentified neighbor. In essence, anyone with a modern computer in this neighborhood could download illegal material, like child pornography. The digital trail would lead only to the Internet user with an unprotected network. That person would likely be someone who lived within a fifty-meter radius of Jonny's flat. If he or she cared for privacy and personal security, that unsuspecting individual needed to protect his or her network more carefully, as handily explained in the how-to section of the newspaper article.

"Jonny, are you just going to read your article all night?" Truls said, offering us more beer.

"Hey, I'm just waiting for the neighbor to turn on his computer," my fiancé replied, nonplussed. "Shall I print 'BOO!' in a gigantic font on his printer? That and a copy of my article?"

"Don't," I said. "We might lose our free Internet connection. Let's hope the neighbor doesn't pick up on it."

"Consequences," Truls said with an unexpected air of gravity. "That's something to consider before putting your picture and street name in the paper." After being mute all week, our landlord was drunk.

Suddenly the doorbell rang, and Jonny and I froze. "Relax, boys, it won't be the neighbor." With a chuckle Truls stood up. "It'll have to be the Hobbits." Truls, who stood only as high as our noses, called Tim and Thom the Hobbits because they were even shorter than he was. Steeling ourselves, Jonny and I touched feet under the table.

"One discovers one's own limits quickly in their company," Truls said. "They just can't help it, but they're harmless. Please believe me. Just establish your standards and you'll be fine."

A short, bald man entered the living room first. "Oh hi, I'm Tim." We stood up to shake hands, but he moved closer, preferring to kiss our cheeks. "We had to come, naturally, after seeing that cute little Northerner in the paper," Tim Høiby said to Truls. "We want one too. Where do you find them?"

Sporting a blond little mustache, his much younger partner, Thom, carried with him a plastic bag of clinking bottles. They'd brought Turkish Pepper candies and vodka for the shots. Truls grabbed the bag. "We'll melt the candies later. Gaysir's fantastic for getting to know new people."

Crashing down on the armrest next to us, Tim wanted Jonny to log on to Gaysir and invite more Northerners over for the party. Skeptically, I glanced at Jonny, who glanced at Truls. "The party?" Jonny asked.

Tim broke in loudly, "The after-dinner party, the pre-going-out party, the all-out sex party! Name it whatever you like. It's your party. "What's your profile name on Gaysir?"

"Why not?" Truls shrugged on his way to the kitchen. "We have enough alcohol for a busload of wild boys right now. Make a party profile and see what happens." I squeezed Jonny's foot. Even if he got the hint he didn't say anything, but at least he didn't log on to Gaysir.

"You have to teach us the trick," Tim shouted after Truls. "Do you just approach any teenage newcomer and ask him to move in?"

The host returned with clean glasses and an unopened card-board box of white wine. "Well, Jonny might be eighteen, but he's very mature for his age. And Kurt turns twenty-one in January."

"Puppy love is so endearing," Thom said, flicking through Truls's CDs. "So did you or did you not pop the big question?" He locked his eyes on Truls.

"Well…" Truls hesitated. "A friendly tone and a clever question can go a long way, don't you think? It intrigues people and gets a dialogue going."

"Oh, this one has such beautiful thick hair." Tim was touching my fiancé. "And such strong teeth!" For a second he held his cheek. "Thom, what do you think? Could we spare a corner for a needy boy?"

"Absolutely."

"Are you two married?" I interjected.

The artist threw up his hand to show me the ring, huge and modern with sharp lines. "Ya da, we married six years ago. This is what I got. Thom wanted something less discreet. Thom, show them yours."

"Already?" Thom was making a face.

My fiancé had never heard of couples with different wedding rings before. "He must've been extremely young," I noted.

"Take a guess at our age."

"You're a bit older than him, aren't you?" Jonny cut in. "So I'll say, he's twenty-five and you're thirty?"

Tim yelled toward Truls in the kitchen, "Truls, I like your boys. They think I'm thirty."

"He must think thirty is young," I muttered into Jonny's ear, fuming at this kind of talk. As Truls was setting out bread and mayonnaise, Tim lowered his voice, and demanded to know how we'd met. Jonny and I looked at each other, awkward.

"Now, don't be boring," he instructed. "You were fourteen, weren't you? And you found each other in a public toilet? In Bodø, right?"

Jonny was staring at the empty bottle in his hands. "Nothing happened in Bodø," I snapped.

Tim gasped. "You had a date in a public toilet in Bodø—and you didn't try a thing?"

Carrying in an enormous platter of shrimp, our landlord was blushing. Obviously Jonny had told him. "They didn't meet in a toilet," he corrected his friend. "I told you they met outside one."

"I don't see how this is any of your business," I burst out, angry at Jonny.

Tim lowered his voice again. "Did you hear from Truls?" I didn't understand the question. "Did he reply to the ad?" This Tim person seemed to think I was dim-witted. He spoke slowly now.

I was speechless. Tim stared at Jonny, who shrugged. "You've got to ask Kurt. It was his ad."

Finally taking a seat next to me, Truls said it was time for Tim to drop the subject altogether, move away from the arm lean, and get to his plate on the other side of the table with Thom. Jonny kept hitting a key to refresh the laptop's screen. "Please, use a paper towel. I don't want mayo on the keys," Truls instructed him.

Thom chuckled.

"What?" Truls snorted.

"I bet you use them a lot these days. To wipe up the mayo."

The comment was kindly ignored. Next, Tim Høiby wanted to know if Jonny was having any success on Gaysir. I shivered when Jonny asked if we were inviting any Gaysir people in particular or certain types.

"We'll take everything on the menu!" Tim replied.

"Don't take from the Hobbits," Truls said. "They eat boys like you for breakfast, lunch, and dinner."

Tim laughed riotously. "That settles it. You're coming over for elk steak next weekend. You boys like elk?"

Jonny explained that we were going up north for Christmas on Thursday. "So this Sunday then," Tim concluded. "You absolutely must." But this Sunday didn't work for Truls—his old folks were coming down for some Christmas shopping. Thom smacked his thighs in frustration—he too was in fact seeing his parents on Sunday. Tim assured his partner, "There will be a Sunday feast whether you and Truls need to entertain your parents or not. Because I need to know how these gorgeous Northerners discovered each other—I want all the juicy details."

"He's on," Jonny yelled, startling us all.

"On?" the three men asked in unison.

The neighbor had turned on his computer, and Jonny now had access to his hard drive. Tim, surprisingly light, landed in my lap the next instant. Examining a letterhead, Jonny read out a name and a social security number. The neighbor had applied for a prolonged deadline on his tax return; Truls recognized him as the tenant downstairs. "He's gay. Why don't we invite him over? Print out an invitation on his printer."

Thom muttered in my ear, "You're the one who flies so much? It must be hard to be away from each other for so long." His cheek, tremendously soft, touched the back of my neck. He didn't even need to bend down from behind the sofa.

"We both travel," I snorted, increasingly worried about Tim's hand searching for support between my legs and about Jonny not paying enough attention.

"This is *boring* as well as ethically objectionable," Tim said. "What's happening at Gaysir? Is anyone coming?"

Taking a mouthful of wine from his glass, his partner studied me up close with a neutral expression. "I want to come," he replied, right in my ear. And then, loud enough for everyone to hear, he declared that he liked my skin.

I brushed Tim off me and was on my feet. Finally registering my alarm, Jonny looked over from the screen. I grabbed his hand. "Jonny, we're going to the bathroom."

Truls didn't say a word, and for a change, the Hobbits looked uncomfortable. Once inside the bathroom, Jonny wanted to comfort me with a kiss, but I brushed his hand away from my trousers. "Hey, take it easy," he said.

"Jonny, I really, really don't want an erection right now. Why are we hanging out with these people? My ear's soaking wet." The door handle moved; someone was trying to get in. "It's taken!" I shouted.

From outside, the same person shouted, "Whose butt's taken?" Jonny couldn't stop laughing.

I shouted, "Go away, you old pig."

"Watch your mouth," Jonny whispered to me. "I sure hope that wasn't Truls."

"Hey, I resent that," the person outside said, rather belatedly. "I've never been called an old pig before. And I'm really not that old!"

"Oh, you are," I shouted back, "you old pig."

"Boys," the voice said, "you've convinced me. Afterwards we're going to play the pig game, all of us. Let's pass the pigs around!"

"The pig game?" I whispered to Jonny. "I don't want to play any dirty game."

"Just ignore him. Pretend you don't notice anything filthy," my fiancé suggested. He wanted us to catch up on our drinking. "We'll make everyone leave with us in an hour. You know ... Truls promised to pay our cover charge at Soho."

"I don't care, I'll pay."

"It's too early, the place will be empty! I don't even think there's a cover charge yet. Kurt—I want you to get the best experience. We should go when it's starting to get busy."

"Please, Jonny. I promise to pay for everything tonight—every-thing whatsoever." Again I shoved his hands off my crotch, but Jonny held on to me.

43

AT THE NEXT tram stop, a young boy of Pakistani origin blocked the rear exit and called for his friends, a group of teenage girls who scampered down the stairs of a nearby 7-Eleven, to follow him aboard.

"To think that Tim and Thom almost held us back by force," I said out loud. "They're pathetic."

Young men with paper hats encircled a redhead who was hand-cuffed to a pole in the aisle. In his free hand, he held a gigantic toothbrush. His eyes were hidden behind a medical mask. Every now and then, they poured more of the contents from a bottle of mouthwash down his throat.

"Do you think that's a bachelor party? I sure hope that's not regular mouthwash," Jonny mumbled near my ear. He moved his thigh toward me. "Mmm, it's nice to sit so close."

The floor was covered in mucky melted snow that everyone tramped on. When the tram finally departed, the new passengers realized one of their own was still missing, and the boy pulled the emergency brake. Pushing open the door, they fled.

"We should get out and walk," I said.

"Too late now," Jonny whispered.

Spotting the bulge in his pants, I couldn't help but develop one of my own, and my heartbeat quickened. But we let go of each other's thighs and tried to act nonchalant when the applause, for the blue-uniformed driver approaching to lift the emergency brake, interrupted us.

Sure enough, we arrived at what appeared to be an almost empty nightclub. A female disc jockey worked in the corner; at the bar, a middle-aged man and woman nursed their drinks; behind the counter, a male bartender was texting on his cell phone. Jonny got the bartender's attention and ordered a beer with my money. Almost at once the woman became utterly absorbed with us. She wanted to know if we were a couple. Jonny nodded. "You look so innocent together," she said. "Do you come here often?"

"It's a first for me," I replied.

"That's good…. It's a first for me too, in fact. How long have you been going out?"

She could have been our mother. "Two and a half months," I said quickly, moving even closer to Jonny. She seemed sympathetic, but from the moment she started talking, I'd been wary of her fervor. Yah, tonight everything seemed to vex me.

"Tell me how you met."

"Oh, we just *did*!"

She pointed to her companion, who was still standing quietly next to her. "We've been married for twenty-six years. I met him in high school. The whole family's here tonight. You should meet the rest of us. Look for an old lady, three girls, and a boy. They're taking an awfully long time in the bathroom."

"I thought this was a gay bar," I whispered to Jonny. "Do you think they're gay?"

"Kurt, if you're really that concerned, just ask her. But I don't think you should be that concerned."

A new person arrived—our age even. He gave Jonny, and then me, an inquisitive look. Bewildered, I poked my fiancé. "You know that guy?"

"No, Kurt, I don't know everyone who comes here."

Clearly my comments irked him. Barking that he wanted to check out the basement, Jonny started to walk away from me, beer in hand. I followed him down the stairs to another empty dance floor. Here a male disc jockey was at work in the corner.

The newcomer darted after us and inquired casually, "Are you two brothers?" He tried to stay close to Jonny, but when Jonny completely disregarded him, the boy wanted my name instead. His breath was exceptionally warm. I swallowed and told him. "Karl?" he asked.

"No, Kurt."

"Knut?"

I gave up and nodded. Then, without introducing himself, he asked Jonny for his name. At least they didn't know each other. "That's a secret," Jonny chose to answer.

"Really? Why?"

Jonny wouldn't tell. He said any explanation would spill the secret.

"What? Why?"

The stranger seemed about to ask again, but my distressed fiancé took off and placed himself alone by the wall, chugging his beer self-consciously. I hurried after him. Undeterred, the other boy followed us. "You two look so familiar," he said to me. "Were you in a reality show?"

"Nope," I answered, unsure of what to do with him.

"Wow, Knut, you look and sound exactly alike. It's so unsettling. Do you want to go someplace where there won't be so many effeminate homos pestering us?"

That was really stretching it. "This place isn't that busy yet," I said. I could tell it annoyed the hanger-on to be so thoroughly ignored by Jonny. But he wasn't giving up on us. As my fiancé physically led me to the nosiest part of the room, our stalker started shouting directly into my ear.

"You see those guys?" Absentmindedly I followed his gaze—two boys our age were on their way to the coat check. "They probably assume we're planning a threesome right now."

The boy instructed me to relocate to his other side and when I hesitated, he stepped between Jonny and me to create the intended result. Upset, Jonny moved to my other side and demanded to know why the stranger was still hounding us. "Tell him to leave."

Before I had time to say anything, our keen pursuer asked Jonny to step back so that his bitter enemies could see that he was busy talking with both of us. I also felt his arm around my waist. When I gazed down at it, he said, "Yah, Knut, that's great, keep looking."

I demonstratively pointed at my fiancé. "You see that boy looking very angry right now?"

"Yah, your bro. He shouldn't be here if he's in such a foul mood. Are you really gay? I mean, both of you?"

I confirmed that, to the best of my knowledge, this was probably the case.

"Do you ever have sex together?"

"Yah, of course, all the time. He's also my fiancé."

After a prolonged delay, he withdrew his hand. "Well ... wow." And with that, he took off abruptly, at long last.

When Jonny lifted his phone to check his messages it brightened with an incoming one, as if he was prescient. He immediately showed me the text. "Look, from Tim—Truls must have given him my number. He's begging us to come back to Marselis Gate."

"Delete it! Or tell him he needs to hurry down here. He shouldn't miss this for the world."

"You're right. I've never seen anything like *that*."

Jonny stared shamelessly at a little old lady who'd taken the dance floor. Three tall girls with Christmas hats on their heads encircled her with their hands in the air. The place no longer seemed so empty.

For some reason, the old lady came over and wanted to hug us. "You're so cute. I'm the grandmother!" she proclaimed. "I haven't seen so many men in a bar since I was a child. I grew up by the army garrison in Sætermoen."

"But you're talking to almost the only ones here," Jonny pointed out, a bit alarmed.

"We were at a pub first... It was full of them."

"Really?"

"Yah, London Pub. Are you boys from Harstad?"

Before we had a chance to answer, the three girls waved her back to the dance floor.

Jonny's phone lit up again and we learned that a whole brigade of visitors from Gaysir were trooping into Truls's apartment.

They'd stay to finish the Turkish Pepper and the vodka. Moments later my fiancé showed me another disturbing message, this one from Truls—they weren't coming after all. They'd decided to play the pig game.

Seeing my anxious expression, Jonny explained it was just a dice game. "It's called Pass the Pigs. Instead of dice, you throw two pigs to try your luck. You gain or lose points depending on how the pigs land in combination with each other."

"I don't want to try my luck with Tim and Thom. I think I know their endgame."

Stroking my back, Jonny wondered if we shouldn't make our trip to town an all-nighter. He was clearly trying to calm me down.

But then the wife from upstairs spoke to me again. "There you are," she said, grabbing my arm. "I was looking for you. What do you think of my mum? It's my three daughters out there with her. We're celebrating my son's birthday. You should meet him. He just turned twenty-five."

She wouldn't let go of my arm. "There he is, the handsome boy in the stairs—Lars, Lars, come over here," she shouted to him. "You have to say hello to some unusually decent boys. They're a couple! Aren't they sweet?"

Jonny's ex turned on his heels and hurried to his siblings. Jonny seized my other arm cautiously as he stared at his former flatmate, who'd become engaged in a rapid discussion with the girls. Lars wore a bright red Christmas hat, like his sisters, and looked much skinnier than I remembered him.

Puzzled by her son's reaction, his mum grew quiet. Was he telling his sisters to get hold of their parents? Jonny didn't appear to be listening when I said his name.

The basement disc jockey had stopped playing music and everyone turned quiet, for a long line of girls, dressed up as dwarves, were marching down the staircase. They held little lanterns and sang, "Heigh-ho, heigh-ho, it's home from work we go."

At the end of the procession, an embarrassed-looking, pale-skinned, and long-limbed young man carried a basket with flowers. An elaborate Disney costume identified him as Snow White.

"*Another* bachelor party," Jonny gasped.

44

UNLICENSED TAXIS SLOWED their tiny cars to solicit us then sped off, spraying us with snowdrift, as we decided to try our luck and walk home.

We unlocked the front door, prepared to flee at a moment's notice. Truls had left the tied-up bag with the shrimp shells in the hall, next to Thom's sneakers and Tim's white boots. Other than that we didn't see any unknown pairs of shoes. The pig game was over. And mercifully, the door to the adults' room was closed.

The lights had been turned off, except in the hallway and the kitchen, where the hum from the refrigerator tickled our eardrums. Somewhere inside Truls's apartment building, a washing machine went through its final stages of centrifugation.

Out scouting, Jonny gesticulated that I should come and take a look in the living room for myself. The coffee table had become a landslide of porn movies: *Buttfucking Buddies*, *Sausage Party*, *Boys Will Be Boys* were just some of the titles. A large dildo, dressed in a rubber, sat in the armchair as if it were a throne. Truls Snøfugl had secrets after all.

"Where does he hide them? I bet no one will notice if we borrow this one," Jonny said, picking up a DVD entitled *Sex Among*

Friends. Begging him to be quiet, I prayed to myself that no one would wake up. I stepped on something soft: one of several rolled-out condoms scattered on the floor. As soon as we'd flushed the toilet, we rushed to unlock the boys' room.

The snow whipped hard against our windowpane, and in spite of my exhaustion, with Jonny my delicate radiator sound asleep against me, I remained awake and alert. In the building across the backyard, a bright flash emitted every few seconds—someone was snapping pictures at this late hour.

Our door handle suddenly moved up and down and then, with a soft click, returned to its resting position. Jonny smacked his lips. Our cell phones lay on the desk—but I didn't dare move. If only we'd turned off the sound and brought our outerwear into our room, no one, unless they'd heard us come in, could have known for sure that we were home.

Struggling with the sheets for a second, Jonny continued his slow, rhythmical breathing. I remained alert, listening. Jonny was quite possibly the only one asleep at this moment. "Hello, are you up?" a man in the hallway, right outside our door, quietly inquired. I wondered if it was Truls, if some kind of emergency had arisen, but more likely someone wanted us to join them in the adults' room or living room. Through the wall, I faintly discerned bizarre patterns of smacking and slapping, whimpers, sighs, and an occasional groan. Feeling cold inside, I couldn't stop searching out the sounds.

An astounding crash rang out, followed by stunned silence. And then, for several long moments, I thought I'd better check on them. Could the closet actually have fallen on top of the three men? Was someone hurt, or stuck? I eventually heard intermittent laughter, rapid footsteps, and doors slamming. At long last came the calm hour when everyone fell asleep—even I did.

As a pinkish-gray daylight entered our window, Truls's apartment once more turned into a flurry of activity. First someone released immense quantities of urine into the toilet bowl. Then the coffee maker started sighing and gurgling in the kitchen. And suddenly Jonny's cell phone beeped four times; it sounded urgent. Still asleep, Jonny made cuddling sounds when I stroked his naked butt to rouse him. Impatient, I checked his device. A total of five unread text messages, all from Tim, one from last night, awaited his response.

As I took the liberty to read Tim's texts, the phone beeped in my hand. It was Truls messaging to apologize. "I'm taking the Hobbits for breakfast in a second and won't bring them back. Just stay where you are."

Well, that was a relief.

My hands shook as I read Tim's messages over again.

After someone had completed a long shower, I finally heard the entrance slam shut and footsteps receding down the stairs. Climbing over my slumbering fiancé, I unlocked the door to inhale the fresh smell of coffee.

The living room had been cleared; the shrimp shells in the entrance, gone. The door to Truls's room stood ajar. A fresh breeze wafted through his window and some planks from his bed frame lay scattered on the carpet.

In the bathroom, a pile of wet towels sat atop the laundry basket. The heating conductors under the floor had been set to maximum. I sat down on the toilet bowl as a cunning plan began to brew deep inside my head.

I couldn't let go of Tim's texts, and the little things he wanted do to Jonny's naked body and the little things Thom apparently wanted to do to my naked body, so easily. You see—Tim and Thom each had their favorite Larsen boy.

Okay then! Please don't shoot me—but if this Tim Høiby character really aspired to behave like an old pig, and he thought himself fit to tamper with the feelings of a North-Norwegian satyr, I'd change my gear at once and play the wolf.

45

"I COULD EAT a whole elk," Jonny said, teasingly.

Mocking our guarded expressions, Tim showed us into a spacious, white-painted living room that held a grand piano, two massive framed photographs, and an ultra-sleek, blue sofa where the three of us took our seats. "Come in further, if you dare. Notice how little we're reflected in the windowpane? It's because it's museum-quality glass. It's dark outside, but you can see a long way down the Oslofjord during the day."

The artist poured champagne into the three flute glasses on the coffee table and watched us taste the fizzy liquid. "Don't look so skeptical, Kurt. I haven't put any drugs in it."

I couldn't stop looking around me. Hanging on opposite walls, two works of art showed huge blocks of concrete stretching far into the horizon. The images depicted panoramic views of aqueducts, in pallid colors—possibly reverse perspectives from the same vantage point.

"I have to say, you have modern taste," I said. "Are those photos your work?"

Come to think of it, the photos must have been taken on separate days. Down in the drains, hard to see at first, the shapes of human beings could be made out: kids sharing a smoke; a solitary boy, unwatched by his group of friends, executing some trick on a skateboard.

At the bottom of the drain with the kids, there was no water in the trail. High pressure had pushed away all the clouds, and the sky shone perfectly clear but saturated with heavy coloration.

In the other image, a man approached with an unleashed dog, perhaps a border collie. The leash was barely visible in his hand. Toward the lone dog walker ran a tiny trickle, and above him, hints of mist could be detected in the air.

"Yah, but they don't belong to me. It's all *hers*. The whole apartment. Even the champagne."

"Whose?"

"The lady who lives here." Jonny put his toes on top of mine. Who was he talking about? We must have looked ill at ease, because Tim added, "Don't worry! She won't be joining us for dinner." Our host was taking me in. "You study art history, don't you?"

Jonny cast me a loving look and put his arm on the sofa behind me. "Yah, that'll be Kurt. Do you often give away art?" he ventured.

Old tennis balls and a shopping trolley occupied the foreground in both images on the walls. Graffiti, juvenile obscenities, were scrawled along the banks.

Tim's eyes glinted mischievously as he ignored the question. "You're adventurous boys, aren't you? I mean, you do certainly seem to enjoy traveling."

He talked and we weren't sure how to answer. "Boys, listen, you should really be *thankful* that Thom and I took care of Truls on Friday. That way, you could do your own thing. You usually do, don't you?" He swallowed a mouthful from his glass. "So when are you two moving in with Thom and me?"

"I don't know about that," Jonny said in haste.

"But aren't you switching flats every few weeks or so?"

"If Kurt ever opens a gallery, would you consider showing something?" Jonny diverted. Our host suddenly coughed.

"Kurt, are you planning to open a gallery? Well, are you? Kurt, you're so quiet."

"No such plans," I lied.

Jonny wouldn't let it go that easily. "Didn't you make some kind of vow about it in a graveyard with your friend Ragnar?"

"Never mind that. It's not going to happen anytime soon—unless we could use our bedroom as a showroom."

"Now, that's interesting," Tim said. "What would you show? And who would your clients be? Random people dropping by?"

"People would pour in if *you* showed your stuff," Jonny countered. "His gallery would get a head start."

Staring at me, the artist paid little attention to my fiancé's prodding. "If you invited family and friends as well, it could prove an interesting collision. A careful merging of isolated elements. What do you think?"

I shuddered at the idea.

"I really like what you have on the walls here. How much would it cost if we'd have to pay the full price?" That of course was Jonny.

Tim challenged me with a look. "Oh, my charge ... what do you think?"

"Eh ... half a million kroner ... each?"

Tim just laughed, and Jonny inquired sweetly, "Can we get a 100% discount? And you really ought to give Truls a piece for Christmas. He'd like that."

Tim refilled our glasses. "Did you know that Truls moved to Oslo because of me? Once upon a time, I gave him so much heartache. And he used to be really handsome, you know. These days he just turns into a closed oyster at bars. He does that thing with his daughter, on the phone, even late at night, and then he's no fun for anyone. Enjoy being young and popular while you can, boys."

"We are," Jonny assured him.

"No, seriously. Enjoy it while you can."

"But we are," Jonny repeated.

"Do you take *any* pleasure in traveling alone?" Our host almost knocked down his glass as he leaned in for emphasis. He was staring at me rather darkly. "I bet you don't."

I asked him to explain himself.

"You feel miserable. You tell your boyfriend how much you *miss* him. You messaged Jonny all the time while you were supposed to explore Hawaii. Truls shares things with me."

"Yah, that's *all* I do."

"Where's your lady friend?" Jonny asked. "Why isn't she here?" She was abroad with her lover, Tim said.

Jonny wanted to hear him play something on the piano. Tim offered to do so after dinner.

"So is it true what you wrote in your text to Jonny last weekend—that Jonny's your favorite and I am Thom's, based on what Truls saw when he surprised us fully entangled on the living room floor?"

"Certainly, boys. And remember that I told you this. Nothing lasts forever. Enjoy it while you can. You're going to kiss at least a hundred princes who turn out to be frogs. Both of you—it's a rite of passage."

"So when are you breaking up with Thom?" I was a sensitive satyr; don't forget.

Jonny piped in anxiously, "I was going to make the same point as Kurt actually. By the way, I'm getting really, really hungry."

"Oh, that's right. You have an appetite. You thought it had slipped my mind? Let's not neglect our honorary guest, the king of the forest."

RAGNAR—I'M NOT particularly proud of what happened next, but I think you need to hear it, even though you've got every reason to be wary. You know I've always struggled to strike the balance between compulsive secrecy and due discretion.

Turning on his chair, Tim Høiby seemed quite stunned when my fiancé, failing to conceal an erection inside his underwear, returned from the bathroom. I'd just finished a third serving of cloudberry dessert and set my spoon down thoughtfully as Jonny stroked himself dreamily. And I heard him say, "Can the piano take two people?"

"Two? Why not three? Are you introducing yourself as the fifth course?"

Bodø Boy nodded.

Wiping his lips, Tim seemed happy to tag along and follow orders. Jonny led me by the hand into the living room. "Kurt's got this theory that you think we're uptight," Jonny said. "He believes the reason you think so is because you can't have your way with us. To you it means that we're in a state of denial—we're not living life to the fullest."

It was my cue. "We'd like to clarify things," I gloated. "We're not denying ourselves anything. You're the one missing out, not we."

Jonny said, "Please remain quiet and play the piano."

"Got it," Tim replied. "Though I'm really not that loose." Enthusiastically, he took a seat at the keys. Although he missed many notes and brusquely skipped from one piece to another, piano music now streamed through the apartment and it somehow made me feel less nervous. It resembled Chopin, Jonny said.

The wooden panel zapped away my body heat when I climbed on top of the grand piano. Then Jonny maneuvered himself onto the musical instrument. And he was on top of me.

"If I'd known you needed that stuff, I'd have left out a tray!" Tim sniggered, as Jonny rolled on the trash bag colored condom he'd kept in his pocket for the occasion. "Let me steer the shaft!"

"Why? I know my way home."

"Then let me at the very least warm up Kurt with a finger. Or my tongue. *Please.*" He was pleading with Jonny now and quick on his feet, fussing with my hair. I struggled to ignore him.

"Shut up, you old pig, and stop touching Kurt," Jonny commanded. I heard him spit in his hand behind me. "Both hands on the piano, please."

"Okay, okay! So you're God's gift to the world but won't share the goodies! Now let me get the camera."

"Just memorize the image. And hold your thoughts—we wouldn't want your brain to short circuit."

We'd certainly triggered something. He'd completely stopped playing. Tim was struggling now.

Clearing my voice, I asked if he knew any Burt Bacharach. It was the first thing in fact I'd said on top of the piano. Although he loved him, alas, he didn't.

"Boys, I should get some sheet music from the hall. Just please be careful so you don't break the panel. The old lady might notice that kind of damage."

"Just play whatever you know by heart," Jonny said, "to the end, and repeat. By the way, are you going to tell Thom? Do you think he'll be jealous?"

"Jealous? He'll be green with envy."

We gave him a good showing of what he and Thom couldn't have. Ever.

Dazed, Jonny let the world-famous artist pull off the condom. Having tied a knot in the contraceptive to restrain his semen, our dinner host cupped his hand around my fiancé's testicles. Jonny didn't approve. "You can remove your hand now, thank you."

"Can I hold on to the condom as a keepsake?"

"It's yours to keep."

We got dressed and took seats at the coffee table once more. "Guess what we're having next—French schoolboys!"

Tim produced a bottle of port wine, three new glasses, and a tray of white chocolate biscuits—apparently the French schoolboys. "It's a slowly detonating bomb, this," I whispered in Jonny's ear. "Hopefully it teaches him not to play with other people's fire."

Tim too wanted to set off a little time bomb—right there between his two works of art. He studied me carefully, then asked, "He popped the Sognsvann question, didn't he?"

Munching a schoolboy, I nodded.

Jonny looked more troubled and hastily replied, "We know that's just an intriguing question he asks to get a conversation going on Gaysir."

"Yah, sure." Obviously Truls Snøfugl hadn't dared to share with us the full story. But we ought to hear it. And Tim volunteered to tell us.

Late in August, our landlord had been surprised by heavy rain at Sognsvann. Or should we say, surprised *in* the rain. Taking hikes up there was his way of chilling down after work. Yah, so he said. Well, this time he got downright soaked. He made it back inside his dry vehicle, into the driver's seat. And then suddenly the other door opened. Into his dirty van jumped this young bouncy boy, a complete stranger, all happy and smiley, wearing bicycle shorts. Tim let us savor the detail for a moment. "Boys," Tim said, "please imagine Truls's surprise."

His front tire was flat. He'd left his bicycle and backpack and fishing rod outside his van. He said he was a student at the university. The poor lad had walked for more than three hours and now he wanted a lift into the city.

So Truls carried his stuff around to the back. The old man happens to store an old mattress in there—but we probably knew that already, didn't we? We looked warily at each other and ran to Truls's defense. "There's nothing strange about that," Jonny said reassuringly. "He sleeps on it when he travels the countryside. He drives around to pick up old car wrecks and auto parts from all over the place, right?"

"Yah, right," Tim said. "It's a perfectly legitimate mattress, of course. Very convenient when he made stopovers in deserted picnic areas. Anyway, the boy hopped in and said, *Excuse me*. Then he took off his wet socks, his jersey, and his drenched bicycle pants. So there you go—there was a naked boy in Truls's van. Truls couldn't believe his own eyes, his luck. There wasn't an ounce of fat on him. This boy had perfectly sculpted calves. Evidently there was no comparison—he was the best-looking boy our landlord had ever laid his eyes on."

Jonny gave an uncomfortable chuckle. Tim just smiled, clearly enjoying the image on his mind. "In front of Truls sat this lanky, light-haired youngster with a tiny, shriveled dick. Straddling it on his knees, he was searching inside his rucksack for a plastic bag with some dry garments.

"'I think you need some privacy,' Truls said. Okay, so those were his words. But then he climbed inside and closed the back door. When a certain alarmed look spread across the boy's face, Truls reassured him, 'I'll keep my clothes on. You just shut your eyes.'"

Jonny and I were tempted to do the same, for then, Tim informed us, he yanked the lad's soggy penis into his face.

"Sounds like one crazy day in the forest," I muttered.

"He seemed inexperienced," Tim went on. "The boy was sweating, heaving, and shivering, and quite abruptly, he made a final thrust down Truls's throat and came. It was all thick and gluey, according to the record. He put on dry clothes and Truls drove him into town, gulping compulsively and trying not to let it show.

"Truls developed a sore throat within a night. For weeks he couldn't get the youngster out of his head. He wanted to continue where they'd left off.

"And so he placed personal ads everywhere, begging the bicycle boy to get back in touch with him." Tim didn't know how many men

Truls inquired of and intrigued—in fact, lots of people offered to go bicycling with him. He had remarkable conversations on Gaysir.

Tim smiled. "I remember the first time he mentioned the two of you. He sounded so excited. Jonny was coming over for meatballs. He thought he was really on to something." We regrettably turned out to be Northerners. "Though I don't doubt for a moment that he's secretly hoping you'll bring that boy around some day. It's a small world, you know. With you being students and all."

"But ... didn't the boy give his name?" Jonny asked.

"No, he never did."

Tim Høiby's borrowed luxury apartment was about to feel smaller than Bus 30.

"Oh yah, there's one more thing. When the boy sat all quiet in the passenger seat, Truls asked, jokingly, 'Was that a seizure, that thing that just happened?' And the kid said, yah, he had a minor case of epilepsy, but at the time it was more of an a-ha moment. That comment has troubled Truls more than anything. He'd always dreamed of teaching someone the pleasures of gay sex. No, he just can't get that boy out of his head."

"Where exactly did he drive him? Where did he drop the kid off?"

"The trace goes cold at the taxi station at Sankthanshaugen. Unless you can help. Do you think you can? Boys, you should help him."

Oslo simply couldn't be *this* small. Yet it was.

47

TO NO EFFECT, on the bus home, I mumbled, "You can't be sure Ragnar's the right guy."

Jonny called me a wimp, asked how many epileptic students who were serious about bicycling and fishing I thought there were that lived at or around Sankthanshaugen.

He knew enough about you to suspect that you were, in fact, the one. More than once he'd teased me about you, questioned why I'd spend so much time with you during the day, when all I'd done was go to the lecture with you and then read in the library. Obviously, Truls and Tim had heard talk of you, too.

"By the way," Jonny said, "you should get to know that lady friend of Tim's. Maybe she'll sponsor your art gallery plans."

Damn it! Tim certainly knew how to mess with us. Of course I wasn't going to take the artist's words at face value. I tried to convince myself that he'd made up the story with bits and pieces of information he'd picked up. I told myself that maybe something had happened in the forest with our landlord, but not with you, Ragnar, my one good friend outside the household.

Yet I couldn't rid myself of the feeling that you were somehow in danger. Truls and Tim clearly talked about everything and everyone, and Jonny wasn't being particularly careful—I told him so.

I demanded to know if he and Tim had ganged up on me. No, there was no conspiracy. He laughed and begged me to invite you over after your shift, to Truls's quarters in Marselis Gate. Why? So we could study the reaction on your face, and on our landlord's face, the moment that the two of you crossed paths—or, at the very least, so Jonny could get to know you better.

He intended to figure you out. Succeed, whatever that meant, where I, according to him, had failed. "No!" I said. "Stop it! Don't drag Ragnar into this!" I didn't understand his obsession. Yet I was somehow curious, too.

When Jonny invited me to Peppe's to celebrate our last night together in Oslo before Christmas, I accepted the offer.

You showed up with a pizza.

Believing that you were meeting my brother, you lingered by our table. Jonny took the liberty to ask about your bicycling habits; he quizzed you as to whether you'd ever punctured a tire in the forest, "because such accidents must be annoying."

It had happened, you admitted.

Jonny insisted that you should come over to our place sometime. I shouldn't be keeping you to himself; that was unfair to everyone else. I was about to pull him out of there. He was seriously pushing it. Fortunately, you had other customers that night.

Between mouthfuls, Jonny told me that you were missing out; you were lagging behind. In keeping you away from several truths, I was basically responsible for slowing down your sexual development. But he promised to take care of it. To repair the damage, he'd invite you over to Marselis Gate without my knowledge, by using my cell phone no less, and pretending to be me—he knew I preferred not to use my phone in order to save money and that I often left it at home.

Fortunately, no one in my household knew your last name. So, still at Peppe's, I excused myself to the bathroom to memorize your phone number and returned to our table to inform him that I'd deleted your entry from my device. Jonny threatened to invite our landlord to the pizza restaurant while I was in Rio. I told my childish fiancé squarely that he shouldn't test my temper over you when I went away.

"I'd forgive you anything but you messing with Ragnar" was how I put it.

"Anything but that then?"

I nodded vigorously.

I'd never seen Bodø Boy like this. He was staring at me with cold, unhappy eyes. Something had been set in motion. A test of sorts.

48

AS PUNISHMENT, HE told me not to get in touch at all over Christmas, for his parents would ask too many questions. He'd certainly stay away from Gaysir and his email account. I thought that we could at least text each other, but he was tense and authoritarian about it. He said that I needed to save my money for my travel.

And finally it was January.

Mum and Dad were probably sound asleep in Bodø, my fiancé was probably sound asleep inside a locked boys' room in Marselis Gate in the Norwegian capital, and you were safe, and probably sound asleep in the mountains with your sister Anniken.

I was again in foreign airspace on my own—the plane was circling above Antonio Carlos Jobim International Airport, waiting for clearance to land. It took another steep turn.

We'd waited forty-five minutes already and the onboard entertainment system remained playing. Most screens showed the same apprehensive face of a relatively well-known African-American actor. The blinking light on the edge of the wing exposed the thick, dark, and wet clouds the large aircraft was charging through.

Absorbed by the in-flight movie, the obese Portuguese passenger next to me inadvertently pushed my elbow off the armrest. The actor looked so anxious I wanted to know what unpleasant news his friend was telling him. Restless and bored with my *Lonely Planet* guidebook on Brazil, I gave in and grabbed my own headset.

The energetic Portuguese dialogue assaulting my eardrums took me aback. I certainly hadn't expected the American actor to speak Portuguese.

I found a way to choose English on my screen, but the dubbed Portuguese continued, so I interrupted my neighbor to ask what language he was listening to. In a grumpy voice, he confirmed that he followed the Portuguese version. Mysteriously, while I was explaining my technical problem to him, I recognized Dennis Haysbert's deep, American accent in my right ear. "I don't know how this happened," I said, embarrassed, "but now I can hear the English."

Then the movie was interrupted. We were informed that permission to land had been granted. The tropical storm had passed; the entertainment system would be switched off shortly, and the headsets collected. However, when the movie came back on, Dennis Haysbert—his character anyway—resumed speaking Portuguese.

Was I losing my mind or on the brink of scientific discovery, hot on the trail of something profound about brains and languages? Maybe so.

I duplicated my previous actions carefully. With both earphones in place, I heard Portuguese. Yet when I lifted the left one, as I'd done to talk to my neighbor, I heard the English in the right earphone. With the left one in place, Portuguese again.

Somehow, the two tongues were transmitted simultaneously, in separate outlets—and my brain chose to listen to the language I didn't understand. I perceived no difference in volume, only in the language spoken in each ear.

I thought of you, Ragnar, and worried, groundlessly, ridiculously, that I was about to have a seizure. And then, to complete my confusion, a loud bang reverberated through the aircraft.

The lights were gone—we rushed downward and the walls creaked with the sudden change of direction. People screamed and my feet gripped the floor. Another bang rang out, this time from below. The lights returned and I felt the aircraft hit the ground. We were making an expedient, controlled landing in Rio.

The voice of the captain emerged over the loudspeakers as we taxied off the landing strip to the terminal. "Some of you may have noticed a loud bang while we were in the air." For a moment he said no more.

My Portuguese neighbor stared at me, dark in the face. "*May have* noticed a loud bang?"

"The plane was hit by lightning," the captain finally pronounced. He said that the plane was built to endure such events—it had special lightning conductors on the wings, among other devices. We could see them for ourselves, along the rear edges. In any case, we had nothing to worry about. This was not a dramatic incident. It happened once a year, on average, to every plane.

My Portuguese seatmate wasn't all that comforted. "I know a few things about lightning; it could cut off the rudder in an instant." He snapped his fingers for dramatic effect. "Then the plane becomes uncontrollable and crumbles into pieces. Guess what? Fuel tanks have ignited a few seconds after lightning." Startling me, he clapped his hands together. "Lightning strikes have led to some of the worst crashes in aviation history."

I wasn't listening to him any longer. I was busy visualizing Jonny's face, clammy and contorted, and shivered at the thought of not being there to console him. I was busy picturing my name on Norwegian television—if we'd been on Thai Airways in April or on Air Canada in June, there would have been two names, in alphabetical order:

Jonny Larsen, 18, Bodø.

Kurt Larsen, 21, Bodø.

Someone needed to comprehend the meaning of those two names juxtaposed. Again I thought of you, Ragnar.

ACT V (2003)

49

MY FIANCÉ, STANDING in the doorway in Marselis Gate, wore nothing but boxers and the shimmering hook around his neck—my secret Christmas gift. The letter J, intermingled with his chest hair, rose and fell, metering his heartbeat and slow, barely audible breaths.

His face lit up every time I looked him over. "You're playing Bacharach," I said, impressed. And he told me that he'd listened to my favorite singer while waiting for me in bed in the boys' room.

He removed my backpack and admitted to taking solarium. He'd felt stark naked since my trip to Hawaii and couldn't let me be the only one with color. He guessed I was the only person in the world to fake a fake tan to his brother and parents. He looked up into my eyes from the floor, still holding on to my foot. "I've been crying for days, listening to this song."

"It's 'Something Big.' One of my favorites. Does it make you sentimental?"

"He makes me miss you so much. You won't be sorry for coming home early. I promise."

He wanted to take things slow and wouldn't let me when I tried to pull off his by now tent-like boxers; instead, he slipped out of my hands and bent down again to remove my brand new sneakers.

"Even I could wear these," he assured me. "As long as you haven't soiled them on the inside. Have you?"

"Of course not! You can borrow them if you're careful."

"Will you ever forgive me for being so mean to you in Bodø?" he wondered. "At least now we can actually celebrate your twenty-first birthday *together*."

Jonny got up and pursued me into the bathroom to watch me pee, something of a ritual-in-the-making on my returns. Unfortunately, the bathroom was in rapid decline. There was no toilet paper, only a bunch of empty rolls, his empty contact lens packages were scattered on the sink, and barely enough toothpaste remained in the tube to cover his brush, which he kindly let me borrow. Jonny and I agreed that housework wasn't his strongest suit. Our landlord had been pretty good at taking care of the stuff.

"Where's Truls?"

"He's disappeared."

"What?"

"Don't worry. Only since yesterday!"

I turned to face Bodø Boy. He seized my hands and pulled me to him, delivering a hard hug. He wouldn't let go. He told me he loved me. And I told him I loved him too. His canine clinginess touched me but also disturbed me a bit. If Truls had disappeared, shouldn't we be calling the police?

"The police? No, he left a note next to the goldfish bowl before he took off."

Jonny had discovered it late last night when he'd started to worry. Truls was out looking for cars somewhere. He thought Truls wanted to give us a little privacy. He and Truls hadn't talked that much lately. Warm and moist, he held on to me. "You're starting to look a little unhappy," he said. "And you just got home. I haven't even shown you my devout gratefulness yet." He caught my gaze with his eyes.

I'd been so keyed up on the train from the airport, feeling tears of delight building as I absorbed the wintery rises along the railway. Yet how could I be happy when Marselis Gate was a mess, and he talked to me, and looked at me, that way? There was something desperate about his smile; it even sounded like he had prepared a little speech. "You know, we promised to be completely open with each other. There's something you need to forgive me."

My first thought was you. I urged him to go on, but Jonny was struggling. I had to remind myself that you were safe in the mountains.

"Well," I burst out, rather impatiently, "something happened to me too. On the plane to Rio. I've been meaning to tell you ever since."

He met my eyes at once. "What? What happened on the plane?"

"First, you tell me what happened *here*."

"It didn't happen here exactly. It happened on Trysil Mountain, last weekend."

We just stared at each other, stupefied, because neither one knew how to continue. I was scrambling to recollect whether you'd told me which mountains you were in. Jonny hadn't mentioned anything about a trip to the mountain. I had to remind myself that he was a teenager and I was not.

Jonny's phone started chiming in our bedroom. He stopped looking at me, for the first time since my return. I followed his steps while he turned down the current song—"Wives and Lovers."

"I don't know," he said, almost whispered, to the caller. "We haven't had time to talk yet. He just came in the door. I'll let you know as soon as we're through." He hung up and I just stared at him. Between begging me to sit down with him in bed, he asked if I wasn't wondering who'd called.

"Of course I am. Who was it?"

"It was *Tim*."

I shivered. "That old pig? What did he want?"

"He's not really a pig."

I couldn't help it; I shivered again, as the silvery hook pounded ceaselessly off his chest.

"He just wants to know how we're doing," he added, softer. "He wishes us well. Both of us. Come closer, please." His voice went thinner. He smelled so good. And he was staring at me with such moist, lovely eyes. "You know, something really happened in Trysil."

Back on topic. "So I hear. What happened?"

"We went to Trysil to … slalom."

"Okay. And?"

"It's so much easier to *contain* oneself when you're around."

I pushed away the dirty socks on the floor and sighed deeply. "You find it hard to contain yourself?"

He said that I was putting words in his mouth. I even detected a touch of irritation in his voice when he said, "It just happened. Okay?"

There it came. I even felt a strange sense of relief. "I don't even know what happened." Yet it had.

"But, Kurt. Please explain that thing in Rio to me first."

"No, Jonny, no. I'm not saying another word until you're done."

"It just happened," my fiancé repeated—as if his mantra made a difference, as if it excused everything. "I don't know why. It was an accident. You must forgive me at once…"

"Let me get things clear. You prefer old pigs to me?"

"I prefer *you*—period!"

"But still things happened?"

"Only twice."

"Twice? Come on, talk! Give him credit where credit is due! Hurray for Tim and his … benevolence!" The words began to pour out of me as if they were pre-programmed.

Jonny gave me one of those longing looks. "Kurt, listen. You've got to understand what I'm talking about since something happened to you on the plane. First, you habituate me to unlimited quantities of sex. Then, you take off on these super-long vacations. Let's face it; you've turned me into this fragile, sex-crazed target."

So I was to blame. "How could you go to Trysil? You don't even have skis."

"Truls rented me a pair."

"Huh, Truls was with you?"

"He organized the trip. If you were here, we could all have gone together. And just for the record," he added, real loud, "*nothing's* changed, except I love you even more."

The phone started ringing again, startling us both. This time when he picked up, he made an effort to comfort me with his free hand, although he wasn't particularly good at multitasking. He soon hung up.

"I'm sorry. Tim's so nervous. He says he wants to speak with you directly. Of course he wants all of us to stay friends."

"Great. I can hardly wait. First you tell me precisely what happened in Trysil."

"We went skiing."

"You already mentioned that."

I was stunned at how sweaty his hand had become. His movements felt mechanical. The sentences had to be dragged out of him, one by one. On the way to the mountain, Jonny had sat in the front of the van, safely ensconced next to Truls. Stuck in the backseat, Tim and Thom resigned themselves to making innuendos about our landlord and his two adopted boy toys.

"Okay, and then?"

Jonny, feeling the need to retaliate, asked if the Hobbits, given their body size, had small penises.

"I see, and?"

He upped the implied insults by inquiring as to whether they could suck their own cocks. "Because that's the only way I'd pass the time while my boyfriend's out of the country," he'd appended for good measure. Next, Tim commanded Truls to stop the car at the nearest picnic stop and get out the mattress in the back, real quick. By now I was shivering badly, but Jonny claimed to have denied them the pleasure. Driving on, Truls ignored his former lover, but the Hobbits ordered Jonny to demonstrate his talent as soon as they reached the cabin.

Again, apparently, nothing had happened.

Yet after a painful fall on the slopes, Tim had noticed Jonny leaving for the cabin alone and had pursued him through the woods with his pocket camera. Once again, no self-fellating had occurred. No naked photos were taken in the snow either. Tim "just happened" to like the way Jonny looked, with his increasingly long curls, in slalom boots and Truls's red mountain anorak. He'd sidled himself up to Jonny under the guise of wanting to shoot a photo series of a regular boy left to his own devices, to essentially idle in and around a mountain cabin. Then finally one thing had led to another and Tim somehow succeeded in jacking off my fiancé (on his knees) under a snow-capped pine tree.

Up until that point, Jonny hadn't quite realized to what extent Tim and Thom shared their experiences as well as their pictures. With Tim and Truls busy preparing lasagna and salad for dinner, Jonny hung out in the cabin sauna with Thom, who needed my fiancé up his ass right away—a wish he made clear in scant few words. I raised my eyebrows considerably. "Yah, of course we used a condom. He's quite adorable—portable, like a laptop computer. We got so sweaty in that sauna. It was surprisingly fun actually." But only until Tim showed up and wanted more pictures.

A short argument had then ensued between the two artists. Needless to say, dinner with Truls had proven awkward. For the rest of the trip, including the drive home, our landlord had remained practically mute.

Nonetheless, after devouring their lasagna, the seemingly insatiable Hobbits tried to have another go on Jonny, this time together. By now, not only embarrassed but also a little mortified, Jonny pretended he didn't understand and hid in his bunk while Truls, for his part, buried himself in front of the old television. The artist couple wouldn't hear of my fiancé's ruse though—it was such an unbearable waste of a perfect weekend, they insisted. They lifted him from under his cover and carried him into their own chamber. Speechless, Truls nonetheless appeared in his pajamas to watch.

There, in the bigger bed, Tim and Thom pulled off Jonny's clothes. Next, Tim emphatically licked my fiancé's ass, while Thom tried to push Jonny's legs over his head. Jonny, now little better than a piece of useless timber, declined to perform the advertised act.

"So it happened three times then."

"No, Kurt. The last time doesn't count, because I wouldn't participate."

There was also a coda. For unexpected reasons, Tim and Thom must have gotten cold feet overnight. Coffee mugs in hand, they sat down the next morning to offer advice on how to handle the boyfriend in Rio.

Most boyfriends, they explained, were prone to jealous tantrums; therefore, any teenager with fresh regrets might want to keep the events that had just transpired a secret. He could simply *bury* them in the past and behave better in the future, they counseled.

"That would be false and disloyal," Jonny snapped. Indeed, he'd become quite edgy during our short time apart. Well, in that case, it was probably better to let me in on the main facts. "Head off any demons right away," they advised. But don't forget, it could take me time to forgive him, and we should take advantage of clearing the air between us to craft a mutually agreeable policy, they warned.

Yah, a formal policy.

Whether a public or private agreement, and no matter what the terms: always play together, anything but kissing, everything but fucking, never without a condom, never without sharing notes, never when both of us were in town, or for that matter don't ask; don't tell. And what have you. Because true monogamy, of course, was also an option.

I moaned. "No wonder Tim's so eager to find out what goes on today in this household." The bottom line was that they'd all agreed at the cabin that if I really loved Jonny, I'd forgive him.

Now cupping my balls on the floor, he gave me an optimistic look. "So do you?"

"Sure! If Tim gives me his pictures and deletes his originals, and I get to read your phone messages immediately, then maybe." Bodø Boy thought it a fair deal.

It would be silly, Tim wrote, if the little things in Trysil ruined the great things Jonny had going for him in Oslo! It did upset Tim though that Jonny and I appeared to be so smug and self-sufficient and behaved like God's gifts to each other, for he loathed feeling unwanted!

I'd gotten to his phone too late though. I was convinced that Jonny had conveniently deleted his replies, although he swore he hadn't even answered his artist stalker. "Come on," he insisted, "I've had more sex with you than with any other person, except for Lars maybe…. By the end of 2003, you'll surely be my all-time high. You're forgetting about Rio again—tell me what happened to you down there. Or was it up in the air?" He lighted up.

"You tell me what kind of relationship you want, first."

"I don't know. I'll go for whatever policy you want…. I suppose we should both begin by airing secrets."

"Define the word *secret*."

"Well, will this do?"

Not knowing what to believe, I let my sinful fiancé jack me off; he used his T-shirt to wipe the viscous lumps off my navel and tried to drag me back into bed. "I want to come too," he begged. But I was already on my feet, looking for my boxers.

I asked him to make me something to eat. "We're out of bread, but I can make you some noodles. Hey, what are you doing with my phone?" He begged me not to bother Tim. I assured him I wouldn't, because I'd probably never talk to that piece of slime again. I took a seat at the work desk and told him to stay away. Not looking much relieved by my answer, he obediently left for the kitchen, his shoulders raised.

"You self-centered, invading pig," I wrote the swine anyway. "I don't want to take your shit. Save it for Thom." I collected my own device from my mountain backpack and wrote another message.

Jonny returned from the kitchen the moment his phone vibrated and beeped on the work desk. "You're extremely well attuned to your ring tone," I muttered accusingly. Breaking up, my voice betrayed my feelings.

"I can turn it off if you'd like..."

"No, by all means: read!"

"It just happened," my message to him read. "I don't know how, but we're not together anymore. Can you forgive me this instant?"

I knew it was a bit harsh and theatrical. Jonny shuddered and looked hurt. A large part of me wanted to console him right away, because he looked so cute and vulnerable as the shimmering hook around his neck rose and fell.

Then, with an unexpected beep in my ex's hand, Tim wrote back to clarify that Thom didn't eat shit. Never had. Red in the face, the eighteen-year-old read his words out loud to me. "But ... hello, Kurt, listen!" he started to protest. "What about Rio?"

50

SITTING TIRELESSLY IN my inner exile on the toilet bowl with my clothes on, I waited until I heard Jonny lock himself out. I then discarded the empty toilet paper rolls, the squeezed-out toothpaste tube, and the twelve contact lens packages that lay strewn around the sink, two for each day I'd been away.

I was too tired after my flight to think much at all, but I had energy to burn. The castle of doom needed thorough cleaning. Although Truls preferred us to save electricity and air dry our clothing on his stand, I turned on the combined washer-dryer function and got my Brazilian laundry going. Our landlord, I reasoned, was in no position to object, running away like that.

Truls's orange blob, Loverboy, greedily attacked the food I tossed into the fish tank in the kitchen. His home was almost as filthy as mine. Excrement swirled around like worms inside the algae-infested walls. Look at him.

Dirty plates greeted me everywhere—Jonny's empty cereal box still lay on the table, as did an additional bowl of another day's soggy cornflakes. On the stove, still hot, I discovered my pot of noodle water, but I was no longer particularly hungry, just eager to tidy things up—and put my stamp on the place before my nap.

The dishwasher was full—everything in it, dirty. For unclear reasons, Jonny had left the empty detergent box in the cupboard, so I placed it under his pillow, perhaps as a reminder or the start of a physical shopping list. I threw my Bacharach CD from his player into the box as well, but only after breaking it—just to remind him my music was ruined. I don't know why, Jonny. These things just happen. I happened to be angry.

Plenty of dish liquid sat by the sink, so repenting a little, I got the dishwasher going. Yah, things kept on happening, everything just *happens*. I should call Tim, check to make sure he was okay with the small, trivial things that had happened in Trysil the moment I left the country. I should shower him with empathy and goodwill.

I imagined our conversation: Tim, are you sure you're okay? I certainly hope you aren't intolerably upset for leading Jonny astray, because I'm perfectly fine about it. Yah, you're totally good, too? Great!

Entertaining this thought, I entered the shower, only to realize we were out of shampoo; although why complain when there was Jonny's conditioner? Furthermore, why spend another day longing and aching in the hot southern sun when I could be more miserable in this frozen mud pit called Oslo, basically for free?

Though knowing my ex would miss my body heat tonight cheered me up a little bit. He needed to explore the feeling of not being my fiancé, or even my boyfriend. Taking my cue from his previous ex, I intended to show off in my underwear, to tempt him, emphasize what he had lost. Foamy bubbles oozed up through the shower's drain, covering my toes. So the drain was a bit clogged then. So what, my feet would get even cleaner!

Outside the shower stall, the bubbles wafted up through the drain by the washing machine as well. Brilliant, my pile of dirty socks was freshening up on the tiles! Yah, the jet of hot water had temporarily carried away my anxieties! Drying myself with a clean towel, I noticed more bubbles in the sink. Those pipes were seriously overwhelmed—how interesting! Never mind the mess, the entire bathroom would soon shine gloriously.

The dishwasher sounded awfully distraught as it made delayed thuds. Entering the hallway stark naked, I felt like I was closing in on an ocean steam-liner.

Okay then, maybe I should have acted less impulsively and gone out and bought dishwasher detergent. A cloud had materialized in the kitchen; thick foam was avalanching to the floor from both the sink and the dishwasher.

About to tear the machine open—the power button lay on the inside—I recalled that it contained boiling water. Then I remembered the cold-blooded vertebrate. As I searched with my hands in low-visibility conditions, I bumped into the warm noodle pot on the stove and then tried not to tip over the aquarium by sheer force. Waves spilled from the sides of the tank in the hallway as I brought Loverboy to safety on the toilet lid, where I shoveled off the foamy top. Utterly composed in spite of the commotion, the fish rested on the dirty pebbles at the bottom, flexing its gills.

I filled water from the tap into a cleaning bucket, but when I attempted to pour him into the new plastic container, the orange creature fought against the current, swam panic-stricken into the walls, and ended up crushed by pebbles. And then, of course, the fuse went out.

51

THE DISHWASHING BUBBLES proved too light to flush down the toilet, so weightless that they were probably still sliding down the frozen building's exterior, creeping slowly from Truls's bedroom window, when Jonny locked himself in the apartment. It had gone dark outside, so it had to be sometime after 4:00 p.m.

Not knowing when Truls would return, I'd gotten second thoughts about spending the night in the adults' room. Instead, I'd placed the camping bed in the middle of the boys' room and retired to your sleeping bag. Carrying shopping bags in each hand, Jonny uttered a sound of surprise when he turned on the light.

"You're still here. And you've cleaned up," he noted. "It smells great in here. Kurt, you must still love me!"

He lay down on top of me and tried to hug my cocooned body. From inside my sack, I found it difficult to kick him away. I told him he had to get up, for he was putting too much pressure on my bladder. He repeated what had become his mantra, "Sorry, sorry, sorry." Pushing him aside, I got up and offered him a murky glare.

"Give me your cell phone."

"Again?"

"Yah! If you can be unfaithful and forgiven, I can be unfaithful and forgiven too!"

"So are we still together then? Because you can't be unfaithful and forgiven if we're not together anymore."

He wanted to know if I'd checked my own phone. "I've sent you twenty-one apologies already. Do you want your birthday gift one day in advance? Kurt, listen!"

Handing his device to me, he looked disgustingly cheerful. I didn't answer. Now he tried to get his hand inside his boxers—the ones I was borrowing. Leaning over my shoulder, he finally took notice of whose phone number I was looking up: Lars, the bus driver.

"What? Are you going to have sex with my crazy ex?"

"I don't know what'll happen. And I can certainly not answer the why part. Just remember to forgive me as soon as it's all over."

Jonny sighed and said I had no reason to feel morally superior, for clearly I'd lied to him. I had no idea what my filthy ex was on about. "That thing you said before Christmas, when we left Tim's," he reminded me. "About you forgiving me anything, except getting in touch with Ragnar, because you loved me so much. Was that just bullshit, or some kind of test?" he challenged. Because nothing would have happened at Trysil, he maintained, if he'd known I wouldn't forgive him.

With a shudder I turned to leave the boys' room. "Sweetheart, come back," he whispered after me. "In Oslo, you aren't allowed to sleep anywhere but in the same bed as me."

Standing in the kitchen doorway, I searched through one of Truls's gay magazines. I was happy to see that Loverboy looked bright and clean in his new and shiny surroundings. Finally my newly dubbed ex realized that I was devouring the meeting place section and cried out, "Seriously, are you going to a gay sauna as well? There'll only be old, desperate guys there. Particularly on a weekday."

"How do you know?" I countered.

"I'm only guessing. What are you planning to do?"

"Where do you think they'll be the most experienced? At My Friend Club or Hercules?"

"This won't be a good experience at either place. You might catch something. And I'll have to quarantine you."

I felt inspired, ingeniously destructive. Perhaps I wouldn't stop at Lars. I might as well do it with you too—I'd pretend you were back in town. And since Jonny had done it with two different Hobbits in a single day, and then two Hobbits in one night at the same time, why shouldn't I look for a bunch of giants at a sex club while I was at it?

"Remember to use a condom." Jonny shouted the words at me, and appalled at myself, I didn't answer him. To feel a little better, I threw a stick of deodorant and a pair of swim trunks, from my backpack, at him. He managed to grab hold of each item, fresh from Rio, and put safely away my back-together-one-week-early gifts for him. "I think you dislike everyone," he accused. "Even me."

"That's not true, I only dislike you and what you did." Tomorrow we'd be even—that's what I told him. On the positive side, both of us would be instantly forgiven. Just as he wanted. But Jonny wouldn't let me put on my scarf, jacket, or winter cap—we struggled with each garment in the entry. He begged me to stay home. Getting nowhere, he changed tactics and insisted on coming along instead; for protection, he said, because he remained forever my loyal watchdog.

I brought Jonny with me into the cold night. The sleeping bag, backpack, and textbooks, and all thoughts of running away to find you in the mountain, I left them behind in Marselis Gate.

52

I FOUND A doorbell emblazoned with the word *Hercules* among other businesses in the building. Jonny caught up on the ice-laced sidewalk outside the run-down address near the Central Station. He was frantically panting frost smoke.

We were buzzed inside. On the winding staircase, a lanky boy, about our own age, was on his way out. He stole a glance at us. "How is it up there?"

He seemed horrified by my question. "Nothing happened! There's almost no one there."

"You want to come upstairs with us? It's nice and warm in there, right?"

When the boy considered for a second, Jonny approached behind me. "Kurt?" My ex looked aghast.

"Yah, Jonny?"

"I don't want this," he said. And that only made things so much easier. I suggested that he should take the tram back home and wait for me in Marselis Gate.

In the meantime, I'd get to know this boy, who suddenly interjected, "Are you two related?" I chuckled unhappily at the question that never went away. I told him to ignore my kid brother, who was only there to make sure I was safe. In fact, I could take perfectly good care of myself.

However, when I attempted to keep walking up the stairs, Jonny grabbed me by the hips and wouldn't let go.

"Oh, come on," I barked. "It'll be fun." I tried to drag him along. But being so much stronger than me, he hugged me from behind and dropped me to the steps with little effort. And then, two floors above us, the door crashed open and a bald, well-built man appeared above the handrail.

"You *kids* down there… Come on up right this minute—or leave! There are other tenants here, so no noise."

Frightened, the other boy immediately ran. I took the opportunity to follow my prey back down the steps. Leaping after me, Jonny pushed me into the wall at the bottom of the stairwell, fell to his knees, and whimpered as he attached himself to my foot, "I can't wait until tomorrow. I need to be with you *now.*"

"But we're not *even* yet," was my reply.

53

I HAD MY suspicions about where the other boy was heading. I acted on impulse and raced down a side street—and Jonny, following some whim of his own, stopped trailing me.

At My Friend Club the staff member gave me a towel, a locker for my clothes, and a much welcome student discount. I could shower as much as I wanted and take as much time in the solarium as I could dream of. Feeling clean and tanned enough, I passed on those opportunities.

In my towel, I roamed through a dimmed labyrinth of rooms. I had no luck locating the other boy though. If I'd caught up with him on my way here, I'd gladly have paid his entrance fee to have someone to hang out with.

Down the hallway, an ancient man droned on, begging for company, for cock. Except for his distressed pleas, I heard nothing but synthesized music and the taped moaning of a porn movie.

I left untouched the complimentary disinfecting spray, lube, condoms, and tissue paper. I locked myself inside a red-lighted cubicle instead, flipped off the switch, and reclined on the cushiony bench. Other activity I filtered out.

I was back on Ipanema Beach and it was incredibly bright.

Hiding behind my smudged sunglasses, I ignored the keen locals, snubbed the eager Americans, restlessly missed Jonny, and relived my decision to call Lufthansa—to see if they could accommodate an early return date. What a stupid mistake. I could have managed to miss him dearly for one more week.

Rowdy laughter awoke me. The music had stopped. The few lingering guests were obviously in good spirits at the dawn of a new day—my twenty-first birthday.

An immense amount of chatting emanated from one of the other rooms. My magnificent boyfriend-in-waiting would probably have told me to make these fellows in towels sing my birthday song.

Sweet little Jonny Boy, don't grieve.

54

IT WASN'T EVEN 7:00 a.m.—yet I had thirty-six new text messages when I left My Friend Club: thirty-five from Jonny and fourteen of them from last night. He believed he'd lost me. What was I doing to him? I couldn't stop picturing Jonny's handsome face, damp with perspiration, contorted with grief. He wanted to know where I was, when I was coming home, when I wanted my birthday present.

The night of trials was over, it was time to console each other and offer reassurance.

There was also an answer from Lars. "Please, don't bother me," it read. I heard a snowplow's blade scraping the asphalt somewhere nearby.

I called out Jonny's name from the entryway but received no answer. His shoes were, in fact, in the hallway—only his jacket was missing from the rack. I headed straight to the boys' room only to find it empty. The kitchen and living room were deserted, too.

He wasn't in the girls' room or the bathroom either, so I finally opened the door to the adults' room. There, his jacket and underwear lay on the floor and, squinting at the light from under the covers in the Murphy bed, his eyes glowered at me.

"So how was it?" he snapped sarcastically. "Go ahead, tell me.

How many pigs sucked you off?"

I noticed another head moving beneath the blankets—without the glasses he usually wore. That head belonged to our landlord, Truls Snøfugl. His hands were gesticulating at me lethargically. "Now that you're both home, why don't you guys stick to your own room and sort things out?"

His deep voice startled me and my own went squeaky. "How was it for *you*, old man? Answer me."

"Nothing happened here," Truls sighed. "You two need to talk."

"Jonny. Let's go to our room. Please. I'll tell you all about Rio."

"I don't want to hear a thing," Jonny screamed from under the comforter.

"But listen… Nothing's happened—anywhere!"

I tried to explain that I went to My Friend Club and locked myself into a cubicle to sleep.

"Didn't you hear what I just said? I don't want to hear a thing, because I have so much stuff on my mind right now. Lots of stuff's happened here tonight while you were on your rampage. Okay?"

I felt a chill down my spine. "I see. So Truls just lied."

Truls scratched his head and told me to listen. He'd driven home in the middle of the night to help Jonny search for me. He'd like to rest for an hour before he left for work now that I was recovered. He also wished me a happy twenty-first. He was sorry about the Hobbits taking their goddamn liberties.

"The Hobbits broke up, after six years," Jonny cut in. "Isn't it dreadful? I don't know what to do. I tell them I'm single and all hell breaks loose. If you don't believe me, call Tim."

"You're not single," I reminded him. "It was a trial separation period and it's over. We're back together."

"Oh, really? You can't decide that for me."

"Guys!" Truls was covering his ears. "Really, why don't you discuss your issues in the boys' room?"

According to Jonny, Tim and Thom had taken turns ringing our doorbell and he'd had to pretend he wasn't home until Truls came to guard him. Tim had been calling every single hour all night. He was begging for sympathy and a shoulder to cry on. Thom, too, had bombarded him with messages. He thought Tim was leading *everyone* astray. They'd told him to choose between them within the day. They both wanted to be Jonny's boyfriend. I guess I wasn't Thom's top choice after all. "Tough shit, just pick the one you want more." I circled the Murphy bed to get to him.

"You're missing the point," Jonny grumbled. "I don't want any of you. All I want is a rest. Why is it so difficult to just stay friends?"

"Jonny, Kurt," Truls repeated. "Please, go to your room."

"No thanks, I'm staying here with you. Kurt, you can leave. And you can delete all my messages. They don't matter anymore."

55

MY HEART SANK further when I found the detergent box and the broken CD still lying under Jonny's pillow. I wasn't alone in the boys' room for long though. Bodø Boy rushed inside and pulled the engagement drawing off the IKEA cupboard. Narrowing his eyes defiantly, he tore the thick, soft paper in two, while I shouted no. He hurled one half at me. "There's your part."

I grabbed hold of both and grew excited when he pushed me into bed. He stared at my crotch—I couldn't help it; it felt like such a tremendous turn-on. "Let's tape them back together," I said. Raising his voice, he demanded that I get out of his boxers immediately. I could dirty my own underwear at sex clubs.

I tried to explain that I'd worn only a towel, but that didn't seem to help. The next instant I was on the floor, with him on top, wrestling his boxers off me. He tried to choke me with the underwear and winced when I grabbed his butt inside his own pair of shorts. "Get your sharp knuckles and protruding bones off me."

"I'm innocent," I mumbled, miffed by his comment. "Jonny, listen. I want us back together. Let's kiss, let's make up."

Obviously there was room for hope. He was practically naked and we were in the same chamber. He broke loose and stood up, hovering over me with his catch. "What about Rio? Start talking now, or I leave."

I began with my rather longwinded account about airline headphones. He didn't seem to think I was being serious. "But you might want to write a newspaper story," I contended.

"There's nothing newsworthy about it."

"Okay, but it's the only thing that happened apart from the plane being hit by lightning. That happens once a year, apparently."

Why couldn't I just tell him about my decision after I'd envisioned our names among the extinct on Norwegian television? Jonny wasn't impressed with my story. To make that much clear, he walked out on me.

I crawled back to bed and tried to listen through the wall. Finally, after a time, I grew confident I heard the smacking of lips—either that or it was foreskin flapping. My body initiated some peculiar, feverish shivering. Wasn't Truls Snøfugl supposed to go to work?

"This is unbearable," I shouted through the wall. "You guys need to get a hotel room, really."

Deciding to intervene, I raced through the living room and yanked his door open. Did they honestly think ignoring my naked body would make me disappear? When I ran inside and attempted to drag off the comforter, they both clung to it fiercely.

"Stop that," Jonny whined, "just leave us alone."

"Take it easy, take it easy, we can't have a civil war at home," Truls cried out.

"Why not?" Jonny sniveled. "I'm not leaving this Murphy bed, ever. I love it here."

A little too late Truls begged me, "Don't slam … the door." I was a satyr with a broken flute, wasn't I?

56

I HID UNDER my bed covers while Truls and Jonny finished their transaction of body fluids. "You're one saucy friend," you wrote in a text message from Sankthanshaugen. "And you get yourself into the strangest situations. But I'll be on my way."

You'd thought I was still in Rio, so you hadn't mentioned that you were, in fact, back from the mountain. I instructed you to wait until the coast was clear. I'd let you know.

Before rushing off to work, Truls audibly swore in the kitchen, rather theatrically, "Does *everything* have to die on me?" For obscure reasons, Jonny was much slower to leave. He took his time reading the paper, turning the pages violently, and clinked his spoon into his bowl with every helping of cornflakes. After he'd engaged in a long shower, he made no attempt to enter our room. Thus, he deprived himself the experience of being locked out.

Jonny's departure served as my last cue—it was time to make a final inspection of the household.

With a pang of guilt, I discovered the goldfish bowl, devoid of its contents, sitting in the kitchen sink. Oh dear, poor Truls; surely the simultaneous death of Loverboy was the clear melodramatic nod goodbye to our current living arrangement.

In the trash bin inside Truls's room, I unearthed four balls of tissue paper. I rolled them out circumspectly and sniffed each one. The fluids they contained were fresh and still sticky. Not snot, by the smell of it. With a shiver, I threw the soiled papers back into the trash.

The landlord and his boy interest could have this side of Marselis Gate to themselves. I ate my bowl of cereal quickly and rushed to remove my bicycle from basement storage. I locked my means of self-reliant transportation with the others across the street, outside the student flats. I needed to buy winter tires with spikes.

Your skin looked mountain fresh that day. Maneuvering past my backpacks, and trash bags, and the office chair covered in Jonny's clothes, you sat down with me, in bed. I apologized about the mess, took in your sunburned face and spiky blond hair. Wondering if that scumbag Tim was right, I stared right at your lower legs. You, my noble rescuer, looked unblemished and stunning, certainly a little more emotionally honest than I was at that moment. You still thought my brother had had sex with our landlord. "You and your little brother shared this room? Isn't that so?"

I nodded. "Is that he?" You'd noticed the drawing on the floor.

"I'm over there. I'm the other half." I pointed at the curled-up piece in the corner.

"You tore it up?"

"No, *he* did."

I momentarily felt your foot move toward mine. Believing the gesture was unintentional, I collected myself. I started talking, fast. "There's something I should tell you. That's our engagement drawing. Our landlord was supposed to be the witness for our civil ceremony. Our plot was to ask you to be the other witness. We didn't really plan to tell anyone else. Do you see? He wasn't really my brother."

At this point my courage disappeared. "Oh … shit," you murmured, staring at the caricature drawing. "Is he *Conny*? I always thought there was something bizarre about her. You must be pretty distressed."

We just sat there together. Minutes may have passed. You finally broke the silence and said, "So where are we taking your things?"

"Back to the university. I'll see if I can find new lockers there since it's the beginning of the semester. I'm calling the girl in the silo. She's got to move out of my flat at once. I don't want to do it, but what are my options? She'll probably talk to Jonny the moment we hang up. They're such good friends."

"Maybe she'll need more than a few days to find a new place."

"She's got to go; it's an illegal sublet."

I told you I'd get us a taxi because I feared that we might be surprised by any of the remaining members of the Marselis sex syndicate. Then I heard myself saying, "There's something I want you to see before we go." I can't explain why I did it—out of fury and recklessness maybe.

"I'm not sniffing anything," you warned, recalling my last text message. Then, in the living room, your complexion turned grave. I, of course, took that as recognition of the seriousness of my situation, as confirmation of incriminating evidence. "You wanted to show me *this*?" We stood so close I could feel your body's warmth. "That's your proposed second witness, your landlord?" You were studying the framed barbeque photo of Truls and his daughter Siri.

"Yah! I thought maybe you'd have seen him before. Since you're from Oslo, I mean."

"And he's been doing it with your … ex?"

"Yup. At least since this morning. That old pig! He's a mechanic and drives around in this scary white van. There's an old mattress in the back. He says he sleeps on it when he's out in the districts. But who knows what he really does on it. I suspect he ravages young, innocent boys. I certainly hope you realize that if only you'd accepted my offer last year, I would've never ended up here... We could have lived happily in your tent somewhere warm."

I stopped there, for your hand lay on my shoulder and you were shaking your head at me. You'd returned to an appallingly peaceful state of being. "We should get you out of here immediately."

All the important documents, including Jonny's remaining travel vouchers and his tickets to Canada and Australia, were still tucked inside my English-Norwegian/Norwegian-English dictionary. I was taking it all with me.

57

IT BECAME AN afternoon of graceless acts. The moment I heard how upset she got on the phone, I offered the silo girl one of Jonny's travel vouchers if she'd move out by the end of the week at the latest. On an inelegant second whim, I removed the chip from my device, broke it into two pieces, and threw the debris in a nearby bin, for I didn't want my crazy ex-boyfriend—or his current boyfriend, whomever he chose—calling every hour to reclaim certain airline tickets and checks.

Third, I entered the computer lab. No students stood in line. Eager to blow off my steam, I sat down to create a brand new Gaysir profile. I was probably the most vindictive, immature, and irresponsible birthday boy on campus that day.

JUSTLINEUP!

I want to explore everything I haven't yet tried with everyone, before it's too late. I'm totally indiscriminate and democratic. Come all over me, now!

A free-for-all ensued. I accepted rendezvous with fatsos, scrawnies, and cripples, married couples, and even a girl who was looking for gay men, all of them ranging from decidedly underage to well past retirement. I scheduled get-togethers, in fifteen-minute time slots, throughout the whole evening. I told everyone to ring the doorbell at Truls's address. "Just be punctual. Ask for Jonny Boy, the stray puppy."

When I ran out of time slots, I provided interested parties with his phone number.

Brimming with destructive energy, I raced across campus and found you holding a seat for me all the way down in the second row. You told me that you had news for me in the break. For the first time, I even raised my hand in class. After finishing his thought, the associate professor gave me the go-ahead. But then he interrupted me. "I can't hear you."

I started over, but before long, he said that I needed to learn to speak up. You tried to repeat my question, but for some reason the lecturer wanted to make a point and took one from the back instead. You whispered in my ear, "I think I know the answer. I'll tell you later." But you wouldn't. For suddenly your upper body started twitching, and the whole class was unable to digest the other student's longwinded question.

The lecturer returned his attention to the second row. "Is his seizure under control, or do we need to call for help?"

"It'll pass. I'll take notes for both of us. Just continue to ignore us, please." Without meaning to, I sounded awfully irritated. The associate professor held my gaze, as if deciding whether he had heard me right. I was holding on to you as best as I could. Your neck was clammy and covered in goosebumps.

You'd stopped shaking and hadn't bitten off or swallowed your tongue, but you remained limp in my arms. We immersed ourselves in the landscape projected on the screen, a fertile pastureland of windy, forested hills—an image of a bygone Italian fantasy world. I didn't realize at the time that my fury too had somewhat subsided.

In the break you mentioned two things. You'd talked to your parents and I could stay in your sister Anniken's room, painted in pale pink and littered with stuffed animals, for the time being. Furthermore, they were short staffed at Peppe's. Would I care to have a go as a pizza delivery boy? Yah, yah!

Needless to say, I badly needed to raise extra money for rent and for winter tires, although as much you probably gathered.

We ate pizza and afterwards your boss hired me on the spot. She gave me simple instructions and car keys and told me to get to work. I planted an insulated bag with four pizzas in the back seat of a small Volkswagen. Even though I'd never driven a car in Oslo, I thought things would be easy, because unlike my parents' station wagon, this one had automatic transmission.

The following moment, searching for the designated delivery wallet to make sure I had change, I selected the wrong gear. And instead of reversing, I crashed headlong into the brick wall, accidentally honking the horn at the same time. All of the employees, including you and the manager, came out to have a look. She was obviously running short on staff, for I wasn't fired on the spot. She said the insurance policy would take care of it. A waiter volunteered to use his own car that night. And swapping duties with him, I ended up serving in the restaurant with you. A much better arrangement.

Your sister Anniken's room reminded me of Siri's chamber across the valley, except the temperature was much more comfortable and the bed bigger. Within the day we'd moved our long bodies from one bed to the next.

"Kurt?"

"Yah?"

"You really are perverse, yah?"

I was squeezing one of your sister's stuffed animals—a squirrel, I think—to a slow death. "No one wants me," I whimpered. "Everyone prefers old pigs to me."

Nonetheless, your lung capacity impressed me. For a long time, you simply inhaled; it must've been all the bicycling and skiing. Then came the longest sigh I believe I've caused in my whole life. "Gosh, Oslo's even smaller than I imagined." I met your eyes at once.

"Okay, Kurt," you whispered, "I really don't know what that guy told you. Seriously, all I really wanted from him was a lift home. I was exhausted. I can't explain it. I just let it happen. He kept his clothes on the whole time. It's the only time I've ever done it with anyone. Man or woman. Ever."

"Want to try again?"

"Please, Kurt. You're family. You're like a brother to me. I mean, a real brother—not the type you sleep with. Let's stay that way until further notice, friends—who keep their clothes on."

I thought for a while. What a choice of words. All sorts of conspiracies crossed my mind. Again I was overcome with rage. I wasn't going to sleep at your place one single night. I'd kick that illegal tenant out of my student flat right now—in person.

You were gently grabbing my lower arm. "Kurt, forget what I just said. You're my closest friend. The one I trust. The one who makes me relaxed. The one I want to be open with and rely on. Feeling better?"

It was hard to overlook your tender gaze. And then you gave in. Tightening your hold, you leaned in and embraced me. Perhaps you'd wanted to prove all along that there really was such a thing as one's own sweet time.

58

I WANTED TO take in the world at my own pace. It was after 6:00 p.m. on one of those late, dusty April days when the sun is always in your eye. People had started summer way too early and I'd just finished my shift, soon after you started yours.

After my bicycle got stolen outside the student silo I'd become a regular bus and tram passenger, but today I couldn't be bothered to wait for public transportation. Youngsters on their way to parties, burdened by plastic bags that clinked with the bottles of alcohol they contained, overtook me as I set out walking.

People just couldn't wait for summer. The smell of broiled meat wafted to my nose from portable barbecues. Music, too, flooded the air. Windows had been set ajar. Resting dangerously far out on the sill, two boys drank beer out of cans, their underwear and butt cleavage clearly visible.

Yet the river was running high with snowmelt. Down by the riverbank, with his knees up and a syringe sticking out of his underarm, a drug addict lay sprawled in the still brown grass—a longhaired girl was stroking his blond curls sweetly. Nearby, dogs, trapped inside adjacently parked cars, barked at each other. Their argument was blunt and syncopated: a tiny woof immediately overshadowed by a much louder howl. I walked the entire way home to my circular student flat.

To let in the day's remaining sunlight, I set my seventh-floor window ajar and spotted, in the rushing river far beneath me, a transient shadow—transformed, moments later, into a glittering flash of silver. The shiny reflection of a sea trout, or a salmon, pushed downstream. Oslo wildlife. A man slept on a ledge along the black rocks. I decided to make sure, in the morning, he was gone. A rat scurried past his foot toward a trash bag stuck in a leafless bush.

My rain-damaged Rio sneakers were going moldy and besides, my neighbor's old pile of shoes proved a constant turnoff. Yet I stripped down to socks and boxer briefs, stretched out on the narrow bed, and tried, as best as I could, to maintain my tan. I flicked through my lecture notes until I dozed off.

It was after sunset. I picked up the wall-mounted phone after eight rings, but following my brief greeting there was no answer. I asked if this person—whoever it was that kept bothering me—might be calling for Ida, the girl who used to live here. But the stranger just wanted to know if I was horny.

I hung up and the doorbell started ringing. The racket reminded me of the false fire alarms in the dorms at night. We'd wait outside by the hundreds for the fire department to allow us to go back to sleep because someone would forget his pizza in the oven—on one occasion twice within the same night. Perhaps it was the same student who'd taken to playing the didgeridoo after midnight—I couldn't exactly be sure where in the massive building that person lived.

I threw on a T-shirt, a pair of training shorts, and the before-mentioned shoewear and took the elevator to the fourth-level entrance. A brawny, Turkish-looking kid stood outside the sliding doors. He held a cell phone to his ear, but his mouth wasn't moving. He seemed to keep an eye on me.

I pressed the unlock button and let the glass doors slide apart. I took a step forward to keep them from closing.

"Whom are you trying to reach?"

Instead of answering me, the boy just stared at me. A sinister expression lighted up his face.

An older male student who was leaving the building gave us

both a long, questioning look, manifestly sensing the tension between us. I let the doors close.

You were working the late shift that night—I wished you were off because I wanted to walk over to your place. I wasn't exactly looking forward to another night of buzzing and chiming.

I took the elevator to the building's nineteenth-floor common area, which rested in darkness. I left the lights off, strode to the row of windows. Way below me, the shapes of the other homes at Grünerløkka looked like tiny coral reefs. No lights appeared in Truls Snøfugl's fourth-floor apartment across the street. I didn't see his white van parked on any of the streets nearby. And no Turk.

What met me instead proved an astounding sight. Swarming under a lantern right outside the row of top-floor windows were literally thousands of insects. A few gigantic wasps idled alongside the hordes of midges and mosquitoes. Hundreds of flies crawled up the exterior pane toward the strong beam of light while others sat there motionless, resting their tiny feet and wings on the thick glass. It looked as if a whole early season's worth of insects was trapped on top of the old grain tower.

And suddenly, a sharp light sliced through the common area. The door to the laundry room opened. I recognized the body, the posture, and the walk well before the fleeting glow vanished.

I'd heard talk among the residents about such druggies.

They'd wake up from sleep and make you jump the second you walked in alone to do your laundry. The moment the elevator doors slid apart, the heroin addict, evidently a trespasser, lit up again, much closer than before. He was wearing a cute beanie. Descending through the building, he left me with powerful afterimages.

Epilogue

I'D COME ACROSS a deserted playground. On the far side of the field, near the forest, hepaticas, wood anemones, and other small wildflowers crowded the banks of a small stream. From there, I could see the rooftop of Jonny's house. Well hidden from the road by giant hogweed, by the looks of it a quickly growing specimen, I was completely alone.

Bodø was wet country—no lack of soft rain. When I left my bicycle in the moist grass, I accidentally walked into a cloud of midges—they were swarming in the shadows above the cool water, ricocheting around me like electric particles. Some stuck to my eyes and my hair.

It didn't matter. I had a dirty condom in my pocket. I'd found it on the ground when I made my way to the post office the previous day.

With luck, Bodø Boy would answer the door himself—if I had extra luck, I might persuade him to come hide with me in the hogweed. I cleaned the rubber in the stream. Removing everything but my gym shoes, I carefully rolled on my condom. If I saw or heard anyone, I'd throw on my shorts, lie down on my stomach, and sunbathe.

Before long, I felt prepared for anything that might happen.

Back in my shorts, on my bicycle, I waited for my erection inside my condom to subside before I exited the hogweed. I rested on my bike across the street from Jonny's terrace house for a moment. A private plane droned a few hundred meters above the Saltenfjord. And then a Volvo station wagon rolled past me, gravel crunching beneath its tires. There was an entire family inside, even a golden retriever, taking me in as they drove on down the road.

When I wheeled toward Jonny's gate, a German shepherd suddenly howled at me through the neighbor's hedge. It spread through the neighborhood like cascading dominos—the persistent sound of dogs barking at me, at each other. Those dogs wouldn't stop until I pedaled away.

I gave up, cycled into town, worrying that the condom would slide off.

When I arrived at my new destination, I didn't even have to pay the five-kroner fee—a stranger in a gray hoodie and red baseball cap let me in on his way out. Leaving the harbor in the distance, the Coastal Voyager sounded its deep horn. Dinner was less than an hour away. I'd be late.

The nameless grown-up came back into the restroom. It was all there for me to observe: the unkempt appearance, the slowed speech, the shrinking muscles, and the crooked posture of a serious heroin addict. Keeping his clothes on, he made me ejaculate into my soiled rubber.

Afterward, he gave me his phone number. He wanted me to repeat it out loud so I wouldn't forget, and he instructed me to call him at the shelter.

Safely home, I washed my sperm out of the condom in the kitchen sink and hid the item in my desk drawer for later use. I reminded myself that things were good because I'd used protection.

Whatever came of my first sex partner, I have no idea. But for now I knew a place in Bodø where I'd be taken care of for a five-kroner fee or less.